TANRY TENERI'S MANUAL FOR YOUNG LADIES

Ash Parker

For Mahdiyah.

VOLUME ONE

CHAPTER ONE

The Matter of Inheritance

After the death of a close family member, young ladies are expected to enter a mourning period appropriate to their relationship with the deceased. For instance, a brother's death requires a year of mourning. A sister's death should be recognised for eight months, four if she is married. — Margrit Bellere's Manual for Young Ladies

Her brother's funeral turned into a tawdry affair. His friends, always enterprising sorts, had found themselves plenty of grieving ladies and bored maids to wander off with. The other guests at the wake had decided to humour her brother's spirit in a way that he would have appreciated: by consuming enough spirits to make a drunkard blush.

Her father, claiming grief, excused himself to attend to his alchemical experiments in his library. Tanry Teneri herself, mildly amused by the young lord vomiting in the log basket, helped herself to one of the finger sandwiches on the refreshment table. She would have liked to thank Trevor for going out so dramatically, because it was providing her with endless entertainment. His school friends sobbed while playing billiards. Five of his sweethearts cursed his name and hurled priceless vases from the first floor landing. His mistress smoked cigarettes while talking politics with the priest. Duke Teneri was no doubt ruing the day that he'd allowed his daughter to organise the event.

Tanry filled her left hand with an assortment of savoury pastries and went to warm herself by the fire. She heard another smash as another vase landed on the marble tiles in the hall, and raised a hand to beckon over her housekeeper, Mrs Button.

"Tell the maids to have a drink to Trevor's memory," Tanry told her. "There's no point in trying to clean just now."

"Very good, ma'am."

Her statement was followed by the sound of the young man retching over the log basket again. At the very least, there seemed to be nothing coming out anymore.

"Let them tire themselves out," Tanry recommended. "But fetch some more wine from the cellar. I can't have any of these people seeing sense."

"And the ceramics?"

"Leave them. If they're going to break things, they may as well walk through the shards. But have Cole move the more expensive items into my wing. He knows which ones."

"Very good." Mrs Button dipped her head and hurried away.

Tanry looked to her left, where another young man was

leaned against the wall.

"How much have you had, Cotterall?" Tanry asked him.

He mumbled a response that she didn't understand. Beck Cotterall was her brother's oldest – though not his favourite – friend. He had spent the morning filling his sketchbook with strange dark drawings of skulls. Now, his ink-stained fingers clutched an empty wine glass.

"I'd say slow down," said Tanry, "but that hardly fits the mood of the occasion."

"Do you not think we should be more sombre?" asked Cotterall.

"Come now, it's like you hardly knew Trevor at all. Have another drink. Pass out on the lawn. Piss on Trevor's grave for all I care." She shoved a pastry whole into her mouth. "It's what he would want, after all."

"Lady Teneri," said a voice.

"Just a moment," she said in between bites. She picked up her glass from the mantel and took a gulp, then considered who was speaking.

It was a footman in livery, but not one of her own. She knew them all too well. This one was far too smart, with white stockings and a powdered wig.

"You belong to my aunt, don't you?" she asked him.

The footman frowned slightly, but not enough to warrant a remark from Tanry.

"The Baroness Vetera requests your presence," he said.

"Oh, it is her, then. Go on, lead the way. This event is getting a little tiresome, even for me."

Behind her, Beck Cotterall was weeping again. He tried to wipe away his tears without a handkerchief, and smeared black ink down his cheeks.

The footman led her away from the revels. Her aunt had taken up rooms on the ground floor and had filled them with her own staff, each servant brought from her estate, and each causing complaints downstairs in the kitchen. The baroness was lucky that she was a relative, or else Tanry would have no patience for such presumption.

Tanry was let into the parlour that the Baroness had fitted for her own use. This meant that she had brought two dozen potted tropical plants with her from her estate, though Tanry could not guess at the reason. They made the air feel humid, and the room smell like grass. Tanry ducked under the waxy leaves of a plant that had branches that dipped to the floor, making her feel like she had been forcibly transported to a jungle dwelling. Tanry tutted as she stepped onto one of her finest rugs and saw that potting soil had been trodden into it.

At a dainty tea table set out for two sat the Baroness Vetera. She was a middle-aged woman who behaved as if she were eighty and knocking on death's door. She wore black, even though her husband had died some twenty years ago, before Tanry was born, and in public she always wore a jet-studded veil. She had foregone the covering to see her only niece, however.

"So kind of you to dress for the funeral," she said with an air of disapproval. Tanry was wearing her best tweed suit and gestured to the black crepe armband she sported. "Come now," she said. "You know Trevor attended Mother's funeral in his jodhpurs."

"I would have thought you were better than your brother."

"Aunt Edna, you know that we were much alike." Tanry sat

down without waiting to be invited. "To what do I owe the invitation?" She crossed her legs and leaned back in the delicate chair, which creaked.

"I needed to distance myself from the festivities that are taking place out there."

"Grief is a complicated thing, auntie."

Tanry lifted the lid of the teapot, sniffed, then set it back down. "I don't care for peppermint," she said. "But why really did you want to speak?"

"You are now your mother's only remaining child, and I am not likely to have children of my own."

"Yes, I was aware of that."

The baroness snorted just a little. "You are about to come into a vital portion of your inheritance."

"I am expecting to inherit the richest estate in the country. I have been managing it long enough," said Tanry. "What more could there be?"

"This is far more important than your estate."

"I doubt it."

The baroness shook her head, then raised her hand to signal her footman. He dashed out and returned with one of his fellows (who wore a matching powdered wig). Between the fronds of imported ferns and the rubbery leaves of plants meant for desert cultures, they wheeled a trolley that was about as tall as they were. It was covered in a green silk cloth, which made Tanry feel as if she were about to partake in a disastrous illusion show.

"This was meant for your brother, but he never took ownership. I trust that you will be far more responsible than he was."

"Why do you trust in such a thing?" asked Tanry. "What makes us so different, truly?" She watched her aunt carefully, daring her to say the unspoken thing, but nothing came. Instead, the baroness stood and walked over to the trolley. Tanry could see four brass wheels sticking out from underneath the cloth.

"My father was the most tremendous inventor," said the baroness. "He never did well in the alchemic field, however. His interest was always in deeper, older magics."

"I remember that he nearly died penniless, until his daughters married well," said Tanry.

Her aunt ignored that comment. "Did you ever learn of the soothsayer of Premure?" she asked.

"Can't say that I did."

"She was a seer. She could tell the truth, even about matters that she had no knowledge of. A talented woman, though reviled. My father understood her completely."

"Ah. Did he know her, then?"

"Hush. He understood her power well enough to replicate it after she had passed. He created this."

She grasped the edge of the green cloth and pulled. It fell artfully, revealing a brass contraption which Tanry could not name. It had so many pieces and moving parts that she did not know how to term it. It was roughly the shape of a cube, and in many ways resembled a birdcage. Inside, it held cogs like the interior of a clock. Tanry stood up and went to examine it more closely.

"Look here," said her aunt. "These are the dials for the input." She indicated a set of about twenty bead-like objects on the front of the machine. "They have twenty-six sides each, so that you may ask a question." She turned one of the dials so that the letter 'T' was displayed proudly. "The output is read here." She pointed to a cog on the interior of the machine, which had twenty-six spokes, each with their own letter.

"I don't understand," said Tanry.

"It is called the discernment engine. It can tell you truth. You can ask it any question, provided it is short, and it will tell you the answer. I shall demonstrate."

She reached up to the dials and turned them deftly to display one question:

WHAT IS MY NAME

When this was finished, she grasped a small lever and pulled it down. The engine sprang into life, though Tanry could not tell where it drew its energy from. Every intricate cog turned and the output dial spun too fast to read.

"When it has an answer, it will stop at the letters in turn. It helps to have a journal nearby."

Tanry watched. The dial stopped at E, then D, then N, then A, then finally stilled altogether. The machine stopped whirring and gave the appearance of never having possessed life at all.

"That is a neat trick," she said to her aunt. "But it is rather elaborate for a parlour game, don't you think?"

"I will not tolerate more insolence," she chided. "This is the most important item possessed by our family. Your mother wanted it passed on to her children. You must take this seriously, as if she were here."

"If you want to prove its worth, you must ask it something that it would not be likely to know. You must make it tell a secret."

The baroness frowned. "I do not know any secrets."

"I can think of one," said Tanry. She reached up to the dials herself and spelled out a new question.

HOW DID TREVOR DIE

The engine began to whir.

The baroness sighed. "Your brother passed from sickness; that is not a secret."

Tanry laughed. "It is hardly in character for him to have died of a stomach complaint. No. He fell from his horse after he had been out drinking. A little embarrassing, especially for the heir to Taltois. Father felt the need to hush it up, especially as Trevor had been having something of a rendezvous with a married woman."

The output dial spun again, then began to spell. Tanry memorised each letter in turn.

FELL FROM HORSE

"Unless this thing has ears, it might just be real. Of course, I can't discount the possibility that it does have ears," said Tanry. "You can consider me impressed."

"I did not intend for you to be impressed. I intend for you to treat this duty responsibly."

"We shall see how that goes," said Tanry. "Have it taken to my wing right away. This is going to be so very useful, Aunt Edna, thank you. I can ask it all sorts of questions about where my life will lead."

"I did not intend for you to make use of it. You must simply guard it carefully. And, you should understand, that the engine cannot tell the future. It cannot know what no one can possibly know."

"I suppose that's a shame, but anyhow, someone makes use of everything, sooner or later," said Tanry.

Three days later, the servants were still attacking the mess. Tanry, after a hearty luncheon with one of her tenants, kicked off her boots by the grand staircase. Her butler, Cole, found her there, inspecting a stone caught in the sole of her boot.

"Your father is wanting to speak to you," he said.

"Then you had better gather the staff tonight to look at the moon."

"Why, my lady?"

"Because it surely must be blue, if my father wants to speak to me."

Cole snorted. "He did imply that it was important."

"I suppose that I had better find out then."

She padded up the grand staircase in her socks and found her father in his library.

"You wanted me," she said, to which Duke Teneri responded with a grunt that indicated he was finishing his page. He was buried, as was customary, in a book. He sat in his most beaten armchair, which was large enough to nearly swallow him, and he held a tome which, Tanry noticed, was not an alchemical treatise, but a book on genealogy. Not content to twiddle her thumbs until he was finished, Tanry went to stand by one of the tall windows and looked out at her estate.

Autumn was browning the world at the edges. She had hoped for at least another hunt before the month was out, but mourning was making a mess of her plans. Apparently wearing an armband was not a good enough show for her truant brother; many seemed to expect the veil and gown ordeal. They also expected her to cancel all her engagements and suspend all her work, as if anyone else were likely to take on care of Taltois.

Her eyes landed on her caravan at the edge of the woods. It was gaily painted, and her favourite refuge. Before she'd possessed her wing, it had been the only place that was hers alone. Her mother – though Tanry had not known her – had apparently been an eccentric sort, who'd bought it from a travelling salesman in exchange for a white lizard she'd raised from an egg. It existed now as an artistic folly, a curious decoration to the grand estate.

"I've been making arrangements for you," said her father in a casual manner that made the statement no less foreboding.

"Well, don't strain yourself," replied Tanry, clasping her hands behind her back. Duke Teneri had taken almost no interest in the life of his only daughter. She had scarcely dined with him, never discussed her own education, or matters of the estate. He had the foresight to hire governesses when Tanry was young, but they left one by one, finding their ward distasteful and wayward. It was Duke Teneri's opinion that the education of daughters was not a priority. That was the duty of wives, he said, though he neglected to imagine what his daughter would do without a mother to teach her.

Instead, Tanry had relied on the dubious wisdom of her elder brother to show her the world. She never quite understood why they were expected to act differently when they spent all their young lives in lockstep, with the same friends, spending their leisure time similarly.

"You're the heir to the estate now." Duke Teneri closed his book with a heavy thump. "And you'll need to change your plans accordingly."

"I'll wear black a little longer, Father, though I can't think what help it will do us. Trevor courts scandal as much in death as he did in life."

Her father tutted and adjusted his glasses, though they hadn't slipped down his nose. "I've made plans for you to get married."

Tanry was so caught off guard that she laughed. "Now that *would* cause a scandal. Imagine, we've only just put Trevor in the ground and some leech is after my inheritance."

He tutted. "I've let you run wild, I admit, but you have to straighten up now. Duke Archibald has set his cap at you. We had drinks last night and drew up the contracts."

"Oh, you're not serious." Tanry wanted to laugh, but there was a pit growing in her stomach. It had to be a joke, because she could not stand the alternative.

"The estate is entailed. You can't inherit the title, but your husband can." He shrugged, as if this were the most obvious thing in the world.

"Why do we need the title? What's the difference, if I have the house and the estate? I don't need the name."

"I hope you enjoy living off your distant relatives, then."

"Come off it."

"If your husband doesn't inherit the title, then you don't get the estate. I've some grand-nephew who gets it instead."

"You have to be full of shit." Tanry had picked up some rather colourful phrases as a child, when she and Trevor played with the tenants' children. It gave her great joy to use them in front of Mrs Button and see her scowl.

"She wants my estate and she curses like a sailor," he said to himself. "The wedding is in six months, after the Duke returns from campaign."

"Like fuck it is. This is the first I've heard about it."

"You're getting married to a duke, or higher. I won't have

my daughter marrying down."

Unfortunately for Duke Teneri, he had not spent enough time around his daughter to recognise the danger that lay in allowing her loopholes.

"Duke or higher, you say?"

"Well, it's only proper. Perhaps if there was an old family, but the arrangement—"

"Duke or higher. Do you agree?"

"What?"

"Do you agree?"

"Yes, that is who you have to marry."

"And you'd accept one who was not Duke Archibald?"

Her father chewed his cheek. "He would have to be higher in rank, and from an older family, and I would have to apologise to old Archie."

Tanry considered. Finding someone of both higher rank and older name would be a tall order, but not impossible. Duke Archibald, on the other hand, was her father's smoking friend, whom she doubted was long for this world. He had his own mistress, an actress, who was pregnant again. In the past, Tanry had heard him wish for a young wife "to show off at parties" so that the actress wouldn't get any ideas about matrimony. Tanry revolted against the idea of being forced into that man's bed. She couldn't imagine herself smiling for him and talk to his friends at parties. Worse still, she couldn't tolerate the idea of forcing children out for such a man. She had been presented an escape, a technicality, and she would take it.

"Done," she said.

"What?"

"I'll find someone higher. Though I suppose there should be a time limit. What was it you said? Six months?"

"That is when the wedding is planned for, yes."

"If I can't find anyone suitable before then, I'll concede and marry Archie." She had no intention of conceding, but an agreement had to be forced somehow.

"You won't find anyone."

"Then why deny me?"

He thought about it for a long moment. Tanry knew he recognised a challenge when he was met with one, but he was not in the field of understanding daughters.

"Fine. You can have six months."

Tanry wasn't one to waste time. She begged to borrow the genealogy book, then fled through the halls of her house to the soft-carpeted corridors of her wing.

It was not her wing in name. Neither her father nor her brother had assigned her more than the sweet little bedroom at the end. They had never been a pair for interior design, however, and after her mother's death they'd let the rooms in the house get shut up one by one. They had no need for receiving rooms, when the billiards room did them just fine. They had no need for guest bedrooms, when they had a few bachelor rooms on the upper floors. In the year since her twentieth birthday, Tanry had transformed the rooms around hers into her own wing.

At first, her ventures had been small. She'd wanted a bathroom with proper plumbing and there was a dressing room next to her bedroom that hadn't been in use for years. She'd picked blue painted tiles and a lavatory with a brass chain. She'd ordered a porcelain tub shipped in from Calness.

The maids changed the flowers there every few days so it always smelled fresh. These were only reasonable requests for the daughter of a duke.

But as time passed, her domain had spread. It transpired that her father did not much care about her activities and where she spent his money. He did not visit her rooms and he did not notice when she gained more of them.

She found a study in her wing that had the most marvellous bureau, so she rolled up her sleeves and helped to dust the whole room down and paint the walls dandelion yellow. She bought new curtains and set up space to work overlooking the parkland.

She also took her brother's papers from his office and sorted them into her new study. Trevor never took care managing Taltois. He did not collect rent regularly, but hiked it up when he needed the money to pay off his debts. He had no idea what assets anyone possessed, nor what game was spread through his woods. Tanry had picked up his work for him before his neck had even cracked.

She kept the estate kicking along. She refurbished her wing until it resembled a proper abode. All the furniture gleamed with fresh polish. All the carpets had the dust beaten out of them. No cobwebs lingered in the moulding on the ceilings. She had her own parlour for receiving visitors, her own guest rooms, her own sitting room, although she didn't often have use for these spaces; she met tenants outdoors and her father in his library. The place was shiny and new and she rattled around in it like a marble in a child's tin.

"Caterina! My trunk!" she called. She had no assurance that Caterina was nearby, but still heard the familiar scuttle of her feet around the corner.

Caterina was dressed in her black maid's dress, but still cut a more elegant figure than any ladies that Tanry had known. "What do you need the trunk for?" she asked.

"We are going to court. I think. I have to look through this." Tanry gestured to the book under her arm.

"I'll have the trunk brought to your dressing room. Why the sudden desire to go to court? The season is over for this year." Caterina led Tanry back to her bedroom, where Tanry slammed the volume down on the dressing table.

"I'm avoiding an unwanted marriage."

"I thought people went to court to *find* unwanted marriages." Caterina bent down in front of the dressing table and examined her reflection. She grimaced as she saw a smudge of dirt along her cheekbone. Carefully, she wiped it aside with her white handkerchief.

Tanry opened the book. "What's higher than a duke?" she murmured.

Caterina laughed. "Aren't you a lady? You're supposed to know."

"Who the hell would have told me? The governess that I sent away, or the father that barely speaks to me?"

"My mother brought me up well," Caterina remarked. "Above dukes, you're looking at princes. Then kings, then emperors. Or archdukes, I suppose, though there's precious few of those left."

Tanry scanned the names in the book. There was a distinct shortage of kings, princes, and emperors.

"Ah. Shit."

"What are you looking for?"

"I've just bet my father that I can find my own match

that's better than his."

"You're an idiot." Caterina rifled around in the drawer of the dressing table. It was filled with make-up and paints that Tanry never used. If a trained eye looked in the drawer, they would see that this was really Caterina's collection of cosmetics: they matched her pale complexion, rather than Tanry's brown skin. Since her employment, Tanry had allowed her to keep whatever she liked in the drawers of the dressing table, and use them at her whim. Caterina was with a needle and had been drastically undervalued by her last mistress. Tanry hired her has soon as she saw the exquisite stitching on her cuffs during the interview, then set Caterina to work running up suits and jackets. Tanry struggled to order them from any other seamstress, who thought it unseemly for a young woman to wear trousers.

Caterina pushed Tanry aside to sit at the velvet stool. She pulled lip paint and brushes from the depths of the drawer.

Tanry moved aside, still poring over the book. "Duke Archibald has a distinguished family line. I should have known."

"You should have checked before you made your bet, more like." Caterina began to apply a deep red lip colour that Mrs Button would no doubt insist she remove later, but which Tanry thought was perfectly fetching.

"I wasn't left with much choice. There's the root of the situation. I've not a great deal of choice in my future, which Trevor never would have stood for, had he been in such a situation."

"It sounds like you might need nothing short of a royal to get the job done."

"Caterina." Tanry tossed the book aside. It landed spine

first on the floor. "Can you get me copies of Pherson's? Going back as far as you can wrangle it?"

"If I search the servants' quarters, I think we can get a few months' worth."

Around twenty minutes later, Caterina returned, without her lip paint, but with six crisp editions of *Pherson's Courtly Hearsay* – the best gossip magazine available for purchase.

"They were all hidden under the mattresses," Caterina said, returning to the mirror. She began taking out the pins that held her hair under her cap and letting her curls fall down.

Tanry fell on the magazines with the urgency of a starved predator. "I really should order these," she said.

Caterina snorted. "I think Mrs Button would confiscate them at the door, even if they were meant for you. She thinks that gossip causes loose morals."

Tanry laughed. There were plenty of morals lying around loose in her house, most left behind by Trevor Teneri.

Tanry flicked through the pages. They were filled with bold text and frothy stories about people at court, accompanied by watercolour portraits.

"Do they have a painter who wanders around, sketching people as they go about their lives at court?"

"That's the general idea." Caterina began pinning up her own curls in the stylish manner Tanry kept seeing inside the magazine. "What are you looking for, then?"

"I don't know exactly, but something better than the alternative."

"What's the alternative?"

"Duke Archibald. One of my father's friends. He'll make

me move to his estate and I'll never come home. He'll be in control of my money and I'll have to beg him for pennies. I'll have no freedoms left in life and no purpose except the birthing of children."

"That's more or less true for every married woman," said Caterina. "It's more or less why the two of us are unwed. There is no one to control us."

"No one except Mrs Button, and me, as your employer."

"Mrs Button I can handle, and you like me too much to dismiss me. But it sounds as if you need someone you have something on. A little control over?"

"If the scales have to be tipped, then they have to be tipped." Tanry closed the first magazine.

"Nothing good?"

"All about fashion and new styles. Hair and fabric choices."

"Ooh – give it here." Caterina held her hand out for it and Tanry tossed it over.

Tanry began flipping through the next magazine but quickly realised that it was the same month's edition. The next one looked more promising. The opening page was taken up by a colour illustration of a royal ball. Princess Athalie, the king's one and only child, was front and centre in an elegant lilac dress and a tiara the same height as her head.

"She's slender, isn't she?"

"I think that the artist is being complimentary. No woman truly looks that way. Not with all the tight lacing in the world."

"I'm sure that Princess Athalie appreciates being trimmed down in paintings. Everyone enjoys being judged so," said Tanry with a ladling of sarcasm.

"Are you finding anything helpful, or are you busy casting aspersions on someone you have not met?"

"It says here that Princess Athalie is a splendid and delicate dancer. You hear that – splendid and *delicate.*" Tanry scoffed.

"I bet she is. Princesses have got to have training just to exist in the world," Caterina proclaimed, as if she, a maid and a daughter of a maid, were an expert on the subject of being a princess. "She'll have been pulled through regimens to seem effortless and graceful since she could walk."

"God, I had it easy. I just had to play football with the tenants' kids and not get mud on the carpet." Tanry flicked to the next page, where the artist had drawn every notable guest at the ball for the purpose of commenting on their clothing.

Resplendent in the centre of a double spread, taking up even more room than the princess, was painted a woman, half-turned away from the viewer. She wore a white dress that had more layers than a wedding cake. Her hair was impossibly long, and braided into a crown that still fell halfway down her back. Her waist was thin in a way that made Tanry assume that the artist was being 'complimentary', as Caterina had said.

"Who's that, then?" Caterina asked, peering over Tanry's shoulder.

"The caption says that this is Imperial Archduchess Lizseta Caela Loreatha Boralda-Solkin. This is what I am looking for."

"It is?"

"Yes. There are plenty of noble families expelled by the revolution in Karda Ven. Some live here now, as their country is a republic. An archduchess would be the sister of an archduke, and the daughter of an emperor."

"What has made you such an expert?"

"I read it in the other book, of course."

Tanry scanned the pages for further mentions of the name Boralda-Solkin. "Look there – she's got a brother." She pointed at a tall man sketched behind Lizseta.

"An imperial archduke is higher than a duke." Caterina clapped her hands in delight.

Tanry flicked through the pages for more mentions of the shy archduke. He was drawn in the corner of another page, behind another of his beautiful sisters.

"His name is Archduke Cezsario Concerto Dalibor Boralda-Solkin." Tanry could feel herself smiling.

"Does he have anything to inherit though? He's an archduke, but an *exiled* archduke." Caterina took the magazine from Tanry, clearly to look over the clothes of the ball guests.

"That's a good thing. If he's nothing to inherit, he has to come live here, and he has to listen to me." Tanry pulled a notebook from her desk drawer and scribbled down the name. "What else do we know about them?"

"Two sisters. Lizseta and Laurina. There are no further family members mentioned in this issue." Caterina said.

"Pack them all up – we're going to need to do our research. And we must figure out how to transport my new machine."

Tanry beckoned Caterina into a carriage and slammed the door shut behind her. Caterina grasped a wicker basket in one hand, which contained two bottles of ginger beer and sandwiches from Cook. They sat in the back of the carriage as it rumbled across Taltois, poring over the magazines.

Tanry had begun to take notes on Archduke Cezsario Boralda-Solkin and his esteemed family. It was an old name, one of the oldest in the world, and of far higher rank than a duke. And – cherry on top of it all – they were poorer than church mice.

"You'll have to dress differently." Caterina gestured to Tanry's tweed suit; there was a dried splash of mud that reached from her trouser hems up to her left knee. "But I can sort that."

"With what dresses? I haven't packed any."

"I've come out ahead of you. Remember when you let me alter your mother's old dresses?"

"Ah. I thought you might get more use out of them than I would." Tanry's mother had been fond of frilly things. She'd liked pastels and flowers and hats with ribbons hanging off them.

"I have been altering them to better suit current fashions. I thought you might let me sell them. But now is the time to show off my work, or so it seems." Caterina sat up straight, satisfied with herself.

"I'll be sure to let you doll me up as you like," Tanry said. She could count half a dozen suitors that wandered in Caterina's wake back at home, entranced by the idea of Caterina, the pretty servant, who might be saved from the drudgery of service. She gained only more of them, like a jam jar left open on a summer's day. Caterina was more dedicated to her work, in reality, than in ensnaring suitors. They were a means to an end, she usually said. A path to better opportunities. She had too much skill to waste on them. It was proven by how she made Tanry's mother's dresses appear fashionable, despite their old styles.

"But don't expect me to wear it well," Tanry continued.

"Yes, yes." Caterina rolled her eyes. "I know how far you

are from the social scene." She reached into a basket next to her and withdrew a small book, which she opened on her lap.

"Another novel?" asked Tanry incredulously.

"I don't know why you're so judgemental. We should all be allowed our enjoyments."

Tanry shrugged, as she supposed there was some sense in that. "Go on then, tell me what it's about."

"There is a young man desperately in love with a woman above his station," said Caterina eagerly.

"That always ends well."

"She is in love with him too, but she has a brother who secretly practices astral projection."

Projectionists could project their consciousness – and a non-corporeal form – across long distances. They were virtually undetectable, and therefore a threat to every government. Anyone in power was paranoid about projectionists, known colloquially as ghosts, and feared that they were being spied on at all hours. The only means of knowing when one was being spied on was looking in a mirror, and seeing if a person was reflected there who did not stand in the room. Ghosts could not hide from mirrors.

Tanry gasped in mock outrage. "I'm assuming he meets some grisly end for that crime."

"Not yet. The young man is lining his house with mirrors, so that he might spot the projection when he comes to spy on him, but he cannot afford all of them. Plus, the brother has paid the washerwoman who lives downstairs to fill the house with steam, so that all of the mirrors are fogged. He sees shadows in the mirrors and thinks that they are the projection, but they are his lover."

"So he harms her in some way?"

"I am still reading." She slouched into the seat of the carriage and turned her attention to the book.

Tanry couldn't count herself as engaged. Worrying about astral projectionists spying on her had never been one of her priorities.

CHAPTER TWO

Princess Athalie

Every noble should spend at least a season at court. It is the only place where bright young people might be introduced to suitable matches. — Pherson's Courtly Hearsay

The royal court of Lyalia was situated in a palace, as one might expect. It was positioned a stretch outside of Albonne, the capital, so that there was a healthy green space in between the aristocrats and the heavy air of the city. There were wings and courtyards and pillars aplenty. There were formal gardens and stables and even a small menagerie for the entertainment of guests. There was a tennis court, which was considered vital to the running of parliament, and three ballrooms, for gatherings of any size. There were steam houses and baths and shooting ranges and dozens and dozens of empty rooms with gilded ceilings.

And every hallway and ballroom and reception room was lined with mirrors to protect the court from astral projectionists, so that residents might look into the mirrors and see people who weren't in the room with them, and know that they were being watched.

It was a strange place. The king had not visited in around seven years; he was busy with his wars. He had played with tin soldiers all his life, and now he had the real thing to keep him entertained on the field and in his tent. His court was run by his daughter.

"Princess Athalie," Tanry said, in the darkness of the carriage. The unplanned nature of their trip had led to them finishing it well after sunset. "What is she like?"

"I haven't met her, in my illustrious career as your maid."

"Did you read anything in Pherson's about her?"

"Not a great deal. Mostly surface stuff. She's elegant. She dances. She is proper. Really nothing of character."

The carriage halted. Tanry peeled back the curtains from the window and saw the flickering lights of Princess Athalie's palace, deserted except for a handful of leaves dancing across the front steps.

"How late is it?" Tanry asked.

Caterina checked the dented watch she kept in her front pocket. "Almost two thirty."

"Do you think they will let us in?"

"*Someone* is awake." Caterina pointed to the front door, which stood ajar.

Tanry, groaning, clambered out of the carriage. "Let's see who."

She flipped a coin from her pocket to the coach man, who

seemed to be dozing off at the reins. He snorted as the coin bounced off his chin. The guards that stood alongside the palace doors did not remark on their presence, as she might have expected from their sudden appearance.

Tanry strode up to the door, pushed on the wood, and saw an impressive entrance hall with marble floors and a painted ceiling. She could not tell the details or the colour, as the alchemic gems in the chandeliers were snuffed out. Only a single light drew Tanry's eye. The gem, glowing orange like an ember, was set in a silver dish on the floor halfway up a carpeted grand staircase.

A young woman sat on the stairs next to it. She had a clothbound book open on her lap, and the gem's light was reflected in her glasses, so bright that Tanry could not see the eyes behind them. Between her lips she held a clay pipe. She puffed on it and released a cloud of purple smoke that drifted above her head.

By Tanry's reckoning, she did not have a particularly memorable face. She had mousy blonde hair that was caught up in a chignon, but strands escaped and stuck to her forehead. She sat, halfway up the steps, legs splayed out like a man sitting on a bench. At their arrival, she looked up.

"Lady Tanry," she said. "Pleased to make your acquaintance." She did not stand.

Tanry gaped for a moment, not quite knowing how to address this stranger.

"Don't stand on ceremony," said the woman. "I wanted to greet you myself, but with no one around there's no point in curtseying."

Tanry, coming to an understanding, said, "Ah. Princess Athalie?"

In the carriage, Caterina had drilled her on the basics of court etiquette. She'd never been herself, but she claimed to have read many informative novels on the matter. Throughout this conversation, dread built in Tanry's stomach. There was no chance of her curtseying correctly, or remembering the right way to address the princess. It was a pleasant surprise to be greeted in privacy, and so casually.

"Yes. I got word that you were coming very late." With delicate movements, Athalie placed a piece of ribbon in between the pages of her book. She watched Tanry with an appraising air, and puffed on her pipe again.

"I do not mean to impose. It was a rather impulsive decision, if I am honest," Tanry explained. It seemed to her that Athalie was looking at her strangely.

Behind Tanry, Caterina smothered a laugh.

"Can I ask the reason for your visit?" said Athalie.

Any pleasure that she found at being greeted privately faded away. If there had been more people, Tanry might have been of less interest. It would not do to let Athalie know all of her affairs. She might have more questions, and Tanry would rather not explain herself. If Caterina had taught her one thing, it was that women weren't *supposed* to hunt for their own husbands, and that it was unseemly.

She needed a quick lie.

"I have simply never been to court. I was not presented, you see. My father – he's a distracted man. I thought I would take the chance to see it while I could."

"We did wonder why you never showed. I can't say I have a taste for court presentations. I was always a little intrigued by you, as you were bold enough to skip your coming out." Athalie looked Tanry up and down in such a pointed way that

Tanry dearly wished she had changed into Caterina's new clothes before they left the carriage. It felt rather as if Tanry was failing a test that she hadn't known was coming. She scolded herself. It was not important what Athalie thought of her. She was not arranging Tanry's marriage.

"I was raised with my brother," she said. "He did not come here, so neither did I."

Athalie frowned a little at this, though Tanry thought that her statement had been rather straightforward. She sighed, glancing back at her book as if it was tugging at her attention.

"In any case, you're welcome here. I have had your mother's old rooms prepared. I'm told she spent most of her childhood here."

"Well, I would not know," Tanry replied, with genuine surprise. She did not know where her mother had spent any of her time, besides the bedroom in her father's wing that she had died in. "Thank you, Your Highness. We must get to bed, I suppose."

"Is it just the two of you?" Athalie asked.

"Yes. Only Caterina and I."

"Fascinating. Yes. I shall see you in the morning, no doubt. If it's a sunny day we will eat on the patio. There is a footman next door waiting to show you to your rooms. Good night, Lady Tanry."

"And you, Your Highness." Tanry nodded her head in lieu of bowing. The princess stood on no further ceremony and returned her reading.

Tanry turned to her left, intending to go to the chamber that Athalie had indicated, but saw a figure lingering in the shadows there. It was too dark for Tanry to see his face clearly. He waited on the threshold, and had the air of someone who had been caught mid-step. He was tall and wore a fine jacket with embellishments that glinted just slightly in the poor light. But before Tanry could truly gather information about him, he stepped out of the way and disappeared into the shadows.

Caterina clicked her fingers at the footmen who had been sent to carry their trunks while Tanry investigated their new rooms. It was panelled in a fresh green colour, which Tanry found particularly tasteful. The furniture had been dusted and there were fresh lilies on the side board; just off the parlour was a washroom, and a cupboard-like bedroom for Caterina, and a much larger bedroom for Tanry.

"Set that over there," said Caterina. Two footmen wheeled the discernment engine, covered in a cloth, into a corner.

"Can I ask what it is?" said one of the serving men. His fellow tried to lift the edge of the cloth and peek underneath.

"Am I not allowed my privacy?" Tanry scolded them. Both of them backed away from the engine so fast one would have assumed there was a wild animal inside of it.

"Our apologies, my lady."

"It's no bother," replied Tanry. "I spoke a little harshly. I only feel no need to explain. Good night, sirs."

They bowed and departed.

Tanry yawned. "I'll see you in the morning."

"No. I need to work on you now."

"What for? Can't I sleep?"

"You are a mess. I can hardly clean you up with the time that I have, let alone in the morning." She directed Tanry to sit on the stool behind the dressing table.

She set to work with more urgency than Tanry had ever seen her apply to her scrubbing and polishing. She made Tanry change into a lacy dress that she did not care for, just to tuck it in and pin it into the right places.

"This is hardly my style," complained Tanry.

"We must all work with what resources we have available. There is not enough time to sew you a dress to suit your sensibilities."

"Fine. It is only for a short while."

"How long do you imagine it will take to seduce an archduke?"

"Gods, I hope not long. I was expecting that my wealth might be a deciding factor."

"Some men want romance."

"We must simply hope that this man isn't one of them." She shrugged out of the dress and shuffled to her bedroom.

"Don't overtax yourself," she said. "I know that you are always sewing half the night."

Caterina mumbled that she would, but as Tanry was falling asleep, she could still hear the rattle of Caterina's sewing machine.

She woke to the soft tweeting of birds and the yelling of Caterina. "Come on! We need to get you ready!" She pulled the covers off of Tanry and threw them onto the floor.

Tanry, with all the energy she could muster (which was not a great deal) clambered out of bed.

She emerged into the parlour and found that Caterina had hung the dress out for her. It was coupled with a hat that was taller than Tanry's entire head. It looked like it was made from rose petals, and would probably be just as robust.

"Do I really have to wear that?" she asked.

"Resign yourself to it now, or you'll never succeed." Caterina helped Tanry into her corset, then layered up a few petticoats, and finally buttoned her into the stiff dress.

"It smells," Tanry complained.

"It's old enough. You're lucky your mother was remarkably forward in her fashion choices."

Tanry snorted at that. Caterina had managed to discern something about her mother that Tanry had never guessed. Her mother apparently wore stylish dresses and kept a secret ancient machine.

"It's a shame that your mother didn't have your skin tone," said Caterina. "I'm not certain that this colour suits you."

"I wish Trevor had talked about her more," said Tanry idly, without much thought. Caterina paused, leaving two buttons undone.

"Do you – do you want to talk about your mother?"

Tanry's heart tightened. She forced out a laugh.

"I was only musing. It's not important."

"You never talk about her."

"Cat – leave it. We have a task to attend to. This charade might just fall at the first hurdle, as I've never been taught any manners."

"Remember what we planned? It's not Archduke Cezsario you need to find first," said Caterina.

"I know – it's the sisters."

It was unconscionable for a young lady to introduce herself to a man, of course. That was far too forward. No, she had to be introduced by a male relative, or a female relative if she had no men kicking about. The only other option was to stage an elaborate accident, where both parties could meet in innocent circumstances. Now, Tanry did not have time to fabricate such a circumstance, as most others did. She also lacked the patience.

She needed a relative to introduce her. Her father remained at home, in the library that he hated to leave. Her brother slumbered in his tomb. Luckily, it didn't have to be *her* relative. In the aristocratic world, most young men married their sister's friends, so Tanry had one good option to get an introduction to Cezsario Boralda-Solkin. He had two sisters left in the world, and Tanry had done her best to research them.

Now, she and Caterina pored over *Pherson's* one final time.

"How accurate are the likenesses, do we think?" Tanry mused.

"Did you see Princess Athalie?" Caterina scoffed. "I do *not* think we can rely on these." She flicked to the portrait of Athalie that omitted her glasses, posture, and pipe.

"There's something we can take from them though." Tanry laid out the page that showed the Boralda-Solkin family, her finger landing on Archduchess Lizseta. "Some things might be exaggerated, but not fabricated. Miss Lizseta here, what are the odds she has this long hair?"

"And what about Archduchess Laurina?" Caterina asked, searching for her picture in the magazine. Laurina did not get as much attention as her sister. From what they could tell, she had the same dark hair, the same pale skin, the same slender figure as her sister. Yet she was plainer. Or at least, she was not paraded by the magazine editor as a great beauty. That was enough to spot them in a crowd, Tanry hoped.

Breakfast was indeed served on the patio in the last gasps of autumn sunshine. Members of the court ate at small circular tables that were shadowed by the voluminous hats the ladies wore. Footmen dressed like penguins bustled in between, brandishing silver trays with caviar and eggs florentine and unbuttered toast. Tanry had arrived to court with no household, so she was shown to a table alone on the edge of proceedings. She ordered eggs and caviar from a passing footman, but kept her eyes trained on the crowd.

She had expected most of Athalie's court to at least be her age. She had this idea that the blonde and pretty princess would be trailed by a series of similar-looking women who'd parrot phrases back to each other. Instead, the horde that Tanry saw at breakfast was mostly families with young children who fidgeted in their seats. There were many stern-faced mothers with big hats sat next to husbands with pencil moustaches who held newspapers as shields against their wives.

Tanry spotted Lizseta at the near centre of the patio. She was not as different to her picture as Princess Athalie had been. Her brown hair was braided on top of her head, but there was so much that the braids could barely contain it. Even the white hat she wore could not hide it. She sat up straight as a ramrod and ate her food in small, delicate bites. This was in contrast to the grey terrier who sat on her lap, yapping and attempting to gain morsels of food from her mistress' plate.

Sitting next to her sister was Laurina; Tanry thought that the editor had not done her justice. She did not have the same incredible volume of hair as her sister, but the colour was a shade or two redder. She wore a pale blue shade that complemented her skin and a hat that was far less fussy. She did not hold her fork in the correct, mannered way, but Tanry thought that was charming – and next to her sat the archduke.

He was tall, perhaps the tallest person in the vicinity even whilst seated. He was clean-shaven, had the same dark hair as his elder sisters, and was dressed in a white pressed suit. There was something familiar about him, and with a jolt, Tanry realised that he had the frame of the young man from the shadows who had been meeting Princess Athalie in the early hours of the morning. For what reason he had done that, and failed to greet her, she could not guess.

They made a solemn trio, altogether. The families around them called after their runaway children and sipped on their imported tea, but the imperial family sat quietly, keeping their eyes on their plates.

"They're a sombre lot, really," Tanry told Caterina later, as the latter was fixing the hairs she had knocked out of place over breakfast. "Didn't speak to anyone, kept themselves to themselves."

"What? Like you did?"

"I mean, it's fair enough. They were run out of their home country. It makes sense that they're a bit nervous of outsiders."

"What makes you think you can make friends with them, then?"

"You make a sound point, Cat." Tanry thought for a moment, then asked Caterina, "What do normal ladies do at this time?"

"They make calls and they take tea."

This was unhelpful. Tanry had no one to make a call on. She usually took tea in a flask while helping the tenants on their plots.

"Let's remember what we know about them - Lizseta and Laurina?" Tanry asked, consulting her journal.

Caterina shrugged. "*Pherson's* has a little. Lizseta enjoys painting, mostly landscapes. Laurina likes music. She's the problem child, or so they say. Ran her father ragged when he was still alive – sneaking out of the palace, having dalliances with young men. Wearing trousers."

Tanry snorted. "Trousers? That counts as scandal?"

"To some." Caterina shrugged. "At court, yes. Unless you are riding a bicycle, but no one here would ever do that."

Tanry put her feet up on the varnished coffee table. "But Laurina courts scandal, yes?" It was the kind of tantalising thread of a statement that could only lead to trouble.

"So the rumours say."

"That might be something that she and I have in common."

CHAPTER THREE

Courting Scandal

Dress is paramount for young ladies. Should a young lady wear a low cut gown before nightfall, or show her ankle in public, her reputation will be ruined. — Margrit Bellere's Manual for Young Ladies

Tanry reread all the magazines that mentioned Archduchess Laurina. In her home country, she had been the gossip magazine's favourite. She was attached to no fewer than three noblemen; she was known to bribe her guards to let her out of the palace; she had been caught in bed with her maids, priests, and once, the ambassador to the Nirillian kingdoms. No fewer than five tirades about her clothing choices were printed.

In short, Tanry found something in Laurina Boralda-Solkin to admire. All that was left was to concoct a meeting. For this, she decided to dispense with Caterina's hard work.

"I finish three dresses for you within a week, and not even a thanks." Caterina huffed, throwing the petticoats over her shoulder. "Don't you even dare go out there dressed in that." She raked her eyes over Tanry's rust-coloured suit.

"Why not?" Tanry adjusted her tie in the mirror, then picked out her standard boater hat, ignoring Caterina's floral concoctions.

"You already risked your reputation with Princess Athalie – you can't go causing scandal now."

"Oh, but that is to our advantage, Cat." Tanry pinned her hat over her hair, and admired her reflection. "I'll see you later." She saluted Caterina, whose mouth was open in outrage, though she did not get a chance to say anything further.

As Tanry walked through the corridors of the palace, she knew she was drawing eyes. She slowed down, basking in each outraged gaze. She even heard a gasp as she entered the library. A lady stared at her and half-covered her open mouth with her hand; Tanry knew she had been the one to make the noise, so she winked and tipped her hat at the noblewoman. That made her gasp again and drop the cards she had been playing with, ruining the game. Tanry put her hands in her trouser pockets and laughed. She had no destination in mind, but wove her way through the court with only the intention of getting as many eyes on herself as possible.

In the third room she crossed, she was caught by Athalie. It was one of those state rooms that had no apparent purpose except to impress a sense of wealth upon the viewer. Athalie had chosen it as her place to read. She caught sight of Tanry walking past, looked over her glasses as if making sure of what she was viewing, and chuckled.

Tanry bowed, feeling that one could never curtsey while wearing trousers.

"I hoped that you would change back," said Athalie. "I thought you were bold, to arrive at court as you did."

"I'm glad you approve," Tanry lied. Earning the ire of the princess would be fuel to any scandal. It might be pleasant to find that she liked Tanry's sartorial choices, but it certainly wasn't convenient.

Tanry walked another circuit of the library and one of the drawing rooms. She had no sign of her quarry. She stepped outdoors, feeling relief as soon as she was under the open sky. The gardens were impressive, with carefully sculpted parklands and an orangery with enough exotic plants to make Baroness Vetera weep. Tanry found a rose garden surrounded by high brick walls and wandered, thinking that she might take a few cuttings back to Taltois.

Just as she was considering calling the whole thing off and going back indoors, but caught sight of Laurina's dark hair at the other end of the walled garden.

The archduchess wore a hat adorned with flowers, with her hair piled up underneath it. Her white dress had a high collar and a blue sash bowed about her waist, and lacy gloves that were deeply fashionable. She looked like any other noblewoman, not an imperial archduchess. She was bent low over a cream-coloured rose, taking in the scent with her eyelids closed.

Tanry stood at the other end of the brick path. The bushes grew over it, making a tunnel over the walkway. Tanry, dressed in the colour of the garden wall, could not have been easy to see.

Laurina pulled back from the flower, and a shadow loomed

behind her. From between the shrubs, a young man appeared. Tanry didn't know him, but he was a lord, or the son of one, judging by the quality of his dress and the smoothness of his hair. He reached for the rose and plucked it. Laurina was unperturbed by the loss of the flower, but a faint blush rose in her cheeks as the young man held it up to her. Tanry thought there was no better time to interrupt. She whistled, put her hands in her pockets again, and sauntered down the path as if she had not rehearsed it in her head.

"Oh," said Laurina. Her voice was high. She reminded Tanry of a nightingale. "I didn't see you there, Lady—"

"Tanry Teneri." She stuck her hand out for either of them to shake.

Laurina clutched her fingers for a moment then let Tanry's hand fall. "We have not seen your family here at court," she said.

"No. Well, my father is something of a hermit and my brother drank himself into an early grave."

Both of them balked at her statement. She let the silence fill in, before saying, "I know who you are, Laurina Boralda-Solkin, but who is this?" She turned to the young lord.

"That is Archduchess Laurina," he said. "You should address her as 'Highness'," he said.

"I do apologise. I was never schooled in manners," said Tanry.

"That much is evident," replied the young man.

"I still did not catch your name."

"Lord Finnlay Tresswell," he said, with a distinct air of self-aggrandisement. Tanry was certain that she was supposed to recognize the name, but she hadn't studied her father's book on genealogy nearly that well. It didn't matter. He wasn't an archduchess, so he was outranked by his companion.

"Well, Lord Tresswell, I shall endeavour to be more polite in the future, though I do wonder why you believe you can speak for the archduchess."

He gaped.

Laurina watched him for a painful moment, then spoke. "Lord Tresswell doesn't speak for me."

"I'm glad to hear it. I was particularly keen to hear that you were still at court, so that I might meet you."

"Oh, well, I can't imagine why you would feel that way," said Laurina, casting her eyes to the path.

"Your reputation precedes you," said Tanry.

Lord Tresswell looked as if he were about to burst.

Tanry puzzled over the interaction for the rest of the day. She made some cursory inquiries as to the character of Lord Tresswell. He was a lord who liked to hunt and gamble, with a sizeable income and a manor house that was far smaller than Tanry's own. All very dull. She needed to catch Laurina alone.

Opportunity arose that evening. Tanry, used to working, found herself rather at a loss of what to do while her peers amused themselves. After dinner was taken, the ladies of the court withdrew to gossip or play cards, while the gentlemen smoked cigars and played billiards. Tanry felt that she belonged in neither space, so wandered into the grand ballroom with only the intention of discovering what it looked like. She walked through the semi-darkness, admiring the cold light that filtered through the windows.

"You did offend Lord Tresswell earlier."

Tanry turned towards the voice, and saw Laurina stood in

one of the ballroom's two-storey doors.

"I don't care much for his opinion, though I suspect you might have guessed that," Tanry replied.

Laurina played with the sleeve of her evening gown. "He's well-respected here," she warned.

"I know his type. He's two-a-penny," Tanry declared. She had seen them trailing in her brother's wake.

"What do you want in this place?" asked Laurina.

"Nothing in particular."

"I know liars well."

"I had heard that there was a young woman in this court with whom I might have something in common," Tanry said, taking a step closer. "Someone who wore trousers and courted scandal and didn't give a damn about decorum. Are you her?"

Laurina stared at the ground. "I am not that person anymore."

"I do have to wonder what might have happened to make a young woman change so greatly in character."

Tanry could have guessed the reason. She had been forced to flee her home country. The house of Boralda-Solkin had been the wealthiest on the continent. They had owned fourteen palaces, each more ornate than Athalie's. Laurina lived now on the whims of a princess who had never been as rich as she once was. She had lost both her parents as she fled home. Tanry thought that a change in character might have been inevitable. Though in her situation, hardly preferable.

But the young woman in front of her hardly seemed the type to arrive to a diplomatic dinner with a bottle of champagne concealed in her skirts.

Laurina glanced around, bashful. "I'm afraid that I have

hardly been myself of late," she said.

"I suppose, then, that it is only fair that we do something to remedy that."

Tanry didn't know how to bond with small talk, or over tea, but she did know how to drink herself silly and make ribald jokes. Perhaps Laurina was altered, but that did not mean she could not be altered back.

"I can't guess what you have in mind," replied Laurina, with a brush of fear in her voice.

Tanry abandoned decorum and grabbed her by the hand. Laurina stumbled, but soon matched Tanry's run. Tanry steered her into the walled garden which was heavy with the scent of a hundred engineered roses.

"What are we doing here?" asked Laurina, stepping through a trellis arch.

"What have you wanted to do here, but been denied?" Tanry asked, taking a brisk walk to the garden's edge.

"I don't know what you mean."

"My brother never denied himself anything that he wanted. To honour his memory, I've decided to do the same." She found the wall and linked her hands together. "I'll give you a leg up."

"You really can't mean to go over." Laurina laughed.

"It's the easiest way out of the palace without going past any guards."

"I can't simply run off," insisted Laurina.

"When did you last leave the palace?"

Laurina lapsed into a silence that Tanry took to mean that it had been far too long.

"You have been dulling your senses in this place, with the

cards and the curtseys and the constitutionals around the parklands," Tanry continued.

"I suppose."

"Live a little, like you used to!"

Laurina smiled a little, though she tried to hide it.

"I am only hunting for a little fun," said Tanry. "Aren't you starved for amusement?"

"I am perfectly amused."

"The girl I read about would not be amused by court dinners and evening card games. If you have not been yourself, now is the time to remember."

Laurina chewed on her lip for a moment.

"Do you promise that we will not go far?"

"I will not spirit you away, I swear it." Tanry motioned a cross over her heart to indicate her sincerity.

Laurina lifted her hand, perhaps to mimic the motion herself. Her face softened.

"I suppose one little drink couldn't hurt," she said, and placed her foot in Tanry's joined hands.

The palace was hardly in an urban centre. It was surrounded by parklands, mostly made of sculpted lawns and lakes that had been well-placed for the view. They took a brisk jaunt across the trimmed grass, and headed towards the lights of the main gate.

"What is this way?" Tanry asked, pointing at a low building along the edge of the palace boundary.

"One of the guards' buildings, I suppose."

As they approached, it became clear that it was a mess hall.

"This should be good," said Tanry. She did not knock, but

pushed her way inside. She was confronted by a wall of bodily odours. All the classics were there: feet, armpits, and breath, accompanied by the scent that can only be generated by cloistering men who have never quite mastered hygiene. The guardsmen, not in full dress, drank, smoked, and gambled as any group of soldiers are likely to do. They didn't notice the cold breeze that accompanied Tanry's arrival at first. Then, as they realised that the door was open, they turned to face her and put down their drinks as if scolded.

"Don't stop on my account," said Tanry. She walked up to the table and took the nearest tankard, finishing the contents in one gulp. It was somehow sour. "My friend and I were looking for some entertainment." She drew Laurina into the room and muttered to her, "There's no place to get into trouble like a guard mess hall."

The next day, Tanry woke with an unsurprising headache. She had made it back to her room, but still had one shoe on while lying in bed.

"Did you enjoy yourself?" asked Caterina, standing in the doorway with her hands on her hips.

"I think I got an invitation to breakfast," groaned Tanry.

"I don't know how you're going to keep any breakfast down."

"Have faith, Cat." Tanry sat up, and in doing so lost a great deal of faith in her own condition.

Caterina made Tanry a hangover cure that she swore by. It contained a great deal of raw eggs and pepper. From the way that Caterina smirked as Tanry drank it, she was certain that it wasn't a real cure, but a petty revenge for something that Tanry didn't recall saying. Her pride dictated that she drank it regardless.

She suffered being dressed in a pinstriped day dress that Caterina had worked on, reasoning that after the night's revelries, she didn't need to stoke further scandal.

The day was bright, maddeningly so, as she made her way to the patio where breakfast was served. The birds that morning had chosen to be astonishingly loud. She wished, for the first time, for a larger hat to block out the sun with.

She caught a footman who held a silver tray that was painfully reflective. "Do you know where I might find the imperials? I'm supposed to eat them. Eat with them."

The footman expressed some mild confusion, but showed Tanry through the crowd to the table where she had seen the little family seated the day before. Tanry sat down before any of them really noticed that she was there.

"Bacon and toast, please," she said to the footman, "and a very strong pot of coffee." Only after she had made her requests known did she register the looks on the faces of the party that she had joined. Two of them were caught in abject shock, while Laurina stared at her plate in rather a sheepish manner.

"Have you got the wrong table?" asked Lizseta, in a tone no one could mistake.

"Ah, no. I was invited," replied Tanry. She unfolded her napkin and spread it over her lap.

In a small voice, Laurina said, "She asked to join. I said she could."

Lizseta snorted.

Tanry welcomed that reaction with a pleasant smile. She turned her attention to Archduke Cezsario. He was not bad looking; she might not have chosen him from a crowd, but he had pretty dark eyes and high cheekbones. He was not a poor choice for a husband.

"I'm afraid that I am new at court, and keen to make new acquaintances." Tanry smiled at them all. "Your sister and I had a good evening last night."

"Oh, I heard all about that," replied Lizseta in a disapproving tone. She set her teacup down on its saucer in such a loud fashion that she made Laurina wince.

"I didn't mean to cause trouble," lied Tanry.

A footman arrived with her breakfast and coffee. Tanry was glad that Caterina had made her stomach turn earlier, so that she felt less queasy around the imperials.

"You'll forgive my sister for being hesitant," Cezsario began. "We have found ourselves in danger more than we would like, and we have trouble accepting strangers."

"I was welcomed to court by Athalie personally, if that helps." Tanry took a sip of her coffee.

"Athalie knows you?" asked Cezsario.

Tanry drank again to avoid the question.

Cezsario looked around the patio and Tanry followed his gaze. She saw Athalie in a mauve dress and matching hat. She stopped at each table she passed, greeting the diners. Tanry might have said that she was exchanging niceties, but Athalie did not construct the false smile that was usually associated with small talk. Cezsario watched her weave among the tables; Athalie noticed him watching, and bypassed the tables nearest her to join them.

"Archduke Cezsario," she greeted him. "I see that you are acquainted with Lady Teneri."

"Yes – uh – Laurina and Lady Teneri got to know each

other last night."

Laurina covered her eyes with her hand.

"I did hear that you had been visiting the guards' quarters," remarked Athalie.

Laurina added another hand to cover her face.

"I do hope they're hale enough to perform their duties this morning." Tanry chuckled to herself.

Athalie made something of a tutting noise. "I expect I shall see you at the gathering this evening," she said, pushing her glasses up the bridge of her nose.

"Gathering?"

"The princess is being humble," replied Cezsario. "She is hosting a ball this eve."

"Part of my courtly duties, I'm afraid." The princess did not look gleeful at the prospect of an impending ball. "Hosting gatherings improves morale, encourages friendly behaviour, and allows for collaboration among different groups."

"How romantic," said Tanry.

"Enjoy your meal." Athalie turned and continued her rounds of the tables.

Tanry watched Cezsario's eyes follow her across the patio.

CHAPTER FOUR

Unreturned Mirth

A young lady might develop an appreciation for art as an ornamentation, though it should never be assumed that she has a formal education, as a woman's place is not at university, as is the way in Lyalia. Other nations are reporting a decrease in focus in classes attended by women. — Margrit Bellere's Manual for Young Ladies

Tanry was sent for that afternoon. She was lazing on the chaise longue in her apartment while Caterina fussed over a ballgown for the evening. A footman in the palace livery arrived, and at Tanry's call entered the room. He brandished a silver tray with a single piece of card placed in the middle.

"A message for you, my lady," he said in a plummy voice.

Tanry rolled off the chaise onto the floor, landing on her hands and knees. She got up, noting the dust that she had got on her skirts, and used her fingernails to peel the card from the tray while the footman stared at Caterina, who swore while trying to thread a needle.

"Good day," he said, and departed.

"I think I'm about to be scolded," said Tanry to Caterina. She held up the card between two fingers. It read only: *The gallery. Two o'clock.*

"Who is it from?" asked Caterina.

"Which person here do we know to have a particular affinity for painting?"

She arrived at the gallery ahead of time. The glass-ceilinged hall housed King Ladarius' extensive – and priceless – art collection, containing some of the continent's most famous artwork. It was also as disordered as a pawn shop. Taxidermy bats hung upside-down over classical marble statues with their paint peeling away; oil portraits of Athalie's ancestors with severe gazes were hung opposite six-foot-high paintings of nude women, accompanied by innumerable silver dishes that had no obvious purpose. A person entering the room to get an education in art history was as likely to gain an understanding of human anatomy and the interior decor of exotic brothels.

Tanry took a moment to admire the collection. She hadn't had a great appreciation for art as a child. It had seemed to her that her father hoarded it with the same vague disinterest that he applied to his tenants. But she had gained more knowledge of it as she refurbished her wing. One had to develop an appreciation of aesthetics for that kind of thing; a taxidermy duck could ruin an otherwise balanced room. The king's gallery was in dire need of help in this field. It had the mood, and smell, of a junk shop. She stopped by a statue of a young woman stood atop a dying lion, and tried to arrange her features to an expression of admiration, but found that the statue was simply too grotesque to pretend otherwise.

"A favourite?"

Tanry turned and found that Lizseta had crept to her side. She had the complexion of the doll that Tanry had owned when she was eleven years old. It had been pale, and therefore not a favourite of Tanry's, who had desired a doll that looked more like her. So the doll had stayed perfect, but without any of the marks that being loved by a child left behind. With Lizseta's dark hair and delicate features, the resemblance was uncanny. Perhaps Lizseta too, was unloved and abandoned. She had that air about her, like a weight dragged on her narrow shoulders.

"I was just thinking how foul it was," replied Tanry. She gazed at the open maw of the lion. A stone tongue lolled out of the lion's maw. It looked uncannily wet.

"What need have you with us?" asked Lizseta, in the clipped voice that she had no doubt learned from her governesses.

"What need have I of anyone?" Tanry laughed.

"We are not in a position to offer anything to you, Lady Teneri."

It seemed that Lizseta suspected something of Tanry's motives, which was inconvenient. Tanry needed to say something to divert her suspicions. Fortunately, Tanry had barely done anything wrong.

"Tanry, please. You simply ask what need have I of friendship, or kind words. I merely saw a kindred spirit in your sister. Judging by her reputation, I suspect that we are not greatly different in character."

"That assertion aside, I must ask that you leave my family alone."

"What right have you to speak for them?"

"I am the eldest. I have taken care of them since we arrived here, when they were still children."

Tanry moved past the statue, no longer having the stomach for it. She came to rest by a landscape painting of a valley with a grand house nestled in the crook of a river. Charming peasants cavorted in the foreground, wrestling donkeys and carrying baskets on their heads, and looking far more pleased with their lot than they ever did in real life.

"Recognise it?" Tanry asked, nodding her head towards the painting.

"I'm afraid that I'm not familiar with the artist. This work is individual among the collection." Lizseta waved a hand around the gallery, then scratched her head in a rather inelegant manner. "You will stay away from my family," she declared.

Lizseta was behaving much like a father with wounded pride, as if Tanry was besmirching her brother's honour. Tanry at least knew how to behave like a father. In such a situation, a father would start a conversation about an exchange of funds. That was the perfect basis for a marriage contract, after all.

"You haven't even considered what *I* could offer *you*," said Tanry.

"I thought that this was only about companionship."

"I admire you for speaking so bluntly, so I should do the same. I am heir to the largest and wealthiest estate in this country. You and your family live by the goodwill of Princess Athalie. Would you not want a bond a little stronger than friendship?"

"Like what?"

"Like a marriage contract, and an entitlement to my father's position."

"For Cezsario?"

"Alas, marrying your sister is not an option."

"Would that not be trading one prison for another? Athalie's goodwill for yours?"

"I'm sure you have an understanding of that, with your history. It would be a gilded cage, if that is what concerns you. I'll even write it into the contract. Marriages for you and Laurina, if that's what you want; manors and tenants if you don't." She had a few spare on Taltois estate, though she was sure they would be a step down from the imperial palaces to which Lizseta was used. Still, the exiles from the old country couldn't ask for much more.

Lizseta stood for a moment, and while Tanry hoped that she was considering the offer, she wasn't quite so optimistic as to believe it.

Lizseta turned away from Tanry and looked at something just over her shoulder. "No," she whispered. "She can't be serious."

Tanry leaned past her, looking for someone hidden just behind Lizseta, but there was naught there. "I am very serious, but who are you talking to?" Tanry asked.

"You, of course," said Lizseta adamantly.

"No – just now, you turned away." Tanry pointed to the spot where she had been looking, but Lizseta did not turn to look, or to explain herself.

"My family will make their own way, without any interference from you."

Her skirts whispered on the gallery floor as she walked away.

"That wasn't the strangest part," Tanry reported to Caterina as she was trussed into her ballgown.

"You mean that she didn't take kindly to your overtures to her brother?" Caterina prodded Tanry with her needle and she yelped. Having run out of time, Caterina had chosen to sew Tanry into her dress rather than finish the buttons.

"It was a good offer," Tanry insisted.

"Because you took it so well when your father gave you a good offer to marry Duke Archibald?"

Tanry had to admit that she had a point, but couldn't afford to let Caterina know that. She would no doubt poke her with the needle again.

"You haven't even asked what the strangest part was," she said instead.

"What was the strangest part, if not her entirely reasonable distaste for your offer?"

"She didn't recognise the painting."

"So she didn't know the artist – what of it?"

"I didn't think she would recognise the artist. I certainly don't. It was the view I thought she would recognise. It's in a different painting at home. It's the hill above the Tenara Palace, in their home country. The imperial family lived there when their children were young. Country retreat. They sold it when they were bleeding money. Lots of paintings of the place, though." The palace had become a symbol of times past, even as the times themselves were in the midst of passing away. "I thought she would have remembered her childhood home."

"Maybe the painting wasn't a good likeness," suggested Caterina.

"I suppose that could be it," replied Tanry, even as she thought that the dark windows and graceful columns of the palace in the painting looked much the same as the painting that hung in the hallway of Taltois, right next to a portrait of Trevor.

Traditionally, ladies of the court were presented to a ball by a male escort. Tanry had left her father at home and her brother in the grave, so she entered alone. The herald, perplexed, remained silent as she stood on the threshold.

"Tanry Teneri," she said to him, nodding to the room at large. She stood atop the stairs, watching the glittering crowd below.

"Um, by what title?" asked the herald.

"Lady Tanry Teneri, if you must. You have to know my family name already."

"Oh. Lady Tanry Teneri!" he shouted, though the room hardly paid him notice.

Tanry marched down the staircase and into the throng. She hadn't attended a ball proper before. Her father had not held any. Thus far, she did not care for it.

Her arms and neck, entirely bare in Caterina's dress, were freezing, but the heavy petticoats made her lower half overheat. A ball seemed to be a lot of people making small talk, which she hated, or taking turns around the dance floor, which she loathed. She stayed on the stairs a moment too long and took stock of the situation.

Athalie was there. Her mousy hair was fashioned into a simple style, and her dress was a pleasant baby blue that suited her complexion. She had a shadow in the shape of Cezsario Boralda-Solkin. He handed her a drink without asking her or meeting her eye; he simply held out the glass and knew that she would take it.

Tanry spotted Lizseta and Laurina together by a table in a corner. Their hair, lustrous and long, was piled high on their heads, and they wore matching white dresses that, while fine, were clearly not recent acquisitions; even from afar, Tanry could spot torn and mended lace. Lizseta had diamond stars pinned in her hair and Laurina wore a glittering pair of ruby earrings. It seemed that they had not left the home country without some of their riches.

Tanry picked up her skirts and descended into the crowd. A young lord tried to grasp her by the elbow. She didn't stop to find out whether it was a polite request or an imposition he intended. Between the glossy heads of the lords and ladies she spotted that Laurina was once again ensconced with Lord Tresswell.

Tanry wove her way through the gathering and unnoticed, she approached Lizseta and whispered in her ear. "That is a little suspect, don't you think?"

Lizseta flinched as Tanry's voice rasped against her eardrums. Lord Tresswell held out a hand for Laurina and guided her to the dancefloor. He wrapped one arm around her waist and pressed his torso against hers.

"A waltz?" said Tanry. "They must truly be familiar."

"What business is it of yours?" Lizseta reached for a glass of champagne and drank a gulp, as if she needed to bolster herself for a conversation with Tanry.

"I do wonder what issue you must have taken with my suit, when you let Laurina entertain this man's attentions." Lord

Tresswell and Laurina danced around the floor, their movements smoother than water, apparently unaware of anyone else around them.

"Lord Tresswell is respectable, and has known Laurina now for several years."

"I was under the impression that Laurina was not that respectable herself."

Lizseta didn't curse Tanry for making such a scandal laden suggestion. The muscles in her neck tensed as if she was all too aware of the problem.

"Any aspersions you want to make, I suggest that you make them to yourself," she said.

"Have you considered his reputation?" asked Tanry. She knew nothing of it, except that he was a rich man, and therefore likely to have something unsavoury squirrelled away.

"What do you care for his reputation?"

"I do wonder what he might mean to your sister, and your family."

Tanry knew that she was scandalous in many ways, but she also knew that she was richer than Lord Tresswell, and money could paper over any indiscretions. The imperials would do better to hitch their wagon to her horse, than rely on someone like Tresswell. What remained was convincing Lizseta of such a truth.

Lizseta tutted. "My family's reputation is unimpeachable," she said with such conviction that Tanry laughed out loud.

"I read about your family's reputation in gossip magazines," said Tanry.

Lizseta, as befitted a wise woman who had escaped a war

that had killed her extended family, left the conversation without baiting Tanry further.

Tanry waved down a footman and procured her own drink from his tray. "She's hardly friendly, wouldn't you say?"

The footman blinked, quite surprised that he was being spoken to. "I daresay I wouldn't know," he replied.

"What do they say about her downstairs? Anything good?"

"Not much, I'm afraid."

"Really? Surely her ladies' maid has a few comments now and then."

"The archduchess does not have a ladies' maid. The imperials refuse to have any servants in their rooms at all."

"Now that *is* interesting. None at all? When their family used to be the richest on the continent."

"I don't like to gossip, my lady, but it is strange."

Tanry retreated to the wall, choosing to observe the theatrics.

Lord Tresswell, a proper gentleman, released Laurina after the waltz ended. He kissed her knuckles and released her to the safety of her sister's side.

Tanry glanced around the dancefloor, expecting to see Cezsario and Athalie taking a turn together, but they were not there. She combed the room, but found neither archduke nor princess were in sight.

Grabbing another drink, she pushed into the crowd and sought out Lord Tresswell. They had technically been introduced, though the interaction had been an accident.

"Lord Tresswell," she began, touching her fingers to his arm to get his attention. "Forgive me, I am unaccompanied and I am looking for Princess Athalie." She felt his arm tense, but he turned to her anyway.

"Is she not here?"

"She was, but now I simply cannot find her."

"Come now, we can look for her," replied Tresswell.

"Yes, you should do that, and I shall stay with Laurina. I do not see the archduke around either, do you?" She walked over to Laurina, while Tresswell, with an air of confusion on his face, wandered off to find the princess. Tanry watched him go, and as soon as he vanished into the crowd, she turned to Laurina.

"You look lovely," said Tanry to Laurina. "White is your colour." She failed to pay the same compliment to Lizseta, though they wore the same fabric.

"Where has Lord Tresswell gone?" asked Laurina in a timid voice.

"I just asked him where to find Princess Athalie. I did want to thank her for hosting, but I can't seem to locate her."

"She's taking some fresh air, no doubt," said Lizseta. Tanry frowned at that. It was suspicious that Athalie had abandoned an event that she was hosting, and it was even more suspicious that Lizseta didn't see it that way. If Athalie had little time to herself, which was likely, given her position, then a ball would be the perfect time for her to steal a moment alone for a foolish dalliance. Perhaps she met with the man who she had been meeting the night that Tanry arrived. That man was tall, just like the archduke.

"In which case, where might I find the archduke? There is also something I need to ask him."

"I'm sure that I could pass on a message," replied Lizseta with an acidic tone.

Laurina looked between them both fearfully.

"Oh, I do think it is polite to speak in person," Tanry remarked. "Look, there is Athalie now. I must go and speak to her."

Athalie had returned on the arm of Lord Tresswell. Tanry marched across the ballroom, cutting through the dancers.

"Princess!" she exclaimed. "I simply could not find you."

"I was outside," Athalie replied. "But you found yourself a messenger."

"Laurina was asking after you," Tanry lied to Tresswell. "You should go and speak to her right away."

"Good day, Your Highness. I shall find my lady." He departed, watched by Tanry.

"His lady? That sounds fairly sincere," she said to Athalie. "Though I would not guess that there is a formal betrothal in the works."

"What business is it of yours?" asked Athalie.

Tanry turned to her with a smile, though the princess did not return her mirth. "Only a passing interest, I assure you."

"Do you want me to believe you genuine?" Athalie's spectacles had fingerprints on the lenses. They were slightly fogged at the edges of the glass, like she had returned indoors in a rush.

"I do not know what else you would believe about me, princess."

Athalie considered Tanry, looking her up and down, but came away with nothing to add. She walked away, and Tanry caught sight of Cezsario. He was alone by the doors to the outside, the curtains fluttering slightly in a breeze. Tanry, by all rights, should have taken the opportunity to seduce the man.

Caterina had tried to coach her in the art of seduction before the ball, but quickly gave it up as a lost cause. It wasn't one of Tanry's strengths. The key to seduction, Caterina said, was to make the other person feel desired, important, and singular. Tanry preferred it when things were the other way around.

She walked up to him anyway.

"It's pleasant to see you again."

"You also." He smiled as if he was really delighted to see her, which Tanry took to mean that he was exceedingly polite. "Are you enjoying the ball?"

"It's my first one. I can't quite see what all the fuss is about." It was a lot of people in one room with music playing, and the effect wasn't as pleasant as many claimed.

"Oh, well I'm aware that these events aren't for everyone." He cast a glance back at his sisters. "Is that why you have come to court? Are you searching for new experiences?"

"I suppose," she said. "Though I could hardly say that I was unhappy with what I had."

"Oh?"

"A large estate. People to be responsible for. Privacy. I'm not one for the social scene."

"Not even the season?"

"No. I was never presented. I prefer it at home. It's safe. There are no big trade routes, no gatherings. If you're there, no one is likely to bother you."

"That does sound pleasant."

"I'm sure it must be, for someone in your position."

"What might you mean by that?" he asked.

"Only that you left your home country in such dire circumstances. The republic of Karda Ven must still pose a threat to you and your sisters, no? I would have thought you might appreciate a touch of privacy."

"Athalie has kept us well," he said, with an air of diplomacy.

"Still, five years in this place – do you not ever get tired?"

"The court caters to our every need. It is the advantage of living amongst the most wealthy."

"Some of them, at least," Tanry remarked. "I still prefer home, of course." She saw that Athalie was watching them.

"She's like a plughole," Tanry told Caterina later, when the latter was tearing into the seam on the back of her dress. "He can't stay away from her. Nearly every time I want to speak to him, Athalie is nearby."

Caterina mumbled, then removed her pins from her mouth to speak. "You don't think that they are attached?"

"I think they definitely are. But they cannot be attached and not engaged, lest there be a scandal."

Caterina peeled away the gown and Tanry stepped out of it, unfastening the hooks on her corset.

"Is Athalie an obstacle then?" asked Caterina.

"Only as far as she intends to be." Tanry fetched a handkerchief and cleaned the cosmetics from her face. "If Athalie wants him, she has to step up and claim him."

She turned to the discernment engine.

"There is one way to be certain of our suspicions."

She spelled out a new message on the dials.

IS CEZSARIO IN LOVE WITH ATHALIE

The dials spun and spun. Caterina leaned over to watch with curiosity.

The machine settled on its answer.

NO

"It might be too specific a question," said Caterina. "Asking if he is in love might be a stretch."

"What might be the better way of putting it?"

"We would have to know exactly how he feels to properly word it."

"That does not help us." Tanry chewed on her lip for a few moments before conjuring a new question.

IS ATHALIE IN LOVE WITH CEZSARIO

YES

"Well that is illuminating," said Tanry. "Though I don't quite know what it means."

CHAPTER FIVE

Competitive Spirit

Even as autumn approaches, Princess Athalie keeps her court well entertained with events, jamborees, and all kinds of novelty. With a princess so adept at hosting, one wonders why she continues with the same group of ladies, who are poor in both funds and noble connections — Pherson's Courtly Hearsay

The ball was cleared away without much fanfare as the court moved on to the next event. A garden party was planned for the day after, to make use of the pleasant weather before it faded away. For the occasion, Caterina produced a cream dress and matching gloves.

"You'll have to dress yourself," she announced. "I have a half-day and I've made plans."

"What has got you busy?" Tanry asked.

"There's a boy in the kitchens who has been sending me

favours," replied Caterina as she fixed her silver earrings into her lobes.

Tanry noticed that she had acquired a new velvet ribbon for her hat. "So you are humouring him?"

"Of course not, he's only a kitchen boy. But he is handsome enough, and his attentions made one of the valets jealous. If someone is taking me somewhere, they had better have enough money to be worth my time." She smoothed the front of the dress, checked herself in the mirror over the mantel, then walked to the servants' door. She closed it, and it melded seamlessly into the panelling.

Tanry dressed herself with a modicum of difficulty; she had no love for gowns that fastened down the back, no hope of fixing her own hair beyond tucking it all underneath her boater hat, and no particular clue what happened at a garden party.

From first appearances it was much like a ball during daylight hours. There were tents made from painted cloth, with folding tables loaded with food underneath. The same footmen from the night before served drinks from the same silver trays. Instead of dancing, the entertainment of the hour was a series of garden games that Tanry had played with her tenants. She recognised a game of horseshoes, but instead of the used and rusted kind that were relegated to playthings at Taltois estate, these shoes were heavy and fresh from the forge. Tanry tested the weight of one in her palm and tossed it. It landed on the pole and spun before thumping onto the grass.

"Yes, I win!" she declared.

Her competition, a pair of young ladies with whom she had just become acquainted, were focused on their own conversation, having lost interest in the game once they started losing.

"I suppose there's no prize anyway," said Tanry, though no one was listening. She glanced across the lawn, where people were gathered in well-knit groups; some playing skittles, a group throwing sacks into buckets, and children knocking down towers made of cans. Tanry was a loose thread with no pattern to follow. She wished that Caterina were there.

She looked for the only people she had met; she had not been able to organise a shoot since leaving Taltois, but she was still on the hunt. Her eyes caught Cezsario, Lizseta, and Laurina playing skittles on a mown stretch of lawn. Lizseta's scruffy terrier gamboled between them, trying to catch the balls as they were bowled. As Tanry approached, the dog ran up and circled her feet excitedly.

"Who's winning?" Tanry asked Cezsario, who looked up in surprise.

"We aren't keeping score. We couldn't find a pencil or paper."

"Well, that's no fun. I could keep score for you, if you like."

Lizseta bowled the ball, knocking down eight of the ten pins. She didn't rush to reset them. "I think we've finished with the game," she declared. "I am going to refresh myself."

Tanry took that to mean that she was going for a piss.

"Idonea-dog!" she called, and the terrier bounded after her.

"Do you want to start a new game?" asked Tanry, while righting the skittles.

"I believe the princess wanted to speak to me," said Cezsario, hesitant.

"She's right there. Princess!" Tanry raised her arm and waved.

Athalie, who had been in the midst of a conversation, looked up and scowled. She excused herself and marched over.

"Did you want a game of skittles?" asked Tanry. "The archduke wanted to play."

"No, I..." he began, but his voice trailed off out of politeness. "I hope you weren't busy."

Athalie turned to Tanry. "Are you good?" she asked.

"At skittles? Not knowingly, but I've never entered a game I didn't think that I could win."

Athalie produced a little notebook from inside a pocket in her skirt. Tanry made an internal note to tell Caterina to sew more pockets on the insides of her clothes.

"You should go first, Lady Teneri. Then Laurina, then myself and Cezsario."

Tanry smiled. "Excellent, I love a competitive spirit." She tossed the ball and caught it a couple of times just to prove that she could.

On her first throw, the ball went too far right and four skittles were left standing. Laurina reset the skittles, but on her throw missed them entirely. Athalie threw the ball without apparent thought, but knocked down all ten. She marked down the score in her little book. Tanry couldn't help but feel the bite of jealousy. It was foolish. They were only playing a game, but she resented how Cezsario cheered at Athalie's success, and the princess glanced back, passing a bashful hand across her face. Their regard for one another was an obstacle to Tanry's goals, and one that could not be overturned with a well-aimed ball.

Cezsario took his turn with good grace, not scoring higher than Athalie. Tanry nearly wrestled the ball from him before he could pass it to her. She made sure to add more power to her throw. She launched it through the skittles and it continued rolling until it hit against the skirts of a lady who yelped.

"I think I understand the game now," she told Athalie, feeling no small satisfaction that all ten skittles were scattered in the grass.

Once the ball was retrieved, Laurina threw again. Once more, she missed entirely.

"I'm sorry," she cried, clutching her hands in front of her mouth. "I'm sorry, I'm terrible at this game."

"Don't worry," Athalie said in a comforting voice.

"It's not a competition," continued Cezsario, despite the fact that it clearly was.

"Why are you apologising?" Tanry asked.

The group fell silent.

"I don't know," said Laurina.

"You're bold. Why do you apologise?"

"What?"

"I've read so much about you. You were the scandal of Karda Ven and you didn't hide in shame. And yet now, you apologise for things you need not mention."

The group was silent enough for them to hear the birds. Athalie dropped the ball, which bounced on the grass and rolled into the bushes. Though Tanry wore the lightweight dress Caterina had chosen, she suddenly felt the full heat of the day.

Lizseta traipsed back into the conversation, blinking at her siblings in confusion. Her famous hair, unable to fit under her hat, fell in its heavy braid down her back. She itched her scalp, then dabbed her perspiring temple with a handkerchief.

"I think I have left my ladies too long," announced Athalie.

"But the game isn't finished," Tanry complained.

"The weather is too hot for skittles," she proclaimed.

That was nonsense to Tanry, as it was hardly a taxing sport. "Say, I have not met any of your ladies. I should like to," Tanry suggested, thinking that Cezsario would join them.

"I suppose," replied Athalie. "Your mother was a lady-in-waiting for my mother. You may as well meet one another."

"I think we shall find refreshment." Lizseta wove her arm through her brother's.

"Won't you come?" Tanry asked.

"Laurina, come along." Lizseta scratched her head again. Tanry had read in *Pherson's* that she secluded herself once every week to comb through her hair and wash it with egg whites. The task was such a trial that it took a full day.

Tanry allowed herself to be led away by Athalie. It would be good to make other acquaintances at court, simply so she never had to breakfast alone. More than that, it would be suspicious to reject the princess' offer, when Tanry had made the suggestion. She could afford to wait. There was time enough to ensnare an archduke. Athalie took her to one of the cream-and-mint pavilions on the lawn, which had tables loaded with fetching cakes and pastries. Four ladies were seated on velvet couches that had been dragged out from the state rooms.

"Ladies, this is Lady Teneri," announced Athalie to the group.

"I prefer Tanry."

"Ah. Well, this is Lady Merrion." Athalie pointed to an elderly woman who had an air that one might describe as dotty, eyes that bulged from her skull, and a head that wobbled atop her shoulders.

"And this is Miss Katydid."

Next in the circle was a young woman, no older than twenty, who smiled widely enough that her teeth seemed to take up half her face.

"Lady Tanry, I'm so pleased to meet you!" She gesticulated enough to punctuate every word. "Your gown is simply splendid, though I did hear that you were wandering about court wearing *trousers*." She shaped the word with fascination, in the way that young girls spoke about kissing.

"Usually I wear trousers everyday."

Miss Katydid gasped in astonishment.

"Never mind about that," Athalie cut her off before she could form another sentence. "This here is Lady Bayard."

The woman she indicated was middle-aged, with kind eyes and hair that had already gone grey. Her dress was old. Tanry felt she was learning a great deal about fabrics from Caterina; she could see that the linen of Lady Bayard's blouse was worn through. It was stained on one sleeve, and the seams were coming apart on one shoulder.

"How do you do?" Lady Bayard asked.

"Well. And you?" replied Tanry, completing the ritual.

"Last of all, this is Lady Moralla." Athalie pointed to the last member of the circle.

Tanry was taken aback by her. She was dressed much like a parrot, in an orange hat adorned with violets and a dress that was lime green with pink trim. The effect was not elegant.

Lady Moralla saw Tanry's eyes roving over her apparel and stood, performing a twirl for her captive audience. "I make sure to always be ahead of the latest fashions," she said.

"I am always behind them, alas," answered Tanry.

Lady Moralla shrugged and sat back down. "I'm sure I could offer you some pointers," she replied. "So you need not wear trousers again."

Tanry decided, quite quickly, that she did not like Lady Moralla. She was quite certain that it showed on her face.

"My maid, Caterina, has all that in hand. She's quite the seamstress. I must allow her time to purchase some new bolts of fabric to show off her skills. She's been making over my mother's dresses for me. But she does make all of my trousers, and they fit beautifully."

Lady Moralla opened a fan and tried to cover her face with it, but Tanry could easily spot her look of bemused indignation.

"Is she good at that? At making things over?" asked Lady Bayard with a greedy look in her eye.

"Sit down, Lady Teneri," instructed Athalie, pushing her towards a satin covered chair.

Tanry nearly stumbled on the hem of her gown, but caught herself in time.

"So, Lady Tanry," began Miss Katydid, "what brings you to court?"

Tanry thought. She couldn't reasonably tell them the truth of the matter. She was certain that Miss Katydid would have romantic notions that Tanry's proposal would disavow.

"I suspected that it was my last chance," she said, forgetting for a moment the truth of the statement.

Athalie settled herself into one of the other seats; Tanry saw the shape of her book in her pocket ruining the lines of her dress. "What can you mean by that?" she asked, rooting through her other pockets to find her pipe.

Lady Merrion and Lady Bayard made disgusted faces, but neither remarked upon it.

"I was never presented, but I find myself on the edge of an engagement. I rather like the freedom of coming here and not having to preen for a husband," Tanry lied, whilst also telling the truth.

Athalie paused, her lit match hovering over the end of her pipe. "You're engaged?" she asked in surprise.

"Not in so many words." Tanry shrugged. "It's hardly a romantic arrangement, nor one of my choosing." She picked at the food table near her, taking a petal-pink macaron. "Why hasn't that got to you?" she asked Athalie.

"What hasn't got me?" She lit the pipe and puffed on it.

"Hasn't your father tried to get you married off?"

"Too busy with his war."

"Is it a good match at least? Is he wealthy?" asked Lady Bayard.

"Yes, but not as wealthy as me."

"You're rich?"

"Yes," said Athalie. "Lady Teneri is the richest heiress in the country."

It was a statement of fact, but Tanry decided to take it as a compliment.

Lady Bayard smiled and leaned closer to Tanry.

When it was time for the party to disperse, Tanry found herself escorted back indoors by Lady Bayard.

"Miss Katydid – does she always speak so much?" Tanry felt as if she had Miss Katydid's chirping voice running around her head.

"Always," promised Lady Bayard, looping her arm through Tanry's. "Yet she is Athalie's oldest friend, so we may never be rid of her. Do you think that your husband will allow you back to court after you are wed? Athalie really should have more ladies-in-waiting. Let's take a turn through the rose garden." She led them past a brick wall and into the garden, which was so pungent that Tanry coughed.

"I was wondering about that," she said. "The princess seems close to the archduchesses. Why aren't they counted among her ladies?"

"That's a question I've often pondered over." Lady Bayard said, as their skirts swished over the path, picking up rotting rose petals. "The imperials keep to themselves. They rarely even speak to the rest of us. I always assumed they were scared of us all."

"Why would they be scared?"

"They left their home country in such fire and brimstone. Father dead, mother dead, all of those other nobles killed. I thought that they must always have feared that someone would find them and finish them off."

"I suppose," said Tanry. "What is Cezsario like?"

"Why do you care to know?"

"Indulge me. I just met the fellow. I am only curious."

"He is good company. He was a skinny young thing when he arrived at fifteen. He was injured terribly and he hid away. But he's grown since. He's had his fair share of interest from young ladies, but their mothers always steer them away. He's no future to commend him. He will end up here forever, an ornament to the court, a curiosity to people who have forgotten the old world."

Tanry stopped to admire a rose that was nearly orange in

hue. "There's no harm in making friends with the man if he is going to be here forever."

"What game are you playing? Are you trying to talk to a young man while you have the chance?"

Tanry laughed along with her. "Oh, don't admonish me. I'm a little vain. Allow me to indulge myself. But is he not attached to Athalie?"

Lady Bayard gasped. "You mustn't talk about such things!" she exclaimed, though there was still laughter in her voice.

"Why not, when it appears evident? She is the princess. She can hardly *not* be attractive."

"It's a childish attachment," said Lady Bayard. "They were young things together, that is all."

"It would of course be scandal for the king's only child to be attached to a penniless exile."

She was hushed by Lady Bayard. They had turned a corner and come across Lizseta and Laurina, deep in conversation at the other end of the path. Lady Bayard tried to steer Tanry away, but Tanry stayed rooted.

"My ladies, I did hope to come across you again. I hoped that we might dine together."

"That won't be appropriate, I'm afraid," replied Lizseta with haste. She tried to brush away an errant hair with one hand. Sweat was beaded on her forehead. She scratched her head again and Tanry saw a slight shift in her hairline.

"Another time, then," she said cheerily, as if she hadn't been insulted. "Good day."

"Why would Lizseta wear a wig?" Tanry asked Caterina that

evening. The latter had laid down on the couch and put her feet up. She claimed exhaustion after an afternoon being doted on by a handsome man.

"Maybe she lost her hair. Stress can do that," Caterina said, between bites of the sandwich she had made herself.

"But why would she get a wig of so much hair? It's so impractical."

"Maybe she was too ashamed of losing her famous hair."

"You can't wear a wig that long everyday."

"You underestimate what people will do in the name of their looks."

CHAPTER SIX

Idonea

For two hundred years, the most sincere crime is to be found capable of projection. Astral projectionists, colloquially known as 'ghosts', able to access any room with which they are familiar, unseen except in mirrors, posed the most sincere threat to national governance. The joint council of 1456 - the only time the continental nations have signed one single treaty - decreed that all astral projectionists be executed, regardless of their alliances. — A Short History of the Continent

The next day, Tanry entertained herself by poring over old editions of Pherson's. They made no mention of Lizseta's illustrious hair being an illusion. She pondered over her problem for a moment, gazing idly around the room. When her eyes alighted on the discernment engine, half concealed with its velvet coverings, she scolded herself internally for not thinking of it sooner. There was no need to ponder over questions. She had all the knowledge in the world available to her. She stood and turned to the machine. As she did so, she heard the clatter of Caterina's sewing machine cease.

She could feel Caterina's eyes on her as she turned the dials to spell:

IS LIZSETAS HAIR REAL

The cogs spun, their brass colours flashing in the sun that streamed from her window. The output dial slowed and spelled out:

YES

"That can't be true," said Tanry.

Caterina laughed. She dashed over to Tanry's side. "All wigs are made from real hair, you have to ask a better question," she said.

"There are only so many letters, and it only ever gives short answers. I have to be circumspect."

"May I ask it a question?"

"If you think you can work it better, then I suppose you must."

Tanry stood aside and Caterina turned the letters.

WILL I OWN A SHOP OF MY OWN

She pulled the lever, but nothing occurred. The output dial refused to spin.

"I believe it cannot answer questions about the future," said Tanry. "Let us turn to the matter at hand."

She turned the dials again.

DOES LIZSETA WEAR A WIG

The dials spun in deliberation, and gave another short answer.

NO

"That still doesn't make any sense," said Tanry.

"You can't force it to give you the answer you want. She may not even wear a wig. Ask it something else."

"I could track down Cezsario, I suppose." She entered another question:

WHERE IS CEZSARIO

She watched the engine do its work, but when it gave her an answer she scoffed. "Cat, it says he's in Rindan. That's ridiculous."

"Maybe it is not the truth-telling device your aunt claimed."

"There is some thought going into it. Rindan is a real place, after all. If the machine had no ability, then it would give me a series of letters that make no sense. It just makes no sense that it is telling me that the archduke is in a farming town in Eastern Lyalia, rather than here, in Albonne."

"It's possible that the machine has made a mistake."

"I don't think it has."

"I don't understand how it works. Neither do you. Onto more important things." Caterina clicked and flashed her scissors. She had turned the main room of the suite into her personal millinery using borrowed mannequins. "I'll have to make a wedding dress if all of this works out."

"You'll have to make one if it doesn't," said Tanry, briefly incapacitated by the vision of having to hold Duke Archibald's hand at the altar. Her stomach turned.

"Yes, well. I'd have to tailor it to the situation. The groom's interests need to be taken into account."

"Don't you dare."

"You want to make a good impression on your husband."

"I have to do nothing of the sort. If I marry Duke Archibald, you sew me a fuchsia dress because that colour looks disastrous on me and he should know that I'm going to be a terrible bride."

"And if you marry Cezsario?"

"Gold, for victory."

Caterina's eyes lit up at this prospect. She spent the next few minutes sketching designs for both wedding gowns.

"You will need to dress well tonight," she said. "If we are going to pull this off."

Tanry attended the evening's symposium in the orangery on the arm of Lady Bayard, who'd sent a calling card inviting her. Caterina had dressed her up in a green silk gown with ruffles that fluttered irritably when Tanry breathed. Lady Bayard arrived in a dress that looked similar to the one she'd worn to the garden party, with new flowers fixed to the bodice, and a matching sash around her waist. There was some discolouration under her armpits.

"I'm so glad you agreed to come," she said, guiding Tanry through the throng of glittering ladies.

The chandeliers were lit with alchemic gems, enhancing the gilded leaf pressed to the walls. There were mirrors everywhere she looked; Tanry caught her reflection and had a moment of confusion. That could not be her in the mirror. There was a fine lady wearing Tanry's face and leaning on Lady Bayard's arm. It was disconcerting. Something about Tanry's image with the frilly, pale gown did not look right. This was how she was meant to appear. She was meant to look like a fine lady, an heiress, but it looked wrong anyhow. Tanry thought that she was meant to wear hunting tweeds, to look like her brother. She shook her head and turned back to her companion.

"I hoped to make friends at court, so it would pay to attend the events where they are."

"Yes, and Lord Bayard and I would love to host you. We are court veterans."

Tanry knew the hungry look in her eye. She did not care for it.

The orangery was lit with a hundred of its own alchemic crystals glowing amber. Plants with waxy leaves reflected the wavering light. It was humid and Tanry could taste dirt on the air. At the centre there was a square pool with dark waters broken by the backs of frolicking fish.

Lady Bayard was speaking to her, but Tanry had no interest in what she was saying. She wandered to the brick edge of the pond and played her hand over the water. The fish scattered, leaving Tanry to look at her own unsettling reflection. She was caught by it, like a character in a fairytale. Behind her, a figure moved to stare into the water. She was tall and pale with dark hair that hung loose around her face. Her look was contrary to courtly fashions, so Tanry met her eyes, intrigued. As Tanry saw more of her, her appearance became stranger. She didn't wear a gown, but a dark purple jacket with two rows of silver buttons. Tanry didn't recognise the uniform, nor the notion of a woman wearing it.

She spun around, looking for the woman, but there was no one of such strange sartorial sensibilities behind her.

"Who are you looking for?" asked Lady Bayard.

"No one. Though look there, it's the archduchess." She pointed across the pond to where she could see Lizseta standing alone, her hair hanging in a heavy braid from her crown.

Lady Bayard clutched Tanry's arm, just above her glove. "Let us not speak to her."

Tanry pulled away. The only reason she was at the damned event was to find the imperials and become friendly with them. It was not working so far, but it couldn't hurt to speak to the archduchess again. Another conversation with the archduchess was another step closer to the archduke. She had no time for Lady Bayard's disapproval.

"I have met her eyes now. I have to say hello at the very least."

Of course Lizseta was pretending that she had not seen Tanry at all. Undeterred, Tanry marched around the pond and struck up a conversation.

"I've no understanding of music," she said. "Is Laurina here to tell me what to listen out for?"

Lizseta grunted. "She is feeling quite under the weather."

"I'm sorry to hear that. I should bring her something to cheer her tomorrow."

Illness was the perfect excuse to stop by. Tanry could bring her some gift – grapes, probably – and seem like a generous, kind-hearted spirit. It was unfortunate, that Lizseta was scowling at Tanry as if she had just threatened to bring her sister a plate of manure.

"I've given instructions that no one is to disturb my sister," said Lizseta.

"I'll make sure not to be too disturbing."

Musicians in black tailcoats filed into the orangery, shining instruments in hand. The court, with an understanding of implicit signals that Tanry could not discern, moved to take their seats in the silver chairs laid out for them. Tanry stuck close to Lizseta's side, like a bee after jam, so they were shuffled into two chairs next to one another. Lizseta glanced around them, no doubt looking for a saviour from her predicament, but found no one to free her from Tanry's company. The orchestra struck up a tune that Tanry didn't recognise. It was grand, like a march, and filled the orangery with an unpleasant din. Tanry winced.

"Can they not play something more mellow?" She resisted the urge to plug her ears with her fingers.

"Hush, I am listening."

Tanry felt a tug on the back of her glove, above the elbow. She turned and saw Lady Bayard seated behind her. She gestured to an empty seat on her right hand side, but Tanry shook her head. The music got louder as a troupe of horns joined the fray.

"How can this be pleasant to listen to?" Tanry muttered.

"How have you not heard this tune before?" asked Lizseta.

"I don't frequent symphonies."

"It's Stallino's most famous piece."

"He's from Karda Ven, isn't he?"

Lizseta nodded. "They're playing it wrong."

"I don't care for it."

"Stop talking and go away," Lizseta whispered. "I want to listen to the music."

"I don't want to sit next to Lady Bayard," complained Tanry.

"You came here with her."

"And I moved away for a reason. I'm not flush with options

for friends."

"If you were more tolerable, I doubt that would be the case."

"You make that sound as if it isn't the work of a lifetime."

Lizseta itched her head again, then dabbed her forehead with the edge of a handkerchief. Tanry suspected that the humidity was making her uncomfortable.

"Please," Liszeta hissed. "What have I done to deserve your attention, Lady Teneri? And what will I have to pay to be divested of it?"

"I have already told you what I seek. It is far more about what I can do for you than what you can do for me."

"My family is not interested in any connection to you."

The flute section trilled so harshly that Tanry did briefly plug her ears. They were joined by an intolerably excitable percussion section, which sent discordant thumps through the floor.

Tanry slumped into her chair. It was useless to be polite to Lizseta, she thought. The archduchess was determined to keep Tanry away. This made little sense. Tanry was the richest heiress in the country, and the imperials had no money. Funds spoke louder than anything else. Yet Lizseta brushed her off persistently. She had her own secrets, though Tanry could not use the engine to guess what they were. She didn't need to ask the engine when she had Lizseta in front of her, and she had never feared the repercussions of being rude.

"Why do you wear a wig?" she asked.

Lizseta caught herself mid-gasp, then tried to pretend that she had been breathing normally. "What rumours are you spreading?" She glanced to her left, to an empty spot of tiled floor. "No," she whispered. "She can't..."

"Who are you speaking to?" asked Tanry.

Lizseta froze. "You, of course," she said, "but I don't care to continue." She stood, although the symphony was far from over. Eyes roved in their direction. Lizseta raised her hand to her forehead, as if to pretend that she was feeling faint. Without delay, she picked up her skirts and rushed towards the door.

Tanry, having run out of patience with the music, darted after her. She followed Lizseta through the bent arms of tropical plants, which cast strange shadows around them. Lizseta broke into a run, passing through the orangery into the mirrored hallway. Footmen lined the room like statues, or suits of armour in an ancient castle. Their eyes flicked as Lizseta dashed past them. Tanry jogged after her, but found her dress was like a net around her legs. She slowed to a halt and watched the train of Lizseta's dress wind across the marble tiles.

"Damn," Tanry said. "She's running in slippers too." She glanced to the nearest footman. "Do you know what's up with her?"

The footman's eyes widened. He glanced to his fellows, though they remained staring straight ahead. "I could not say, Lady Teneri."

"That's very diplomatic of you. I'm supposed to win her over, but I think it's a lost cause."

"Can I fetch something for you?" asked the footman.

"Oh, nothing. I'm just going to get away from that racket."

She already felt better, only a room away from the orchestra. She nodded at the footman, and once more caught her unsettling reflection in the mirror. In the corner of her eye, she saw movement. It was only for a moment, but she swore it was the woman in the purple uniform.

Her suite was thankfully quiet, apart from the rattle of Caterina's sewing machine. Tanry nearly tore her dress in her rush to get out of it. She pulled on her velvet dressing gown, hearing the rhythmic tap of Caterina's pedal against the floor.

She stood in front of the discernment engine. Her notebook, open on a nearby table, was covered in dozens of questions about Lizseta's hair, none of which had borne fruit. She considered the sight of the woman in the mirror. She turned the dials on the engine to say:

WHO IS THE GHOST

The machine came alive, twisting and spinning its cogs until the question disappeared, and a word appeared on the output dial.

IDONEA

Tanry snorted. For reasons she couldn't discern, There was an astral projectionist spying on the court, one with the same name as Lizseta's dog. That was a connection, though Tanry couldn't be sure of what it meant.

IS SHE WATCHING LIZSETA

The dials spun. When the machine did this, Tanry imagined that the machine was deep in thought, though she supposed it had little resembling a brain. The answer it decided on was short.

NO

Tanry turned to Caterina. "If you had a dog, what would you call it?" she asked.

"Bobbin," Caterina replied.

"That was fast."

"I've thought about it before."

"Would you name a dog Idonea?"

"A four-syllable name for a dog? Feels a little clunky, but it's not entirely strange, I suppose."

"Why would Lizseta name her dog Idonea, when that is the name of an astral projectionist?"

"Where did you see this projectionist, exactly?"

"In the water in the orangerie, and then in the mirrors. She was looking at me, I could have sworn.

"If someone else were to see her in the mirror, she would be executed no doubt. It must be worth the risk for her," said Caterina.

Tanry returned to the engine, lost in thought. She entered a new question:

WHY IS THE DOG NAMED IDONEA

The engine spun satisfyingly, but the output dial whirred so fast that Tanry could not read the answer it gave her.

"What does that mean?" asked Caterina.

"I think that I've asked a question too complex for it to properly answer. It's no good at giving any opinions." She pulled the lever down and the machine went still.

"Do you ever think that you are asking the wrong questions?"

"Constantly," said Tanry. "But there's some exact things I can find out."

She found a notebook, then returned to the machine.

WHAT IS IDONEAS SURNAME

STRADER, it replied.

That wasn't a noble name, but it proved that she was a real person.

WHERE IS SHE

VENI

Tanry laughed aloud.

"Someone from home must be bringing them messages," she said. "Who can say why – I didn't think they had any friends left in the capital of the republic. And she didn't look like a noble."

"What did she look like?"

"She was wearing a uniform, I think. Military."

"A woman? In the military?"

"They do that sort of thing in their home country," said Tanry. "They let them attend universities too."

"How radical of them."

"Don't believe what you hear. They barely fund the poor girls who attend. It is still a question as to why there is an astral projectionist consorting with Lizseta at all, when that is the most reviled crime on the continent."

"Ask the engine. I certainly don't know." Caterina returned to her sewing. She paused, her scissors hovering over a thread that was about to meet its doom. "How can you be sure that the ghost is consorting with Lizseta? Didn't the machine just say otherwise?"

"I cannot think of another reason for the dog and the projectionist to be named the same thing, but I may as well prove it."

She arranged the dials once more.

WAS THE DOG NAMED AFTER IDONEA STRADER
YES

"There you go. Sometimes it is merely a case of asking the right questions."

"I suppose," said Caterina, "though that hardly proves that

they know one another."

"Then I merely shall have to ask again."

She arranged a new message, and pulled the lever.

IS IDONEA KNOWN TO THE IMPERIALS

YES

"There you have it," said Tanry. "She's involved with them somehow."

Caterina nodded to show that she understood, but turned back to her work. She had sourced a rich, golden fabric that shone under her fingers. She pored over it when it arrived, like a king with a chest of freshly minted coins, like she was entranced. She could get like this, sometimes, when there was a project that diverted her attention more than others. Any other subject of interest was ignored, in favour of whatever gown had captured her heart.

"In your novel..." Tanry began.

"I am busy," said Caterina.

"Just quickly – in your novel with the astral projectionist, what did the hero do to escape?"

"Nothing."

"What?"

"There was nothing he could do. He was watched every moment. It only ended when the ghost fell down a staircase because he was projecting somewhere and he couldn't see where he was actually walking. It wasn't a very good ending."

That wasn't helpful to Tanry, but there was another thought in there that disquieted her.

"If there was a ghost watching us right now, would I know?" Tanry asked. Caterina looked around the room.

"You'd need more mirrors to be sure of that. But unless

someone knows the interior of this room well, then you're unlikely to be watched."

Tanry suspected that she was trying to be comforting, but Tanry couldn't shake the idea that Idonea Strader might be staring over her shoulder as she covered the discernment engine.

CHAPTER SEVEN

A Mutually Beneficial Arrangement

Young ladies should never attempt to enhance their beauty through artificial means. Gentlemen want to know exactly what kind of lady they are engaging with, and use of powders, rouges, wigs, and tinctures are grievances as sincere as lying to a gentleman directly. — Margrit Bellere's Manual for Young Ladies

Athalie's birthday rolled around with more pomp and splendour than Tanry could understand. Athalie herself seemed unmoved by the lavish decorations and expensive gifts delivered to her. The palace filled up with foreign dignitaries, diplomats, and every member of the gentility who could afford the journey. Tanry found no good excuses to spend time with the imperials, and instead found herself sought out by Athalie's inner circle.

Miss Katydid insisted that she eat breakfast with her everyday while she nattered on about her horses, her brother's new wife, and her maid's way of speaking that confused her. She was escorted to social events by Lady Bayard, who had a lot of questions about the size of Taltois, and the breadth of Tanry's income, and invited to play cards with Lady Moralla, who only ever opened her mouth to talk about whatever confection she was dressed in.

One evening, after failing to spot Lizseta or Laurina at the card table, she asked the discernment engine another question:

IS ATHALIE WATCHING ME

It turned and spun and landed on an answer quickly.

YES

She trudged back to the parlour, where Caterina was working hard at her two wedding dresses, which looked like unfortunate, headless twins on their mannequins.

"Athalie is having me monitored. That's why her ladies are everywhere I try to go."

"It would make sense," admitted Caterina. "You are still convinced that Cezsario is her beau, correct?"

"Yes, though the machine still won't confirm it." All possible combinations came back with useless spinning or dull silence.

"Have you tried simplifying the question?"

"Don't you think that was my first port of call?"

"Try again. Stop touching that." Caterina batted Tanry's hand away from the golden dress.

"I'm beginning to think it doesn't work. Since we arrived, it had barely given out an answer that makes sense. It might just give out words in a random combination, and sometimes they're right. It's a probability engine, nothing more. There's no mind behind the cogs."

"I wouldn't know anything about that," said Caterina, in a manner that meant she considered the conversation over. Tanry frowned. Caterina turned the wheel of her machine and fed the fabric through so fast that Tanry feared that she was about to sew through her hand.

"Do you not have any idea of the engine's ability?" she asked.

"I'm not an expert in machines, you know that."

Tanry watched her for a moment more, hoping that Caterina might say something else, and offer some opinion on the discernment engine, and help her work through the problem. Now she had her dresses to distract her, and Tanry held less interest.

Tanry couldn't help but feel glum about it.

"I'll have to rely on my own skills," said Tanry. "Tonight, at the ball, I'll wager that Athalie and Cezsario will wander off alone. I'll have to make sure that they get caught in the act."

The ball, another grandiose affair, featured no fewer than three musical quartets, so wherever the guests walked, there was no escape from noise and chatter. Tanry once again found herself in the company of Athalie's ladies, who sat on the edge of the dance floor. Word had apparently travelled – no doubt via Miss Katydid – about Tanry's engagement. Or so Tanry assumed, because she was not asked to dance by any young or eligible men. Lord Bayard, in all his gallantry, asked her to dance, though she turned him down. Miss Katydid sat on the edge of her seat, tapping her foot, chewing on the inside of her cheek, and watching the dancers with a distinctly worried air.

"Take Annabilla to the floor," Tanry told Lord Bayard. "She's far too pretty to stay here being a wallflower all evening."

He agreed, and Miss Katydid leaped up and followed him to the dance floor. Beside Tanry, Lady Merrion cackled.

"I know," said Tanry. "Dancing with a married man is hardly what she was looking for, but I couldn't stand how she was bouncing her leg."

Lady Merrion snorted. Tanry watched Miss Katydid, who danced in a group with Lord Tresswell and Laurina.

"Now, why aren't they betrothed?" asked Tanry, "Lord Tresswell and the archduchess?"

"No money," said Lady Merrion. She smiled widely enough that Tanry could count her missing teeth.

"If Cezsario made a good match, that could be solved, of course," said Tanry.

An idea sprang into Tanry's mind. She waited for the dance to be over, and for the partners to perform their obligatory bows to the ladies. Then she cast a glance around for Lizseta, who sat at a table with only the company of her dog, who ate foie gras off her plate. Tanry skirted the dance floor until she was behind Laurina and Lord Tresswell, who departed the floor leaning on one another. Tanry picked up her pace until she was in step with them.

Lord Tresswell sighed when he saw her. "To what do we owe the pleasure, Lady Teneri?"

"I was simply wondering why the two of you still find yourselves unattached."

Laurina blushed.

"I'm sure that it's no business of yours," replied Tresswell.

Tanry steered them close to a flute quartet, so their conversation, while terribly impolite, would not be overheard.

"I've no interest in your opinion, Lady Teneri," said Lord Tresswell, holding Laurina's arm tightly. "Please do return to your companions."

"Is it money?" asked Tanry.

"What can you mean?"

"The imperials have no money. Does your father require a wealthy bride?" Tanry laughed. "My father requires an old name and a high rank."

Lord Tresswell bristled.

Laurina rubbed her thumb over his arm in a comforting manner, though it did little to improve his mood.

"Again, I need to remind you that this has naught to do with you." he said.

"I doubt that. But Laurina – must he continue to speak for you? I have a proposal that would interest you."

"There is nothing of interest you can propose," insisted Tresswell.

"I know of a way for you to be married, if that is what you desire."

Laurina's face brightened.

"She's not speaking truthfully, darling," said Tresswell.

"What would your father say if Lady Laurina had a connection to a wealthy family? Say, one residing in Taltois. He might be far more inclined to allow you to wed."

Lord Tresswell was stunned into silence, though he continued to scowl at Tanry.

Laurina found her voice. "How would I get that connection?"

"Taltois is one of the richest estates in the country. My father might not be prominent at court, but he is a wealthier man than any of the people at the ball. All that you need is a Teneri to wed a Boralda-Solkin. Such a thing would have seemed impossible a decade ago."

"You are already engaged, Lady Teneri," hissed Tresswell.

"An engagement is not marriage. There's no certificate, and there have been no banns. My father has agreed to my choice, provided the candidate matches his requirements. The archduke fits the bill."

"This is terribly forward of you," said Laurina, though she did not seem disturbed. She was maybe even impressed.

"I consider myself a terribly forward person. Where is Cezsario? Is he enjoying the ball?"

Laurina gave a cursory glance around the ballroom. "I can't see him."

"Convey my proposal to him, won't you? Bless you both."

She did her own circuit of the ballroom at pace to make sure that Cezsario was not there. Neither was Athalie, though Tanry didn't expect her to appear. She didn't waste time asking people where Athalie had gone.

Among the flood of people moving back and forth, Tanry went unnoticed as she dashed through the halls and back to her suite. Caterina was not there, having taken advantage of Tanry's absence to bother another gentleman caller, so Tanry went right to the discernment engine and in a rush turned the dials to ask:

WHERE IS CEZSARIO

The dials swirled. Tanry waited, half-expecting them to turn endlessly as they sometimes did. Then they settled into one word:

RINDAN

Once more, the discernment engine was giving her the name of that backwater town, which made no sense. By all means, Cezsario could not have flown there from Albonne. She did not believe, not really, that the machine was making a mistake, but it was not being helpful either. If she lingered on this question, she would not be able to find the archduke as quickly as she needed.

She changed tack, and asked:

WHERE IS ATHALIE

The machine stirred, but rather quickly it settled on:

LIBRARY

This answer made sense. Tanry picked up her skirts and dashed back to the ballroom. She was out of breath and sweating, but she didn't need to make a good impression for her to scheme to work.

"Lord Bayard!" She caught him as he was leaving the dance floor. "I find myself quite in need of fresh air – would you and your wife accompany me out?"

"Of course!" he replied eagerly, beckoning to Lady Bayard.

Tanry grasped her by the arm and steered her away from the doors to the terrace.

"Did you not want to step outdoors?" asked Lady Bayard in confusion.

"There are ever so many people out there still, and smoking mostly. The library should be a bit more quiet, don't you think?"

"That's very wise of you, Lady Teneri."

Together, they departed the revelry and delved into the quiet sea of the palace corridors. It was but two turns to reach the library, which had been shut tight to defend against the celebrations. Tanry pressed on the handle and slipped inside.

"Are you a keen reader?" asked Lady Bayard in a hushed tone, though she didn't know there was anyone else nearby.

"Only on some subjects," admitted Tanry. "Agriculture, hunting, horse breeding."

"That's so... fascinating."

Tanry marched into the room on the pretense of looking for books, mahogany bookshelves rising around her like trees in a forest.

"Let me find that section," she announced. She had no notion of where that section might be, but she gazed down every aisle until she heard the hum of muttered voices.

They were ensconced among the historical books, seated in the crook of a window, knees touching. Their only light was the ember in Athalie's pipe, so they could not have been reading.

Tanry didn't know how to gasp dramatically or convincingly, but she sucked in air between her teeth in a clear attempt. It was not loud enough that Cezsario and Athalie heard her, but it did not matter; Lord and Lady Bayard caught up and saw what had made her pause.

Lady Bayard gasped properly. "Princess!" she cried. "Our apologies, we did not expect to see you here."

Athalie stood. Cezsario moved away from her as quickly as he could without running. He picked up a book and flicked through the pages, as if to pretend that he was there to peruse it and naught else.

"I needed a moment from the ball. I ran into the archduke by mistake." Athalie's lie sounded rehearsed. She didn't stumble over the words once, as someone taken by surprise might have.

"Of course," said Lady Bayard.

"No," replied Tanry. Now came the test. Who would Lady Bayard defer to, her princess, or her new line of credit? Tanry continued. "It is most improper that you were alone with a man. Though you can trust, princess, that loyal subjects such as we can keep your secret." She caught Lady Bayard's eye.

"Yes," said Lady Bayard. "You can rely on our discretion."

"There is naught to be discreet about," said Athalie.

"We would not want to damage your reputation, Your Highness," said Lord Bayard. "But we should leave, regardless."

"Yes," said Tanry. "Happy birthday, Your Highness."

Once they were free of the library's hold, Lady Bayard looped her arm back into Tanry's and giggled. "That was quite shocking, wasn't it?"

They turned back to the ballroom, Lord Bayard in their wake.

"You mean to tell me that you did not guess that already? They are hardly subtle with their affections." Tanry laughed.

"I suppose I did know, but it was far easier to turn a blind eye when they were not in front of us."

"You know, I thought that might be the case," said Tanry.

In the ballroom, they found Miss Katydid sitting at a table alone. "What has got you so entertained?" she asked as they sat down.

"Oh, we should not tell you," said Lady Bayard.

"It was about Athalie," said Tanry in a low voice.

"No!" Lady Bayard hissed, her former deference vanishing

for the moment.

"Was it the archduke?" Miss Katydid asked, a glint in her eye.

"See, Lady Bayard, she guessed it right away. No need to keep the secret."

"It isn't proper," insisted Lady Bayard.

"They are always going off alone," muttered Miss Katydid, "but she is the princess, and they are more discreet than others." She nodded at Laurina and Lord Tresswell, who were dancing another waltz.

Across the ballroom, Tanry saw Cezsario enter alone. He wove among the tables and the dancers to find Lizseta. He scratched the terrier under the chin and sat down next to his sister.

"Don't mind me," Tanry said to her companions. "Lord Bayard, your wife has not danced in quite some time."

He smiled and reached for his wife, and Tanry used their distraction to hurry away, making it to the imperials' table before either of them could make a hasty exit.

"Lady Teneri," said Cezsario, standing out of politeness.

"Archduke, archduchess." She nodded at Lizseta, who pretended that she hadn't noticed Tanry's arrival. "I do so hope we didn't cause you and the princess a great disturbance."

"The princess is not easily rattled, you must know," declared Cezsario with a hint of pride in his voice.

"Be that as it may, I would hate for her reputation to be ruined. Of course, there is quite a simple way to undo all this."

Cezsario furrowed his brow. Lizseta, meanwhile, turned her attention fully to Tanry.

"Do not listen to her, Cezsario," she instructed him. "She is full of madcap schemes."

"You mean to tell me that you have not even informed your brother of my proposal?" Tanry laughed in disbelief.

"It was such a triviality that I felt no need to inform him of it."

"If you should change your mind, the archduke should know what his options are. I, were I married to the archduke, would provide your family with funds to live in luxury."

Cezsario gaped. "That's kind of you, Lady Teneri, but—"

"It isn't meant to be kind. It's meant to be a mutually beneficial arrangement. It deserves thinking about, does it not?"

"I— I do suppose so."

"Very good. I shall depart, I think. You know where to find me, should you come to a decision."

Tanry spun, ready to get back to her room and sink into a tub, but something caught the back of her skirts. She turned back, but Lizseta had let go of her dress only a moment after she had grabbed it. She stood, her terrier in her arms, and drew close to Tanry's side.

"I think I shall walk you back to your rooms, Lady Teneri. I shall retire for the night myself."

"Oh, splendid," said Tanry, though she found the change in Liszeta's demeanour disquieting.

They walked back together through the ballroom, briefly drawing the eyes of the Bayards, before arriving in the mirrored corridor. Lizseta's arm was wound tightly around Tanry's, so that there was no chance of escape.

Tanry glanced into the mirrors. She saw a shadow, though only for a moment, passing behind them. It was too fleeting to be certain, but Tanry knew, without perhaps knowing for certain, that they were being watched.

"Say," Tanry began, "what fault do you truly find in me?"

"Such a question reveals your lack of perception."

"No, I know there is more to it than my supposed rudeness, my brash nature, and my unseemly request."

"You cannot know all of that and still act as you do."

"You imagine me to act with shame, which I have sworn an oath never to do. No, I know that I have been uncouth, because that is my way, but I also know that there is more to these proceedings."

Lizseta glanced at the footmen that lined the walls. Though they did not stare back, Lizseta cringed away as if they bore the eyes of demons. She grasped Tanry and dragged her along with surprising strength; Tanry was caught in her wake.

Lizseta led her to the orangery, which, without the alchemic lanterns lit, was enthroned in shadow. Tanry could see the lampposts beyond the windows, casting long orange lights on the surface of the fountain. Moonlight streamed through the roof, adding a cool glamour to Lizseta's pale skin and dark hair. She set the dog on the floor. It had a velvet collar and leash that was quite at odds with its scruffy hide.

"I have more sway with Athalie than you know," she said. "I would take care not to threaten me, Tanry Teneri."

"Because Cezsario has an eye for Athalie? Would she protect him over her honour – when she will need her father's permission to marry him? If her reputation meant less than his affection, they would already be wed."

"You have no understanding of the situation at hand."

"I understand enough. If a scandal brews, do you imagine that your family will come away unscathed? At what point do you think that Athalie will find you to be more of a burden than a curiosity?"

"What makes you think that you are more valuable than I? Scandal can touch you just as easily."

Tanry laughed. "Do you imagine that I care? I would die for a good scandal right now. Anything big enough to end an engagement."

"I don't want to be part of your game."

It was useless. Lizseta was resolute. Tanry needed her unnerved. She needed to make Lizseta scared. She would not think that Tanry's offer was her best option if she was comfortable, if she thought that no one knew her secrets.

"Why do you wear a wig, Lizseta?" Tanry asked.

"Archduchess," she insisted, though her voice lacked any conviction.

"Is it really?"

Lizseta snorted. "You should not pry, Lady Teneri. I lost my hair five years ago. If you had seen the things that I had seen, hair would be the least of your concerns."

"You see, that is what Caterina – my maid – said, but I had a different opinion. I just wondered why you would choose to wear such a heavy wig."

"It's none of your concern." She looped the dog's lead around her hand and turned around the corner, ready to hide among the jungle plants.

She should not have turned her back on Tanry. She could not have realised how serious Tanry was, or she would not have done so.

Tanry's hand darted out and grasped one of Lizseta's plaits. It was soft in her hand, like a silk ribbon. Her hair was so long that she didn't notice until the cap over her head was already slipping. Tanry put both of her hands on the hair and pulled. It was held on with pins that burst free. They fell across the floor and danced like stars, and were lost among the flower pots. The cap came off with the wig. Both landed in a soft puddle on the floor, with barely a sound to mark their passing.

Tanry had one moment of fear, thinking that Lizseta had been truthful in her proclamation. Yet when she looked, Tanry saw that Lizseta's head was not bare. Instead, she was crowned with bright blonde curls. This was not a false blonde, either. Caterina had once fried her hair with bleach; it had come out orange, and within a week there had been a line of darkness at the roots.

Lizseta threw her hands over her head, though the idea of covering her secret was laughable.

"You did not see anything," she said.

Tanry resolved that no reply was needed. Lizseta already knew all that there was to know about Tanry, and could guess her actions from that very moment.

She picked up her wig and with clumsy hands, she set it poorly on her head. She turned, using the dark glass of the orangery window to set her hairline straight. Idonea-dog worried at her feet, running back and forth under her skirts. She could not right the heavy wig without help; Tanry thought for a moment about reaching over and holding the wig in place, but could not think of a kind way to do it.

Tanry watched Lizseta tuck blonde pieces of hair away. Her eyes shone, and Tanry suspected that she was holding in a sob.

Tanry turned away, feeling absurdly like she was intruding on Lizseta's privacy by seeing her so. She watched her own reflection, until something moved in front of her. Though no one stood in between herself and Lizseta, and no shadow was cast over the floor, a face leaned over Lizseta's shoulder, dark eyes were fixed on Tanry. The figure's skin was pale, like a real ghost, and her hair dark. If not for the uniform, she would have looked like an imperial.

For the first moment since meeting them, Tanry understood the fear that the imperials had once struck in their people, and the fervour which had fuelled their extermination.

CHAPTER EIGHT

The Beast Inside the Machine

Emperor Cezsario Boralda-Solkin III was executed with his wife in the morning, in the main square of Veni, to a cheering crowd of thousands. Agents were sent promptly to retrieve the three surviving imperial children, though they were unsuccessful. The monarchies of the continent would do well to remember this tragedy, and never ally themselves with the murderous republic.
— Rackham's Treatise on Continuing Monarchy

"Destroy that fuchsia gown," ordered Tanry.

Caterina did not jump to her command, but rather stared at her, perplexed, her mouth full of pins.

"I am going to marry the archduke," declared Tanry. "Because now I know what is wrong with him."

"Is it his liaison with the princess?"

"It is far worse than that." Tanry tore the coverings off the discernment engine. She didn't quite know what to ask it. She was confronting someone nameless, voiceless, who always wore a mask. Yet the engine tended to interpret things literally, without explanation. She turned the dials.

WHO PLAYS LIZSETA

"What can that mean?" asked Caterina, having dispensed with her work to peer over Tanry's shoulder. It seemed that Tanry had finally found a question interesting enough to distract her from her work.

"You'll understand," said Tanry. The dials spun, as if the machine was in thought. They danced before her eyes, and she chewed on her cheek, uncertain of whether the beast inside the machine understood her meaning.

Without warning, the output dial spun and gave its answer. It produced another single word, though it held little meaning for Tanry.

"Bridget," she read aloud. "Her name is Bridget. There aren't many imperials named Bridget."

"What does that mean?"

"The imperials – such as we call them – have never encountered the king, have they?" asked Tanry.

"The imperials have been in residence for five years, and the king has been on campaign for six."

"That fits together rather neatly. The king is the only man at court who knew the imperials well. He fought with the Emperor Cezsario when they were youths. He met the family several times. He has never verified the identity of the imperial children here. They have only been received by Athalie, who might have no way of understanding who was an imperial, and who was not."

"What reason would any impostor have to take the place of

the imperials, especially when they're in exile?"

"Why would anyone do anything? Riches, wealth, a con beyond compare. It is one thing to arrive, take the place of the imperials fleeing their home country, but why stay for five years, and not even squirrel a jewel away from the palace?"

"Do you know all this for certain?"

"I know that Lizseta – that is to say, Bridget – wears a wig over her natural blonde hair. I know that she is watched over by a projection, though where it comes from I cannot tell. I know that Athalie and Cezsario have an attachment but refuse to wed."

"Is that not on account of his poverty?"

"I do suppose it could be, but Athalie strikes me as someone who would have her way regardless."

"And you would know," said Caterina.

"There is only one way to be certain that they are impostors."

"Torture them until they reveal their true selves?"

Tanry ignored her and rearranged the dials on the engine. She asked it:

ARE THE IMPERIALS IMPOSTORS

It replied:

YES.

Tanry didn't let Caterina dress her for bed. Instead, she changed into one of her hunting suits and her softest pair of boots. She departed into the palace corridors, followed by her reflection in the walls, like she was haunted by her own personal projection.

She knew the way to the imperial chambers, having

learned their location from Caterina, who had a liaison with a footman who brought books to Lizseta on occasion. It was in an out-of-the-way part of the palace, close to the gardens. Tanry waited, rocking back and forth on the balls of her feet. She knew that she stood on a precipice, as she was about to do the most significant and risky thing she had ever done.

No footmen passed her. No maids. The alchemic lanterns on the wall faded and died.

She straightened her jacket, then seized the door handle. She didn't know what she would have done had it been locked.

Knowing how unwelcome she was, she was quite surprised to find that no one awaited her. She stood in a rather cluttered parlour. There was a pianoforte that had gathered dust on its closed lid. A mirror hung over the mantel with a piece of brocade thrown lazily across it. On a desk by the window, there was a smattering of writing papers, upon which were scrawled childish sums. There were books, all cloth-bound and inexpensive. Tanry flipped over the cover of one and saw that it was a book of poetry, a subject of which Tanry knew little. The cushions on the armchairs and couches were all collapsed or moth-eaten.

"Hello?" called Tanry into the space. "Have I blundered into an empty room?"

There was a crash, followed by a flurry of footsteps. From one of the doorways, Laurina sped into the room. Her long hair had come loose from its pins. She hadn't changed out of her ballgown, but it was creased on one side, as if she had been lying down.

"Oh, I quite forgot about you," admitted Tanry. "I was looking for your brother, or failing that, your sister."

"But you didn't knock." Laurina gaped at her.

"I do not think that I am welcome, so knocking seemed rather a pointless endeavour."

"My siblings aren't here."

Tanry considered Laurina in the new light she had discovered. Her hair seemed real enough. Her eyes were dark, just as they should have been, her figure slight, her chin narrow. The only thing that gave Tanry pause was her character. The girl who had been caught drinking port during a church service had become so demure that she did not even have the will to order Tanry out of her quarters.

"Do you know where they went?" asked Tanry.

"They were still at the ball, I thought."

"I'm going to wait here for them."

"I really don't think that you should."

Tanry ignored her and sat down on the couch under the window. "Why aren't you out dancing with Lord Tresswell?"

Laurina shrugged in lieu of an answer, then asked, "Do you mean what you said? About helping Lord Tresswell and I get married?"

"I'll make it happen. After tonight, anything will be possible."

Laurina shifted on her feet.

"Why don't you go and find your siblings?" Tanry asked.

"I think I won't."

They were interrupted, thankfully, by the door opening. Cezsario stood there with his arm around Lizseta's shoulders. She was tearful, and held a handkerchief to her face. Idonea-dog escaped from her arms and ran to Tanry, jumping at her knees, then sticking out its pink tongue and licking her boot. Following the path of her dog, Lizseta saw Tanry. She did not stare with a look of abject horror, but rather an expression of resignation.

"You changed," she said.

"Yes, Bridget," replied Tanry. "I did."

Cezsario gasped, but Bridget was far from surprised. She peeled her wig back from her scalp and dumped it on the floor, then shook out her blonde curls.

"What do you think you know?" she asked.

"See, that depends," said Tanry.

"On what?"

Tanry looked at Cezsario. "On what you are willing to offer me."

Bridget sat down opposite Tanry. Behind her, Cezsario covered his face with shaking hands.

"Not a chance," said Bridget.

Her refusal didn't matter anymore. Tanry had quizzed the discernment engine for half an hour and learned everything she needed to know. The engine had never lied to her, she just didn't understand what it was saying. Now she knew everything about them, and she could use it against them.

"Your name is Bridget Mathieson. You are twenty-five years old. His name is Valentin." She pointed at Cezsario. "Couldn't find a surname. That was odd. But her name is Matfey D'Aubey. You are from Karda Ven, but you aren't the imperial family. Based on your behaviour, I would wager that no one knows."

"What proof do you have?"

"I don't need proof to start a rumour. I have persistence."

"How do you know all this?" Valentin asked. He ran his hands through his tidy hair, despite the oil holding it in place.

"I have my methods. That's not important. I have a deadline and I am getting impatient. I'm willing to keep your secret once we wed. Otherwise, the secrecy won't be worth my while," declared Tanry.

"No," said Bridget.

"Shouldn't we consider this?" asked Valentin. He put an arm around a crying Matfey.

"You are not marrying yourself off for us. It's too great a price," insisted Bridget.

"And what happens if she tells?"

"I won't let you do it."

"I'm not fifteen anymore, Bridget. I can protect this family," said Valentin.

"No."

"I'll do it Lady Teneri. I'll marry you."

Tanry stood and held her hand out.

Valentin looked at her, blinking.

"Go on, shake it."

He took her hand and shook it, though his grip was uncertain.

"I'll draw up the contract before noon," she said. "Wedding before the month is out."

VOLUME TWO

CHAPTER NINE

The Heir to the Empire

The last emperor of Karda Ven lacked an heir for many years, the empress having only produced daughters. This made for an uncertain future for the empire, a fact which was easily weaponised by its opponents. It was easy to argue that a republic was for the better when there was no heir to inherit the empire. When Cezsario Concerto was born, it was to become the heir of an empire that many had long decided should cease to exist. — Gara Thien's Treatise on the Republic of Karda Ven

The foolish Lyalian summer refused to end. Back home, it would have been cold already, with the first frost of winter on the ground.

The harvest was underway, and Rindan swelled with passing farm hands. There were thrice as many people in the farming town as usual. Like Zsari, most of them were travelling souls, coming across the plains for occasional work, before they went back to their cities. They assumed that Zsari too came from Martois or Albonne, and none of them suspected that he had walked over the mountains from Karda Ven.

Zsari liked the crowds. It was easier to hide among them. He could talk to dozens of people and not tell a single one his name.

The evening dawdled into nighttime, and the Ridgeways held a dinner at their farm. They had a surplus of potatoes and made a stew for all the farmhands. There was some festival approaching that Zsari didn't understand, and all the village girls were chattering and glancing at young men over their hands.

"What is happening?" Zsari asked of the man next to him. They were seated at folding tables on the field next to the farmhouse. Zsari had eaten one bowl of stew and stolen another. "Why are there so many young women whispering and giggling?"

The farm hand next to him was from three villages over. He was a burly sort, with a scar on his upper lip that he'd got from falling on a fence as a child.

"They want to make choices for the festival," he said.

"What?"

"Haven't you had a harvest festival before?"

"Forgive me – I'm from Karda Ven," said Zsari.

"My condolences. At the festival, the girls get to pick a partner for the night. They get tied together with ribbons at the wrist. There's a lot of marriages in early winter."

Zsari grimaced, which made his companion laugh.

"You can always refuse. But it does look like you're attracting some interest." He nodded to another table where Milla sat with two other young women. Their heads were leaned close, and they made surreptitious glances in Zsari's direction. Milla was a farmer's daughter, and Zsari was sleeping in her parents' hayloft.

"God," said Zsari. "There's no chance she's looking at you, is there?"

"I'm married. She knows that."

Zsari set down his spoon. "I'll be leaving then," he said.

"I'd love to have your problems."

"You wouldn't," Zsari warned him.

He walked across the fields to the farm as the sun was going down between the mountains. The sky was coloured pink and there was a chill to the air that made Zsari believe autumn might finally make itself known. The farm was deserted when he arrived, marked only by the noise of chickens just out of view.

In the barn, he climbed the ladder into the hayloft and took stock of his possessions. Once he'd gotten his coin, it was best to be on his way, so it was wise not to carry too much. He only had clothes with holes in them, and one pair of boots that he'd repaired as many times as possible. His blanket and pallet he'd borrowed from the family.

He figured that he would travel north for the winter, find a tavern on the highway that needed more hands, and try to sleep somewhere indoors.

He laid down on his pallet and wished for a bath to soothe his aching limbs. He was about to put out his lantern, when he heard the creak of the barn door.

"Hello, Val?" called Milla. Zsari had been sentimental when he'd chosen a false name in Rindan. Until recently, he had avoided using any names of friends from the home country.

Zsari leaned over the edge of the hayloft and saw her standing on the barn floor.

"What?" he asked.

"I was looking for you," she replied.

"What for?"

"I'm sure you've heard about the festival next week."

"I am thinking that I should be on my way before then."

Milla looked at the ground, crestfallen. "Oh," she said. "Well. You would have been welcome to stay."

"I can't stay in a barn over the winter."

"You wouldn't have to stay in the barn, necessarily," said Milla in a way that Zsari could only describe as suggestive.

"I will be moving on," said Zsari.

"I understand," she replied. "I – I just need to put something in here."

Zsari furrowed his brow. There was nothing that Milla needed to put in the barn. It was nearly dark and his lantern didn't throw enough light for him to see what she was doing. She went into the dark at the other end of the barn, where he knew there were crates lined against the wall. Milla was down there for a moment, then she returned, casting a guilty glance up at Zsari in the hayloft.

He waited until she was gone before he dashed to the ladder, lantern in hand. He shuffled down the middle of the barn until he found the piled crates at the other end. At first glance, there was nothing amiss, but when he looked behind the crates, there was a small, hand-sewn bag hung on a nail. He could tell that Milla had made it. It had careful stitches along the handle in yellow thread. He felt as if he were about to intrude on something sacred and private. He reasoned that if it were her diary, he would simply not read it. He opened the top of the bag and saw a small packet of paper. Setting down the lantern, he spread the pages on top of a crate. It was a collection of three pamphlets, each preserved by Milla's careful hands. He read the title: *Pherson's Courtly Hearsay.*

A gossip magazine. He understood why Milla was hiding it. Her mother was obsessed with her daughter's propriety, and no doubt Milla would be scolded even for looking at such an item. Such things had existed in Karda Ven, but they had stopped being fun once the tensions became too fraught. He flicked through the pages of one issue, looking at the carefully printed illustrations. They were mostly pictures of beautiful people in beautiful clothes, with captions that praised their humility or their grace.

Zsari wasn't greatly interested in the fashions of court. This was a world he could leave to Milla, for whatever fascination it held for her. He was about to close the pamphlet when he saw his own name printed on the page. It was in a caption under a drawing of a young man.

The Archduke Cezsario Boralda-Solkin.

That was his name, but that was not his picture. The man in the drawing was taller, leaner. It was not a perfect likeness, but Zsari could guess who he was looking at.

"Valentin," he muttered. "I thought you were dead."

CHAPTER TEN

The Most Thrilling of Gossip

A young lady on the cusp of engagement should not indulge in smugness, or glee. The task of marriage is a daunting one, and requires careful preparation. — Margrit Bellere's Manual for Young Ladies

Tanry didn't know the proper decorum for announcing an engagement.

"Typically we would have the princess' permission to wed, and she would make the announcement at her leisure," said Valentin over their breakfast.

Tanry was enjoying wearing her own clothes again. She had her dark spectacles on, and the brightness of the patio was pleasant, rather than painful. "Why should the princess protest our engagement? No part of this is amiss."

"Except for your lack of courting," said Bridget. Idonea-dog sunbathed in her lap, completely at odds with the powerful rage possessed by her owner.

"Hardly the most thrilling of gossip. I'm rich and he's not. The most classic of marriages," said Tanry.

"People will talk."

"Oh no. How terrifying."

"You will draw attention to us," hissed Bridget.

"Only for a moment, then we will depart to my estate and live in relative anonymity."

"You don't know what you do."

Tanry sighed, and turned to Cezsario. "Archduke, there is the princess. Best make your announcement now." She nodded at Athalie, who was performing her morning rounds of nodding at the diners on the patio.

"I really don't think this is wise," he complained.

"Go on, you want to get it over and done with."

Valentin stood and cleared his throat, but he hardly cut through the hubbub.

Tanry sighed. She picked up her crystal glass and rang her knife against the side. Across the patio, heads turned in her direction, most shooting expressions of disgust. She stayed seated and nodded at Valentin. He understood the instruction, though she could tell he railed against it.

"I hope you are all having a good morning," he began. "I have a small announcement that I care to make."

Now all of the court were turned on him with looks of curiosity. The ladies in their wide hats and the gentlemen with their slicked back hair bore their eyes into Valentin, who adjusted his neckerchief for no reason.

"Lady Teneri and I have become engaged."

The court was not prone to great fits of drama. They only engaged in dramatics behind closed doors, in hushed tones, with one eye trained on the exit. They didn't gasp in the manner of actors in a play, but performed dark looks to their next door neighbours. There was an unenthusiastic round of applause.

"Thank you," said Valentin. "Lady Teneri and I do appreciate your recognition and your support."

He looked at none of the people to whom he spoke. His gaze was drawn, like a fish on a line, to Athalie.

The princess didn't betray any hysterics. If she did love the man, Tanry could not tell by looking at her in that moment. She turned about and walked through the palace doors. Two guards followed behind her at a respectful distance, and she was gone.

"He needs to be a bit more excited, or people will start asking questions," Tanry told Caterina.

The fuchsia gown had been removed from its mannequin and lay in Caterina's scrap basket. She was now concentrating on the gold wedding gown, which was mercifully high-necked and loose. Caterina had somehow sourced a matching gold veil to complete the ensemble.

Tanry could only dread the expense of the thing.

"It's hard to imagine why he's so anxious, seeing as he's madly in love with you," said Caterina sarcastically.

"It's not as if most aristocratic marriages contain an ounce of love," replied Tanry. She straightened the collar of her jacket and smoothed down the lapels. "It's really a wonder how they haven't gotten caught before. Bridget especially, with the ghost, and the dog, and the wig. She's a liability."

"Work on her, then."

"What?"

"Get rid of the wig, get rid of the ghost, get rid of the dog. If those are the things that will give her away, get rid of them."

"I'm not going to kill her dog. I'm not a monster. But the rest – it's not a bad plan. I'll have to think on how to get rid of an astral projection. The other sister is easily dealt with. I've lined it all up. She wants to get married to this young man whose father wants her to have a dowry. That I can provide."

Caterina sighed.

"I suppose you'll be wanting a trousseau for the young woman and all."

"Couldn't hurt to provide one. It'll be a show of good faith. I have a trunk with the Teneri crest that will really emphasise the connection."

"And I suppose I'll have to be in charge of sorting that," said Caterina.

"It can't be me. We want her to *like* her trousseau."

Tanry got to work on what she considered the simplest task she had to fulfill. She knew even at that early hour, Lord Tresswell would be playing billiards (the discernment engine had informed her).

There was no explicit rule against women entering, but Tanry felt the taboo in the air like the haze of blue cigar smoke. She steeled herself. She knew how to play billiards. At Taltois, it was her domain. There was no reason for her to be cut out on account of being a woman. She played better than Trevor, after all.

The room was panelled in mahogany, including the ceiling, which gave it a cave-like atmosphere. This was enhanced by the brass lamps which hung over the billiards table, which Tanry felt were akin to stalactites. It was not busy, but four or so gentlemen played with Lord Tresswell, who was taking a shot so ambitious that Tanry laughed. The cue shook in Tresswell's hand and glanced off the side of the ball.

"Do you mind?" asked Tresswell, enraged.

"My apologies, but I needed a moment with Lord Tresswell." She looked at the gentlemen who circled the table, leaning on their cues. They gave her identical confused expressions.

"Go on, then," she instructed them. "Give us the room." They continued to stare at her. "I will not leave until you let me speak to Lord Tresswell alone."

They made a calculation. Perhaps Tanry's oddity unnerved them, or perhaps her reputation had preceded her. They left while Lord Tresswell turned to the arduous task of chalking his cue.

"Lord Tresswell, I'm sure you heard the news from Archduke Cezsario."

"Yes, it was rather a surprise to us all," he said.

"You do understand how this improves your position."

"I'm afraid that I don't."

"You want to marry Archduchess Laurina. Now, you can do it. Tell your father."

"I think that is a touch premature," said Lord Tresswell.

"How so?"

"You aren't wed yet. Forgive me, but this may fall apart before long."

"Consider it, at the very least. I don't know what else you can do in your situation."

As it stood, he was unconvinced, but Tanry was not concerned. She had a feeling that Laurina might do all the convincing for her.

She departed, hoping that she might tell Laurina the good news. She didn't know where to find her, but supposed that she might begin at the imperial suite. She had to make good on her entitlement to visit them, after all.

She knocked on the door but didn't wait for a response. A footman stationed along the corridor stared at her like he witnessed her kicking an old dog.

"Laurina?" she called to the room, though it was empty. She knew that the footman was no doubt listening at the door. "Laurina? I have good news."

She counted the doors in the suite. There was a tiled bathroom, of the modern variety, with brass taps and a flushing lavatory. There were three bedrooms, all empty and all cluttered. One was panelled in dark wood: a young gentleman's room with books of poetry on the dressing table. There was an adjoining dressing room, though it was missing the bed where a valet might sleep. Tanry already knew that they kept no servants, though she supposed that she now also knew why.

She took a cursory look around the other bedrooms, which were light and airy, much like the occupants lived inside a meringue. In Bridget's room, Tanry ran her finger along the edge of a box of paints. The brushes had fine, unstained hair, and the watercolours were smooth and unmarred by droplets. A sheet hung over the mirror. Tanry picked up the edge of the fabric and pulled, and the fabric fell in rivulets. Like a child, she was mesmerised by the motion of it, so much so that she did not look at her own reflection.

When she caught her own eye, she noticed the face that loomed over her shoulder and her heart leapt with shock. An instinct, born in her by hunting, made her close her hand tightly and throw her fist into the glass. Cracks split from her knuckles, and Idonea's face broke into pieces. Tanry swore. She spun around, but of course there was no one behind her. She heard the door open and a voice called out:

"Who is there?"

Tanry knew from the sombre tone that Bridget had arrived. Tanry felt her hand sting as she flexed it, and imagined that shards of glass were creeping in below the skin. She marched back into the parlour, where Bridget stood perplexed, playing with the frayed sleeve of her dress.

"What do you think that you're doing here?" she asked.

"I was looking for your sister, but the ghost has to go."

"Ghost? I don't know what you mean."

"Don't play coy; you are infuriatingly unsubtle. You are in contact with an astral projectionist, and that makes you close to revealing yourself."

"You are making no sense."

"What kind of archduchess consorts with a projection? Let alone one that looks like that. Get rid of her, or I will be forced to take action."

"What action could that be?"

"Don't tempt me. I can get creative," Tanry warned. She was eager to leave before Bridget noticed the broken mirror.

"I would caution you, Lady Teneri," said Bridget, "against

causing so much ire when you have few lasting connections at court."

"Because *you* have so many connections, Bridget. What can you possibly do to me?"

She inspected her hand in the corridor, with the nosy footman looking on. She had indeed gained several small cuts, though there was no long shard buried in the soft spot between her knuckles.

"There's a broken mirror in there," she told the footman. "Have someone remove it."

She went back to her own suite, hoping that Caterina had not had the poor thought to go out.

"You got your needle to hand?" she called to the room at large, trying to examine her knuckles in the better light.

"I daresay your maid always has a needle in her hand. She is quite the accomplished seamstress."

Dread grew in Tanry's stomach as her gaze was drawn to the couch. Princess Athalie was there, wearing a plain lilac gown and seated on Tanry's couch, her hands folded neatly in her lap.

"I had her fetch some tea," continued Athalie. "She went off to the kitchen."

"You didn't send your card. So forgive my surprise."

"You must forgive my own surprise at breakfast." Athalie shook out a handkerchief and held it out for Tanry, who took it cautiously, as if she were facing down a wildcat.

"I do suppose that a little surprise is warranted," said Tanry. "We have hardly been courting openly."

"Yes. Quite. Well, I wanted to rectify the mistake so I came for tea. Sit down; we can talk about arrangements."

Tanry sat down, folding the handkerchief around her hand, feeling as if it were more than odd to be speaking so casually with shards of glass in her hand. It was even more odd, she supposed, that Athalie had failed to comment on her injury.

"What arrangements?"

"For the wedding, of course. There's your other fiancé to deal with, but I suppose that you've a plan to sort that unpleasantness. I'm happy to take the matter in hand. A letter with my seal, and Duke Archibald would never dream of spreading scandal."

Tanry chuckled. "I don't care about scandal, Your Highness. I'm well used to it, and therefore it isn't good fun for the scandalmongers."

"Well, I suppose that is sound news for you. I have sent a missive to your father already, as I suspect it will take him a little time to get here."

"Why would he come here? He has not visited court since he played with a wooden sword."

"I insist on hosting the wedding for you. Archduke Cezsario is such a dear friend, it would only be right that I threw an event worthy of our friendship."

"Oh, Your Highness, that's really not necessary. I am certain that we don't need a lavish affair."

"Nonsense! It's only what you deserve. I will have my tailor run you up a gown, and for the archduchesses as well."

Though her words seemed friendly, there was a strange harshness to Athalie's tone, as if she was threatening Tanry with talks of new gowns.

"There will be no need for that. Caterina is almost done with my wedding dress." She gestured to the golden gown on its mannequin.

"Let me do this for you. A bride can have two gowns. I'll throw you a ball for your wedding eve, and you can wear a new gown then."

"Oh, well if you insist. Anything but fuchsia."

"Wonderful. We shall throw an event worthy of this town. Your love deserves to be celebrated, does it not?"

"I swear, we are humble people. We don't need a fuss."

"The wheels are already in motion. Do let me know when your father writes back. I shall have a suite prepared for him and his household." She stood without needing to be excused. "I shall be in touch."

Before Tanry could protest further, she swept from the room. Tanry sat there, feeling the blood drip from her hand, and was surprised from her reverie by Caterina returning through the servant's door with a tea tray holding a steaming pot and a platter of small pink cakes.

"Where did the princess go?" she asked.

Tanry shook her head. "She didn't stay for tea. She only came here to tell me that she'd written to my father and that she plans on hosting the wedding."

"That's good news, isn't it?"

"Why would a princess, who is perhaps in love with my betrothed, want to host my wedding? She wants me where she can keep me, and she wants my father here too. She wants me curtailed, Caterina."

CHAPTER ELEVEN

Mirrored the Stars

In the last days of the empire of Karda Ven, the imperial family reduced their public appearances. For some years, they faced threats from their populace; their eldest daughter was once shot whilst on parade. Her resilient blood pulled through, and she survived, but Emperor Cezsario became more determined to ensure his family's safety. His corps were successful, to the point that when the emperor was executed, his children could not be found. — The History of an Empire: Karda Ven

Athalie was relentless. For two days, Tanry could not step out of her suite without a footman arriving with some missive from her. She was dragged to the offices of Athalie's tailor, who resided permanently near the princess' apartments. He made Tanry stand in her chemise and pantaloons while he ran a measuring tape all over her body. Athalie insisted on taking meals with Tanry and agonising over the details of flowers, seating, and cutlery arrangements; Tanry came away with none of her wishes recognised. The guest list ballooned, as Athalie thought it pertinent to invite every exiled member of the imperial court of Karda Ven who now resided in Lyalia. Many of them had never even set eyes on Archduke Cezsario. Of course, now they never would.

Tanry was convinced that this was an elaborate battle of wills. With every arrangement, every decision made, Athalie pointed out that it was not too late to turn back.

"If you're overwhelmed planning a wedding," she said after Tanry sniped at the tailor, "you have to remember a marriage is much more toil."

"I wish that she would just tell me right out," said Tanry to Caterina that evening. "I wish she would tell me that she wants me to back out of it."

"She wouldn't do that. She was born in this place and bred by it. She knows that politeness is the only currency she possesses. She will never be so blunt as you," replied Caterina.

However, Athalie was not nearly so much of a problem as the ghost. Her name, it seemed, had been given to Bridget's dog in a clever ruse to allow Bridget to address her astral companion in front of others. Released from her veil of secrecy around Tanry, Idonea no longer solely appeared when Tanry caught glances of her in a mirror, but she appeared, purposefully, leaping into Tanry's view, as solid as any other person, though no one else could see her. She always wore her purple uniform with the brass buttons that shone. Sometimes she had a matching cape and a helmet tucked under one arm. Tanry couldn't help but imagine who she was. Caterina's novel had illustrated some of the finer points of astral projection. Usually, an astral projectionist appeared as a ghost wearing whatever clothes they happened to be wearing at the moment.

"That aspect was a problem in the novel," said Caterina, focused on sewing a hem, but filled with energy at talking about her favourite entertainment. "The young man appeared to the heroine in a state of undress when she was not expecting it."

"And she fainted?"

"She fainted."

Absent-mindedly, Tanry turned the dials on the discernment engine, though she didn't know what question to ask of it.

"Why was he projecting to her while he was naked, anyhow?" Tanry asked. Caterina rolled her eyes.

"He wasn't naked, but he was missing a few buttons."

"Scandalous."

"It was a little contrived, I admit. Idonea Strader must be always wearing the same clothes, if she is always appearing in them. She must go somewhere in Karda Ven, have some sort of life. We have to assume that she is always wearing the same clothes, wherever she goes."

"What sort of person never changes their clothes?"

Caterina shrugged. "Maids," she said with a grimace.

"No," said Tanry. "If she was a maid, she would be far too busy doing her work to project herself to another country."

"That's probably true. One has to assume she makes some sort of living. There are no nobles in Karda Ven anymore. She must be a very talented projectionist to be doing something else with her body, and have her mind watching things over here."

That gave Tanry an idea. She turned back to the discernment engine and spelled out a new question:

WHAT IS IDONEA DOING NOW

She pulled the lever and the dials spun. The output dial gave her one, unsatisfying word:

PATROL

Though Tanry didn't know how to interpret the engine's response, it soon became apparent that Idonea was alert enough to follow Tanry around. It began that evening when she walked to dinner, and saw a flash of purple in the corner of her eye. She saw her again in the dark glass of the windows as Tanry returned to her suite. There were footmen positioned at every corner and she didn't dare address Idonea in front of them. She needed somewhere private and she had no desire to bring Idonea's attention to the discernment engine.

She wandered outside. The night air was still oddly balmy, and Tanry wondered when autumn would finally make itself known in Albonne. She strode into the rose garden, which was deserted except for a few nocturnal bugs.

"Show yourself," said Tanry. Her words fell empty on the air. There were a few alchemic lights hung on the walls of the garden; the rocks inside of them were blue and needed changing. The effect of the dim light was that every plant cast long, sharp shadows. Despite her good sense, Tanry's imagination conjured horrors about what could be hiding behind the rose bushes.

As a child she'd been frightened of the dark, until Trevor had taken her outside with a collection of alchemic rocks. He broke the seals on them all at once, then used his slingshot to catapult them into the flowerbeds around Taltois so the gardens mirrored the stars in the night sky. Tanry thought it was wondrous. The next day, Mrs Button made them both collect all the rocks, because if they broke any further, they would set fire to all the shrubs.

"Come out!" Tanry shouted. She spun around but saw no sign of Idonea. There were no mirrors nor pools of water. The ghost was invisible to her, but Tanry had the uncanny feeling that she was being watched, and that Idonea was enjoying her misery.

"You have to show yourself eventually."

"Do I, now?"

Tanry was so startled by the voice that she jolted. She spun around, looking for its owner, but saw no one in the dark. It was only a moment later that she remembered that Idonea didn't need to show herself. She could hide herself, should she choose, and Tanry would never know that she was being watched. The only thing she could hear was the wheeze of breath between her teeth.

"I thought you were tough," hissed a voice in her ear, and Tanry flinched. She swatted the air near her ear, but of course there was nothing there. She heard Idonea's soft laugh.

When Tanry turned again, Idonea was standing there, a polished helmet under her arm, a gleaming pistol holstered on her hip.

"You are easy to frighten, it must be said."

"Anyone is easy to frighten if you follow them in the dark," said Tanry, defensively. "Don't you have things to do in Karda Ven?"

"Everyone needs a hobby."

"What business does any of this have to do with you?

What concern is it of yours that I would marry?"

"You are inserting yourself into our business. Don't pretend otherwise."

"Who are you? Who are you to them?" She tried to reach forward and strike Idonea, but her hand passed directly through her shoulder, as if Tanry had touched nothing but a shaft of light.

"I am family, don't you understand? I made them safe when they left Karda Ven, and I have been keeping them safe ever since. They are mine, as much as anyone can belong to anyone else." She said this, strange as it was, with an easy smile. She was confident of her power over Tanry, that much was clear, but Tanry's attempt at touching her had cemented a notion in her mind.

"If you want to own them, Bridget, Matfey and Valentin, then you must leave Karda Ven and claim them. You may see all, but what else can you do?"

"You'd be surprised, Tanry Teneri," said Idonea, "how much I am willing to torment you."

Idonea was, unfortunately, right.

Tanry was playing chess with Lady Bayard in the library when Idonea appeared behind Lady Bayard's shoulder. Tanry jolted so hard that her chair scraped along the floor, making the most intolerable noise. Then, when she was undressing to step into a steaming bath, she saw Idonea's dark eyes reflected in the water. Tanry yelped and spun around, but as she turned, Idonea appeared in front of her nose. She reeled and collided with the side of the porcelain tub, cracking her injured knuckles on the tiles. She cried out, and had to face the embarrassment of being found naked and nursing her hand by

Caterina, who, rather tactlessly, found the tableau a touch amusing.

She was woken in the night by a high-pitched whining. She rolled over to see Idonea's head disembodied upon her mattress, bloodless and strange. As soon as Idonea saw Tanry's groggy expression, laughter burst from her mouth. This happened three further times in one night. The last time that it happened, Tanry found that she could not return to sleep.

She tried to consult the discernment engine, but could not conjure a question short enough for the problem at hand. Instead, she wrote to her father, praying that he was reluctant to leave his experiments at Taltois. She begged him to bring books pertaining to astral projection, though refused to offer an explanation.

On the third day of this torment, Tanry stepped out for a game of court-mandated croquet. Safely engaged, she was free of the long skirts and pigeon bodices, and Caterina had allowed her to wear cricket whites and her straw boater. She felt no need to play the game, so breezed past the footman who held out a gaily painted croquet mallet for her. She found the imperials – or the impostors, she should term them – cloistered at the edge of the game, wearing their threadbare summer clothes, which Tanry had seen before at Athalie's garden party.

Tanry saw Idonea, like a beetle in her purple uniform, among the white linens and silks. She had no compunctions about letting Tanry see her now, and the outdoors suited her. There were no mirrors in which she could be spotted by unsuspecting croquet players. Bridget's gaze was also dragged to Idonea, though she attempted to pretend that she was staring idly into the crowd.

"This cannot stand," Tanry announced as she arrived to the party.

"What can't? Our loss at the game?" Bridget pointed at her ball, which was languishing under a rhododendron bush.

"Idonea cannot stay," said Tanry.

Bridget blanched. She wrapped her dog's lead around her hand. "You have no right to take my dog away from me."

"I do, when your dog risks revealing you everyday in this intensely mirrored palace. We have a great deal of work to do, as Athalie is turning this into a monstrous affair."

"She is?" asked Valentin, who had previously been disengaged in their conversation.

"I can't be certain, but I am half-convinced that she is trying to scare me out of continuing. She's invited half the country."

"We can't see half the country. What if the king attends?" gasped Matfey.

Bridget hushed her with a hiss. "My thinking exactly. I don't want to see the whole country. I don't want dozens of nobles from the old country arriving and recognising that you are not who you say you are. I need you – Archduke – to talk her out of such ridiculous plans," said Tanry.

"What can I do?"

"Don't play the fool. I caught you in the library with her, and what is more, I knew that you would be there. Convince her to scale back these plans, or be prepared to be arrested as an impersonator."

Across the green, Miss Katydid shrieked and hopped up and down as her ball struck the central post.

"She will not listen to me," said Valentin softly. "She feels betrayed."

"Then make an effusive apology. You're a charming young man; I'm sure you'll figure it out."

"Don't speak to him like that," said Bridget.

"I shall speak to him how I like, because Princess Athalie is visiting me so frequently, I might let something slip."

Bridget's eyes widened in fury, but her mouth remained tightly shut.

"I am perfectly willing to hold up my side of the bargain. I do want to offer you better lives than you currently possess. I have spoken to Lord Tresswell already," declared Tanry.

"You have?" asked Matfey, her eyes glistening.

"I am willing to pay your dowry," said Tanry. "You can marry the man, though I cannot see the appeal."

Bridget held her hand up to stop her talking. "You cannot marry that man," she said with her hand on Matfey's arm. "It would endanger us."

Tanry groaned. "No more than you are already. Hitch your horse to his carriage and he will have to protect you. It's in the vows."

"If you marry under a false name, you'll find that the law isn't so kind," Bridget warned.

"Who is using a false name now? Laurina, tell Lord Tresswell that his solicitor should draw up a contract. My father is on his way – he will add his stamp to the document."

"Lady Teneri, this is not wise."

"Lizseta, I have heard your advice. Deal with Idonea, won't you?"

She did not. Tanry woke past midnight, her sheets damp from

sweat. She rolled over, expecting to see a head on the other pillow. It was empty, but the sense of disquiet didn't leave her. She sat up.

Idonea was there, dark hair falling over her face, her pale skin ghastly in the cool light. She smiled.

"Get out," whispered Tanry.

Idonea shook her head.

"Get out!" Tanry shouted. She grasped the edge of her pillow and threw it. It soared through Idonea's stomach and thumped against the wall.

The ghost gave a little snort and the edges of her mouth curled.

"What can I do to get rid of you?" asked Tanry.

"You have a wonderful estate, Lady Teneri," said Idonea. Her accent was common, her voice deep.

"I have worked hard for it."

"Go back there, and leave what's mine alone."

Tanry had no opportunity to tell Idonea that keeping her estate relied on a marriage to Valentin, as she vanished before her eyes.

CHAPTER TWELVE

Too Many Variables

It is recommended that young ladies do not overburden themselves with mirrors. Seeing their reflection only serves to promote vanity.
- Margrit Bellere's Manual for Young Ladies

She ordered a footman to fetch her as many mirrors as possible and claimed that Caterina needed them for a dress fitting.

Before long, they appeared with long mirrors and Athalie's tailor, who glared at Caterina as the footmen carried the mirrors into the suite.

"I am happy to help you with the fitting, Lady Teneri," he said.

"We will be fine, thank you," said Tanry.

"Yes. All is well here," added Caterina. "And you should attend to your sleeve. You are missing a few stitches there."

He furrowed his brow, but refused to answer her. "Will

you need them for long?" he asked Tanry.

"I'll send them back as soon as we are done." Tanry ushered him from the suite. They emptied the dressing room of standing furniture.

More than once, Tanry saw Caterina stand still, hands on her hips, mouth open to ask a question, but she abandoned the words before they formed. They knew each other well enough now, Tanry supposed, that Caterina could tell when it was worth asking questions, and when it wasn't.

They laid the mirrors facing up on the floor of the dressing room. Tanry filled in spaces with the mirror from above the mantel, the triumvirate of glass from her dressing table, and a silver-backed hand mirror.

"Close the door," she ordered Caterina, then pulled the ember out from the alchemic light and broke it in her fist. It had a greenish hue, and gave herself and Caterina a sickly colour.

"Dare I ask what this is about?"

"I'm being pestered by the astral projection, and we need a place to speak unwatched."

"What will this do about it?"

"Wasn't it in your book? They can't trick mirrors. They appear in them. They get caught in them. Astral projections – I think by nature – appear to everyone in the room. Everyone, everything. But they use their power to disappear. They disguise themselves from the people who observe them. Idonea can appear to me, but be seen by no one else in a crowd. But she cannot hide from mirrors. She cannot come into this room without being seen."

Caterina nodded, though her face betrayed her concern.

"I can't use the discernment engine without the possibility

of her knowing what I ask," Tanry continued. "I can't make a single move without her knowing. From this moment I have to assume that I am always being watched. She can hide herself from me, and I can only hide myself in here." Tanry raked her eyes across the floor, but saw no sign of Idonea.

"Do you still plan to get rid of her?"

"Yes, though I've nowhere to begin. I don't even know who she is."

"Why not start with what you do know? What does she look like?" Caterina asked.

"Dark hair, dark eyes, pale skin. I thought she looked like a Boralda-Solkin."

"Could she be? We know that they aren't here."

"It's a question for the discernment engine. She would be a distant relative. She doesn't have their surname, and the engine has not lied about their names so far."

"I suspect not an imperial, then. None of them were called Strader, at least as far as Pherson's tells us. Her dress is perhaps more significant," said Caterina, predictably. "How does she dress?"

"She wears a uniform. Sometimes she has a hat, more of a helmet, perhaps, with a silver badge. She's a purple felt coat – not violet, but darker. Shiny belt and boots. Silver buttons in two lines down the front."

"Police."

"What?"

"That's the uniform of the republic police."

"How do you know that?" Tanry asked.

"I saw a picture. I thought they were very flattering."

"And that stuck in your mind for no particular reason?"

"Who hasn't admired a good uniform from time to time? Why are they being watched by someone who works for the republic?"

"We haven't an answer to why they are here. They could have been sent with a monitor of some kind. Bridget wants Idonea here. Perhaps they have some sort of friendship."

"Another question for the discernment engine, I suppose."

It was a vague enough question that Tanry felt there was no harm in Idonea knowing that she was asking. She turned the wheels.

WHY ARE THEY HERE

She feared, as she set the final dial, that the query contained too many variables for the machine to understand. It spun, and Tanry was ready to turn back the lever, before the engine settled on a word:

WAITING

She chewed on the inside of her cheek, feeling less than satisfied with the answer. Her hand hovered above the dials, ready to ask another question, but she wasn't sure of how to phrase it. People were so tricky with their phrasing when it came to love. For Tanry, it made little sense worrying about what it meant to be attached but not engaged, or what holding affection for another truly looked like. She was engaged, and the matter was entirely legal in nature. Still, she needed to solve a mystery, so she posed a question:

DOES IDONEA LOVE BRIDGET

Quickly after the lever was pulled, the engine came to a decision.

YES

"I suppose that clarifies things a little," said Tanry, though she was uncertain that was true.

Later on, a footman appeared with a dossier from Lord Tresswell. It was the beginnings of a marriage contract with an eye-watering figure for a dowry.

"You may inform Lord Tresswell and his father," she told the footman as she returned the dossier to him, "that I should not be expected to pay Laurina's dowry as if she were still the daughter of an emperor. I think that the new figure I've suggested should be more than fair."

She sent a card to the imperial suite inviting Laurina to meet her at the tailor. Out of all the imperials, she harboured the least ill will towards Tanry, so there was no harm in helping her get married off. It was one less dependent to take care of at Taltois.

Not twenty minutes later, she was met by Matfey in the tailor's suite. The tailor showed little surprise at Tanry's arrival.

"Do you have my mirrors?" he asked.

"No. The archduchess might be in need of a wedding dress soon, and she needs a new gown for my nuptials, anyhow."

He welcomed them inside and had a maid fetch them tea. Matfey sat on one of the armchairs, blushing and holding in a smile.

"I would wager you haven't had a new frock in some time," said Tanry.

Matfey shook her head.

Tanry gestured to the rolls of fabric that lined the walls and boxes of trimmings on the tables. "Pick anything you like," she said. "I rarely spend money on gowns."

"Athalie gives us an allowance, but Lizseta says that we

must not squander it," said Matfey.

"None of that. I've got income to spare. I can move you all to Taltois – though I expect that you'll go to Tresswell's manor eventually."

"Is that really going to happen?"

"I'm in the midst of negotiations. You don't have any parents to ask permission from, so there are few barriers should you wish to wed."

The tailor returned with a sketchbook of designs, each with swatches pinned to the page. Matfey pored over them with the fascination of a doctor seeing inside the body. She found a gown she adored within five minutes. A grin lit up her face and she stroked the page like it was a miniature of her lover.

"I will take your measurements," said the tailor, and a moment later he summoned three maids to do it for him.

"Be glad I am organising this and not Athalie, because her plans are lavish to the point of intolerance," said Tanry.

"I don't mind a spot of lavishness."

"A spot, yes, but not half the country."

After the measurements were taken, Tanry suggested that they take a promenade in the park. Matfey accepted with an eagerness that was almost embarrassing. She had a lace parasol that she set on her shoulder and spun whenever the mood took her. She wove her arm into Tanry's as they walked among the fountains and the rose bushes. Beyond the manicured garden, a brook played and rolling fields kept the sight of Albonne proper from the court. Tanry knew without having to ask that the parklands were sculpted by hand, rather than by the whims of Mother Nature. She was half-certain that it was the work of the same artist who had wrought Taltois a century ago.

Tanry steered Matfey off the beaten path and down a wandering trail towards a folly on a hillock, which was round and sported crenellations like a military castle.

"I have been meaning to get a moment alone with you," said Tanry. "I feel that I am on the back foot, and your siblings will hardly talk to me."

"Lizseta, well, I can't say that she approves of you."

"I did not think that she did. I can try a little to earn her approval, though I shan't pretend it's a priority. No, I need to talk Athalie down from her grandiose plans, and I need to get rid of Idonea."

Matfey paled and she pulled her arm out of Tanry's as they reached the folly. She perched on the steps and looked back at the palace, with its dark glass eyes staring at her.

Matfey did not sit next to her, but held her arms tightly across her front, the breeze making her skirts dance around her legs. "I can ask Idonea not to bother you anymore," she said meekly.

"I'm afraid that that cat is out of the bag. Now I can never be certain that I am not being overheard. I suspect that is why astral projection is so harshly punished."

"Idonea helps us. She can help you too."

"I suppose what I don't understand is who she is, or where she came from. Or who you are, for that matter."

"She – she was one of us."

"Forgive me, but I do not know who any of you are. I was ready to accept the tale that I had been told until very recently."

"I shouldn't tell you," said Matfey. Her lower lip quivered

and she wrung her hands.

"I've already lifted the stone, Matfey. What does it matter if I count the lice underneath?"

Matfey seemed half-startled by her own name. She glanced around, though they were not in company. The day had become overcast and Tanry could smell rain in the air. They were not likely to attract a crowd.

"We weren't supposed to stay here," admitted Matfey in a voice so low that Tanry could barely hear it over the wind. "They said a month, at the most," she finished.

"Who said?"

"The imperial protection corps."

There was a name that Tanry hadn't read in Pherson's magazine. She had heard it some five years past while her father read to Trevor from his ironed newspaper.

"Good lord," he'd exclaimed. Grand emotions were so out of character for him that Tanry wouldn't have been surprised if he'd dropped dead at that moment. "They've executed the emperor," he'd said, his mouth hanging open. "His wife too."

The news came out later that the revolutionaries had imprisoned the imperial protection corps, the organisation responsible for guarding the members of the imperial family. The archduke and his sisters were missing. Duke Teneri had reacted to all of this news as if his own family were placed on the chopping block; he'd had some grand notions that the nobility as a whole would soon be forfeit. At the time, Tanry hadn't been able to find an attachment to the ordeal. People she had never met had died in a country far away. There was no need for hysterics.

"So who are the corps – soldiers?" Tanry asked.

Matfey sighed. She peeled off her glove and wound it

between her hands. "Spies, really. I never even knew how many of them there were. They were all over the palace. They had training grounds in every city. They were different from the army, because they worked in secret. They could be in disguise, if they wanted."

Tanry leaned back, setting her elbow on the step and mulling over this notion for a couple of moments.

"Why were you with them?" she asked. If there was anyone who seemed ill-suited to be mingling with powerful, malicious spies, then it was someone as meek and polite as Matfey.

Matfey shrugged. She held her hands wide and looked about, as if searching for the right words. "I – I don't think I've ever had to explain this," she said.

"Be that as it may, I'd like to hear it."

"I – I was twelve when the IPC found me. Valentin was younger, but I can't remember how long he'd been there for."

"They *found* you?"

"Yes. They had lookouts. People who found kids who were the right age, had the right look, or close enough. They had a list of them, I think, candidates for decoys for the imperial children. They found me and told me that my family would be provided for if I went with them, so I did. I went on a lot of parades."

"That can't be right."

"No, it happened."

"No, it's not *right*, meaning that it was wrong. They told you they'd pay off your family, and then they kept you from them?"

"Yes, but only because I was so busy. I went to lessons with Laurina. I was fed and warm, which wouldn't have been the case at home. It was better that way."

It was the sort of militant thinking that never had really affected Tanry, who had never gone hungry a day in her life, so she brushed past the comment. "So, you worked for them, sort of, by pretending to be Laurina in parades?"

Matfey nodded. "Yes, at first that was all it was. Idonea was there as well, but then she got hurt."

"Idonea was there?"

"Yes. She was there the longest of all of us. She was Lizseta's decoy before Bridget. Idonea was shot when we were on parade, and they hired Bridget after that. She had the right face, the right build, and they could cover her hair with a wig. It was tricky, because Lizseta was a young woman, and they didn't know how to train someone who was grown up. They found Bridget because she had too much debt to continue studying. They paid it off for her, in exchange for a few years work for them, posing as Lizseta. By then, Laurina was older. She used to get drunk before diplomatic banquets. There was one time where Idonea convinced some of the IPC that I should take Laurina's place at dinner because Laurina was passed out. It would have been funny, but it kept happening."

"It's good to know that Laurina really earned her reputation," said Tanry. "Why did Idonea stick around, if she was shot?"

Matfey rolled her eyes. "It was only her shoulder. She joined the IPC. They couldn't rightly let her go, knowing what she knew."

"I take it that they never knew she was an astral projectionist."

"Of course. She would have been executed. You mustn't tell anyone. She is such a help to us, and Bridget loves her so dearly."

"If only Bridget were more subtle. Idonea is a liability, that much is clear. How was it that the three of you ended up here, when you aren't the imperial family, and the IPC were mostly arrested along with the emperor?"

"There were more assassination attempts towards the end. The IPC moved us to a palace near the border. It was isolated, so they figured we would be safe there. We stayed for one summer, just us, Idonea, and the real imperial children. Then we got news that they'd killed the emperor. We really didn't think that they would, but the IPC knew that they'd be coming for us next. Or coming for Laurina, Lizseta, and Zsari, at least."

Tanry tried to picture them, the real imperials, but found herself thinking of Bridget, Matfey, and Valentin in their place. The imperials were strange and foreign ghosts, long gone, or so it seemed.

Matfey continued. "The spies wanted to move them somewhere safe, I suppose. I don't know where. They thought fleeing into Lyalia was too obvious. They dressed us up in their clothes, gave us their jewels, and put us in their carriage. I had a feeling that something bad was going to happen, because Idonea was staying behind. I knew that they were sending us to die right as we were leaving."

"How?"

"The archduke chased after the carriage as it was drawing away. He called after us, and I think he knew what was happening. Valentin didn't understand. I don't think they imagined that we'd make it across the mountains. The rebels did find us. It was only Idonea's advice that let us escape," she said, frantic. "The instructions they gave us were to wait in

Albonne for the real imperials to arrive. Idonea told us the same thing."

"So you were trained to take their place in an emergency, and said emergency arrived, and they only instructed you to wait here?"

Matfey nodded thoroughly. "Wait for the real imperials to arrive, and then, well, I don't know what was planned after."

Tanry didn't reply to that. She presumed that, as the IPC had not expected them to survive, that there had never been any plan for after. The IPC had intended the rebels to catch their decoys. Perhaps someone had even thought to tip them off, but Idonea's astral projection abilities had changed things.

"Where was Idonea, if not with the real imperials?" Tanry asked. The notion struck her as odd. Would Idonea not be in charge of protecting them, as a member of the imperial protection corps?

"She ran away, she told us," admitted Matfey. "She saw them get into carriages and she got out of there. She knew the rebels were on their way."

Tanry supposed that her actions, while cowardly, were sensible in their own way. Idonea, perhaps never truly loyal to the imperials she once impersonated, abandoned them and joined the republic police. The real imperial children were carried away in their carriages, and naught knew what happened to them.

Many people in Karda Ven had wanted to kill them, who was to say they hadn't succeeded? The real archduke and archduchesses, whatever the plan had been, were probably as dead as Trevor Teneri.

That evening, Tanry pondered over the discernment engine

while Caterina embroidered nightgowns for Matfey. There was too much to ask of a machine that could barely give a sentence in response. She started simply.

WHO WAS BRIDGET BEFORE

The wheels and cogs spun in thought before giving her an answer.

ALCHEMIST

She noted the revelation down. It conjured the image of Bridget with her bouncy blonde hair, pouring fizzy liquid in her father's laboratory.

Tanry tried another question.

WHO WAS MATFEY BEFORE

The answer was even less satisfying than the previous one. The machine simply said:

SISTER

Shaking her head, she switched out Matfey's name for Valentin's.

WHO WAS VALENTIN BEFORE

This answer, while no more revealing, at least was more intriguing.

BASTARD, read the machine.

CHAPTER THIRTEEN

A Bastard or a Venereal Disease

It is unseemly for young ladies to speak of dowries or financial arrangements. Such matters should only be discussed in privacy by their male relatives. If no male relatives are available, a neighbour or clergyman will suffice. — Margrit Bellere's Manual for Young Ladies

Lord Tresswell Sr, known as the Duke of Angill, met with Tanry for the official signing of the marriage contract. His quarters were not more sumptuous than Tanry's, she noted, though he seemed to have a proliferation of servants. There were footmen to linger, maids to fetch and carry, a valet to lean over his master's shoulder and whisper, and footsteps behind the walls to indicate the presence of servants too foul to be seen.

"I expected your father to be here," said Angill.

Tanry sat on a couch that had been left open for the negotiating party, which had been expected to be greater in number than the sole person who had arrived. "He is on his way," assured Tanry. "Though he doesn't have a great hand in these negotiations."

Angill blanched. He ran a finger along the inside of his collar. "Does he entrust you with these agreements? Do you have that in writing?"

"Not in so many words, but practically speaking, he is not the one who runs his estate."

"Lady Teneri—"

"Tanry, please."

"Lady Teneri, there is quite a difference between the choosing of a few new wallpapers, or the purchasing of furniture, than in the negotiation of a marriage contract."

"I think you misunderstand my role at Taltois." There was no real way to treat with the man without demeaning herself, she realised.

"Your father should be here," insisted Angill. "This is most eccentric."

"I take it you would prefer to begin negotiations when he arrives."

"I think that is only suitable."

"You'll be disappointed when he arrives, at least. I'll still do most of the talking."

"I doubt that."

Tanry left the suite swearing, causing a great disturbance to the gentlefolk who milled through the corridors. She marched back to the imperial suite, noting as she went that the purple shadow of Idonea followed her. She appeared in flashes and glances in the mirrors that might have been mistaken for a swishing curtain, if one didn't know what to look for. The shock of seeing Idonea still made Tanry jolt, despite how frequent it had become.

She was stopped in her path when Athalie turned into the corridor, accompanied by her attendants. The princess reached for Tanry's arm and made a claw-like grip appear as if she had merely slipped her arm into Tanry's.

"I have some floral arrangements for you to peruse," she announced.

"Oh, we don't need anything quite so time consuming."

Athalie failed to heed Tanry's pleas, though, and led her to the royal greenhouses, which were large enough to be considered a village. They were devoted to all sorts of botany, with plants of every exotic variety that Tanry couldn't name. One boasted a proud herd of pineapples, an expense that no one else in Lyalia could manage. Its walls were wiped clean of condensation, if only for passers-by to peer inside and know that Athalie was rich enough to eat pineapples for breakfast.

Athalie took Tanry to a hothouse that contained an explosion of out-of-season flowers. The air felt solid as they stepped inside, perfumed with unbearable scents that made Tanry cough. Athalie, heedless of the existing discomforting smells, put her pipe between her lips and lit it. Lilac smoke rose and made a halo around her head. She removed her spectacles, which had become cloudy as soon as they stepped inside, and cleaned them with the edge of her silk sleeve.

"I thought these were perfect, as orange is very much your colour." She pointed to a collection of ember-coloured lilies.

"Lilies? Aren't they a bit funereal?"

Athalie let a trail of smoke escape from her mouth. "When

have you cared for social standards?" She gestured at Tanry's tweed suit, which would be inappropriate even for a gentleman to wear on a sunny day at court. "The lilies will suit you perfectly. Now for your bouquet."

"Your Highness," Tanry interrupted her. "Do you not think this is a little extravagant? It is hardly as if we are planning your own wedding."

"No, we are not," she snapped. "But how else am I to send a dear friend such as Cezsario off to his new life?"

"Of course. I only mean to warn that he feels such extravagance is wasted on him."

"That seems so very odd, given how paltry this affair is compared to what he would have expected in Karda Ven."

"It is only that – well – he has said as much."

"And not to my face?" She snorted. "Why does he choose now to speak only to you? What hold do you have over him? He has scarcely known you a month and he chooses now to marry you. What was your courtship like, to bewitch him so?"

"I will not lie to you, Your Highness."

"You had best not. I cannot stand liars."

"It is not a matter of love. This marriage is convenient to us both. A romantic affair, with such a large audience, would be inappropriate for the match we have made."

Athalie snapped a fledgling rosebud off a nearby bush. "Not romantic?" she asked.

"No. There was no courtship, so to speak."

"What could he possibly want from you, if not love? What could he possibly require that he does not already have access to?"

"I don't rightly know," said Tanry. She could feel her palms becoming damp. "Most marriages are arranged for money."

"I have offered the imperial family more funds every month that they have been in residence. They have always refused. Your money does not smell different to mine. It does not look different. What have you to offer that I do not?"

Her eyes were glazed with more ferocity than Tanry had seen in her life. She feared that her sweat would show through her suit. She knew, even as her heart raced, that there was naught she could say to calm Athalie.

"I am afraid that might be a question for the archduke," she said. "I cannot speak for him. I must get back. I promised to speak with Lizseta."

She knew Athalie could make her stay, so she strode as fast as was proper from the greenhouse. She marched all the way back to her suite, where she fell into an armchair, gasping, before realising how guilty she had made herself appear.

Duke Teneri arrived at the court that evening, with all the pomp and circumstance that such an occasion warranted. Athalie went to stand on the front steps, and all her retainers were summoned to flank her. Tanry was shunted to the front. She could feel Athalie's eyes on her as she stood in the middle of the long drive alone. Behind her, the imperials stood in a line, dressed in sombre navy blues. They looked a great deal like they belonged to one another, though Tanry knew they rightly didn't. They were painted by the same doll maker. Each was crafted in perfect form and poise. They made Tanry wish idly that she had worn the same colour as they did.

They were forced to wait for longer than was comfortable. Tanry glanced down the long drive. It was gravel, with edges so neat that there must have been a team who weeded it daily.

The drive was lined with the most majestic breed of trees that Tanry had ever seen. No doubt they had been shipped from across the sea at great expense to grow in orderly lines, taller than the highest towers of the palace. Tanry wondered what they were called and where she might acquire them for Taltois.

Her father's carriage, with its matching team of black stallions, lumbered towards them. Tanry became aware of how her shoes pinched her toes. Her neck ached from turning her head to watch the carriage's approach.

By the time the carriage drew up to her, the horses sweating and bobbing their heads, she was picturing the iced drink she would have once she was back indoors. She could see her own face in the lacquered wood of the carriage, and the imperials, pale and haunting behind her. For just a moment, she made out the murky shape of Idonea behind Bridget, her dark eyes trained on Tanry.

Tanry had little time to watch her, as a prompt footman strode forth and opened the carriage door. He was expressionless, understanding that his place was merely as furniture to the people of the court.

Compared to his gleaming carriage, Duke Teneri looked a mess. His hair, grey now, was uncombed and flattened on one side from where he had been sleeping. His clothes, while rich, were disordered; his necktie was loose and one wing of his collar stuck up. Ink stained the cuffs of his coat sleeves, which made Tanry imagine that he had attempted to write while inside a moving carriage. He looked at the crowd with a sneer that well communicated how little he thought of them.

"Father," said Tanry in lieu of a greeting as she held up an arm to help him down.

He stepped heavily out of the carriage, refusing her arm. "I was surprised to receive a summons," he said.

"I did what I said I would do."

"This isn't proper, Tanry."

"Archduke. Higher than a duke by definition. The family name is older too. By several centuries."

"He is not landed."

"That was not specified in our arrangement. What are you to do now? Turn down the match in front of the princess? When she has been putting so much thought into arranging the celebrations? That would be poor form."

He snorted. "Let us get this over with." It was as good a concession of defeat as she was likely to get.

With Duke Teneri now in evidence, negotiations began again with the Duke of Angill. Both Dukes got on swimmingly with each other, causing Tanry to grind her teeth until her jaw ached, as they jested and drank and had to be cajoled into writing the agreements. Despite this, within the day, they had agreed to a small parcel of land, a reasonable sum, and a joint hunt to celebrate. Tanry conveyed the good news to Matfey at supper in the imperial suite.

"Your wedding will have to be after ours, of course, and at the Tresswell family chapel, rather than at court," said Tanry as she sat at the table, ostensibly, with her new family. The impostors were eating a supper of beef stew and asparagus, while Tanry sat at an unset place, having already supped with Caterina.

"This isn't wise," hissed Bridget across the table. "Marrying Lord Tresswell will separate you from us."

"Yes," said Tanry, "that's the order of things. Girls are

meant to leave their families to start new ones. Matfey is more than old enough. She is older than I. Of course, I don't necessarily agree with the way of things, but if she wants it, I'm only happy to oblige."

Bridget threw down her silverware in a manner most unsuitable for the daughter of an emperor. "Matfey—" she reached for her sister's hand, to punctuate her entreaty "—if you marry Lord Tresswell, you will have to pretend all by yourself. You won't have us every time you make a mistake as Laurina."

"But – what if I told him?" asked Matfey in a small voice.

Valentin let out a hiss of air through his teeth. Tanry could see him clench his hands together under the table.

"Under no circumstances can you tell him," said Bridget.

"Matfey, you really shouldn't. He might react poorly," said Valentin, in his best attempt at a soothing manner.

"There can be no question of telling him before you are wed," declared Tanry. "After, maybe. He will be legally attached to you. Although a match under a false name would be easy to dissolve. He would take a significant blow to his reputation, however. He would not want to seem like a man who is easily tricked. It would do, if you intend to tell him, to make sure that we know something of his that he could not stand being made public. A bastard, or a venereal disease. Something of that ilk."

Matfey gasped and covered her mouth with her hand. Tanry wanted to ask her who was watching her performance. Valentin reached across the table to touch her arm. It was meant as a comfort, Tanry was sure, but it also served to cut off Matfey from her at the head of the table.

"No one is going to do that. I'm sure that Lord Tresswell

has not done anything like that," he said. "But what if he does not react in the way you hope he will?"

"He – he loves me, and he will want to be with me."

"If he loved you that much, he would have asked you to elope, rather than waiting for you to have money," said Tanry.

"He never knew you would come along, Tanry," replied Valentin.

"Perhaps he was stringing Matfey along until someone better turned up." Tanry shrugged. She hooked her legs over the arm of her chair. "There really is no telling what his thoughts are."

Matfey looked down at her bowl, tears brimming in her eyes.

"Suppose that there was a way to test his mettle," said Valentin, with an edge of unhelpful optimism.

"We cannot tell him anything. We cannot tell him, Valentin, you *know*." Bridget spoke in a hurried yet demanding way, and Valentin quailed as if admonished by a schoolmistress.

Tanry's own governess had been dismissed within a week of her employment. Tanry never had patience for her kind; she had tried to instill shame within Tanry, who would not stand for it.

"Let him speak," she ordered.

Bridget stared at Tanry, her cooling meal abandoned. Perhaps she was wishing that she could throw it in Tanry's face and remain respectable.

Valentin cut across them. "We would not need to tell Lord Tresswell who we are. We would just need to measure whether he is keen for Tanry's money – or – uh – for Matfey."

"He has told me he loves me," said Matfey.

"It's just a question of how much," said Tanry.

Bridget put an arm around Matfey's shoulders. "This is unkind," she said.

"Their love is real," declared Valentin. "You know that, Matfey, but like all living things, it can't thrive under some conditions. Lord Tresswell might love you. He might be sincere, but he is also sincere about his love for his father. He knows that he cannot marry a common girl and have his father in his life. You should not have to compete for his affection, but you will have to."

She seemed to enjoy his platitude, because her breathing slowed.

Later, Tanry and Caterina spoke in the dressing room, the alchemic light reflected in the floor between their feet.

"I'm afraid that she is serious," complained Tanry. "I pushed this marriage to get her off my plate, but once she is out of my sight, I will have no means of making sure she doesn't reveal the secret."

"It is selfish to hope that she marries, if only to make use of the trousseau I'm making for her?"

"Yes."

"Oh, well. Then you should reconsider. Even if you convince her to hold her tongue now, who is to say that she will when she goes on her honeymoon? Or any time in the next twenty years?" Caterina's voice was laden with concern.

"I don't want that dread hanging over me, wondering if the cat's out the damn bag. I have to stop this wedding."

"How will you do that? You will cause such upset. What

will you tell Athalie?"

"For fuck's sake, I've no idea. She's already close to something, though I've no telling what. She will find any reason to doubt me and sink her teeth in. I'll have to keep the whole thing as quiet as can be. Let us find out what the engine has to say."

As was habit by now, Tanry confronted a gap in her knowledge by approaching the discernment engine. She led Caterina out of the dressing room, hoping once more that Idonea had not chosen that moment to project to her suite. Carefully, Tanry lifted the velvet covering away from the front of the engine. Since her privacy had become so directly challenged, she had stopped uncovering the machine entirely every time she used it.

She arranged the dials to form a new question.

WHAT DOES ATHALIE SUSPECT

This time, after she pulled the lever, the output dial spun for a full minute, revealing nothing. Tanry swore.

"That's not a useful phrase. She could suspect any number of things."

"You could ask it what Tresswell will do," suggested Caterina.

"The engine cannot predict the future. No, we need something more illuminating."

DOES TRESSWELL LOVE LAURINA

This time, the answer was swift.

YES

Tanry sighed. "That doesn't mean much, alas. He could love her and still love money more. The engine doesn't know a great deal about human emotion."

"Could you not convince either of them to call the whole thing off? There would be few questions then," said Caterina.

"It would not be difficult. Valentin wanted to test Tresswell's love. I can test him too hard."

CHAPTER FOURTEEN

If You Would Rather Be Rich, Don't Bother

Nessa Spa is a pleasant enough town, with ancient pools known for improving one's health, and delightful countryside to walk through, yet it is chiefly known for one particular business: marital laws in Calness allow young couples to marry without the permission of their parents, or without a contract at all. Nessa Spa is merely the first town across the border from Lyalia, and thus happened into this scandalous reputation. — Jean Trier's Travels in Calness

Tanry and Valentin could not speak unobserved. Tanry thought that Idonea must fear that Valentin's reputation would be besmirched if there was not a ghost hanging over his shoulder at all of their meetings. They were ensconced in the library, on the upper level. Valentin was framed by one of the round windows, the slate roofs of the palace behind him. Tanry could see Idonea's face reflected in the glass. She stood behind Tanry, unmoving. Tanry had resolved to not give Idonea any satisfaction, so pretended that she had not seen the ghost there at all.

"What do you think Tresswell's reaction will be?" asked Tanry.

"Of course, one hopes," began Valentin, "that he will shake off the loss and confess his love for Laurina."

"She isn't here," replied Tanry. "What do you think his real reaction will be?"

"Oh, I suspect that he will call off the engagement."

"We all wish that he'll fall on his knees and beg Laurina to run away with him," lied Tanry, perhaps less than convincingly, "though should the alternative occur, let him be embarrassed enough to scuttle home straight away. Then Laurina would be afforded the privilege of being able to insult him without the risk of him walking into the room."

Their scheme, simple as it was, rattled into action that evening. The day was hot, despite the oncoming approach of autumn, and dinner was served on the patio. The servants lit citrus-scented candles to wage an ineffectual war on the summer's last insects. Tanry sat with the imperials at their white-painted table. In the half-light, the court looked like a painting. The colours were off, rich in places and mild in others.

Despite being outdoors, the ladies wore no hats. Their hair glittered with jewelled fans and combs; Bridget wore three dozen diamond stars, each pinned to her plaits. Apparently, she had escaped from the home country with them tucked down the front of her corset. They looked a constellation in the dark tresses of her wig, and it barely mattered that the bodice of her white gown was frayed. She rested her elbows on the table and leaned her head in her hands. Her eyes shone in the candlelight.

Tanry was struck for a moment by her particular beauty. She understood how it had been for citizens of Karda Ven, when they saw her on the steps of the imperial palace. They would have been enchanted. Perhaps they would not even have worried that she did not look quite like the archduchess did in her paintings.

It was a tough feat for Bridget to recreate that beauty, and to wear it as her own shield. She did it with aplomb. It was a wonder that she did not draw every wandering eye from across the patio.

Valentin, in his charming guise, rang his knife against his crystal glass and stood. Tanry's eyes sought out Athalie at her own table. A look of dread crossed her face, as if she imagined that Valentin were about to announce his engagement for the second time.

"I must beg all of your attention again," he said. "I am pleased to announced that my sister, Archduchess Laurina, is engaged to Lord Tresswell. She has been determined to upstage Lady Teneri and I." He gave a snorting little laugh of the sort that people made when they wanted to indicate that they had made a joke, but didn't want to lose decorum over it.

Lord Tresswell, only mildly surprised by the announcement, duly stood and accepted a light round of applause. Matfey blushed and stole a glance at him. Valentin sat back down and the chatter of cutlery against crockery built again around them.

"We will catch him later, when he withdraws," muttered Valentin.

This remark did not go uncaught by Bridget. "Who are you catching?" she asked.

"Nothing for you to worry about," said Tanry. "I merely need a word with Lord Tresswell about arrangements."

"What kind of word?"

"Merely a matter of bureaucracy. All is well in hand, Lizseta."

The matter was dropped until all of the silver forks had been used and taken away again. When the bell on the clock tower rang out ten o'clock, Valentin plucked Tanry's sleeve and pointed. At the Duke of Angill's table, Lord Tresswell had stood in congruence with a handful of other men his age. They were headed to the billiards room, no doubt, and Tanry knew how to catch them there. She and Valentin stood.

Bridget raised her voice in protest. Valentin placed a hand on her shoulder in an attempt to placate her, though it was ineffective. Tanry rushed away instead of listening to her reply. Valentin was on her heels, but as they passed the dark windows of the orangery, she saw Idonea walking between them. They hurried through the hushed palace corridors in the wake of their quarry.

They interrupted the party before a game had been set in the billiards room. Valentin seemed as much a stranger in that space as Tanry was. He stood back from the table, as if there was a boundary that he dare not cross.

Tanry did not wait for him to speak first. "Lord Tresswell, might I have a word?"

At the sound of her voice, Tresswell scowled. "Is there a concern?" he asked.

"Speak to me and find out." She turned around and left, grabbing Valentin by the arm to ensure that he followed.

"Will he understand?" asked Valentin.

"I gave him a very specific instruction. He can come out here, or he can wonder what I was going to say."

Lord Tresswell did emerge, but not so quickly that he couldn't have dawdled.

"What could not wait until the morning?" he asked harshly.

"Well," Valentin began, "we had something to run by you."

"Be direct," Tanry cautioned him.

"We had some questions for you about your feelings for Laurina."

"What questions? Get on with it, man."

"Well – I suppose – how much do you love her?" asked Valentin.

"What do you mean by that?"

Tanry could not stand the direction they were headed in. "What is she worth to you?" she asked.

Tresswell blinked and moved his tongue around in his mouth for no reason.

"Tanry, that isn't what we discussed," muttered Valentin.

Tanry ignored him.

"Pack a bag, Lord Tresswell. My father has rescinded the dowry. If you want to marry Laurina, you'll meet us by the musician's folly at midnight. We will have horses ready to take you to Nessa Spa. If you would rather be rich, don't bother to come."

"This isn't what I intended," complained Valentin as they stood on the steps of the musician's folly. It was at the edge of the parklands, and placed out of the way of any significant guards' barracks. It was built like a temple of the classic age, though no sacrifices had marred its floors, and only musicians attended it regularly. They played on sunny days just for the delight of passers-by.

Tanry was less interested in Valentin than she was in the mural on the back wall of the folly, upon which the old gods were painted wearing hoop skirts and top hats.

"I think they dressed in far less clothing, you know," said Tanry. A similar painting adorned the ceiling of her father's library, though in that the gods only wore carefully placed sheets.

"Athalie told me her grandfather believed in modesty. He had all the murals in the palace repainted like this," explained Valentin. He ducked through one of the arches, his head nearly brushing the ceiling, and stood next to Tanry.

"His son has hardly followed in his footsteps," said Tanry. "Or is it just rumour that King Ladarius is a connoisseur of pornography?"

"I wouldn't know," said Valentin. "I've never met the man."

"Of course. The war."

"It's a good thing. He met – well, us – he met the imperials in Karda Ven."

"Ah, and I do suppose that you all look a little different now."

"I'm a lot taller than I should have been."

"What should you have been?" asked Tanry, finding the comment preposterous. No one, as far as she knew, had a designated height they had to fulfill. "The emperor?" She laughed.

Valentin didn't find it amusing. "I should have been shorter, stockier. I should answer to Zsari. We looked the same when we were young, but I hit a growth spurt not long after we arrived here."

"When you were young? When did the imperial protection corps take you?"

"I was ten." He shrugged. "They didn't take me. Lord Taybury gave me up."

"I didn't know they took you that young."

"A gunman shot at Zsari in a park when he was five years old. They killed his governess."

Tanry whistled. "And they didn't see the revolution coming? The malcontent has to be fairly strong to try and kill a five year old."

Valentin tutted and shook his head. He raised his voice in a way that he had not before. "Don't make light of him, Tanry."

"Don't speak ill of the dead, you mean," she said. "Is that it? You're still waiting here because you still feel guilty for taking his place?"

"Why shouldn't I? And you do not know that he is dead."

"He was the richest fuck in your entire country, and some lord signed you over to die for him. If he is not dead, why has he not appeared in five years? They must be dead, you have to agree."

He did not. His jaw was tight, and he refused to meet her eye. The empty night briefly rang with bells from the clock tower.

"It's midnight," said Valentin. "I don't think Lord Tresswell is coming."

They looked out at the empty park together. There were

no signs that a young lord was on his way, ready to elope with his blushing young bride.

"Give it ten minutes. His watch might be slow."

They stood side by side on the steps like a pair of guardsmen. Valentin shivered, while Tanry was fine in the wool greatcoat she had thought to bring.

"When we are married..." began Valentin.

"Don't worry," said Tanry. "We shan't have children. You shall have your own wing of the house. You can only see me at functions, if you like. You can have an allowance and start your own projects. I won't care what you do."

"Ah, that's good," he said.

Tanry suspected that he had only cared about the first sentence.

The next morning, Tanry was summoned by her father. He had turned his suite into an approximation of his library with the number of books he had brought. She stood by the window, as was her custom, even in a new place.

"The bastard Angill tore up the contract. Apparently because of something you said."

"I'm sure that you were only too happy to oblige, Father." She rocked on her feet, watching the parties wander through the walled garden.

"Can't say that I need the alliance with the fellow. I don't want the expense. Happy to see him go."

"As am I. If he comes crawling back, warn him off."

"I don't think that's likely."

At dinner time, Matfey looked around the terrace for her beau, but could not catch his eye. She asked a number of people if they had seen Lord Tresswell, until Lord Bayard informed her that the Duke of Angill and his son had departed for their family estate.

"Why wouldn't he tell me that he was leaving?" she asked tearfully, of their table.

"Perhaps it was an emergency."

"And he could not leave a note?"

Valentin looked at his plate and shuffled his food around with a fork.

"He's not coming back," said Tanry. "If he wanted to marry you, he would find a way. He has not. Put him out of your mind."

That night, Tanry carried the alchemic gem from her bedside into the parlour, and lifted the cover from the discernment engine. It was a balm, having the engine. She was never tormented by curiosity. She asked the engine:

WHO IS LORD TAYBURY

The output dial spun and she held her alchemic gem close to it, so the brass cogs gleamed with a pinkish light.

VALENTINS GRANDFATHER

The machine's reply gave her pause. Lord Taybury - Valentin's own grandfather - had given him away to the imperial protection corps. Matfey and Bridget had gone willingly, or as willingly as anyone in need of funds could. Valentin had been a mere decade old, betrayed by an elder. There were more pieces to the story.

WHO WAS VALENTINS MOTHER
GENEVIEVE TAYBURY

Tanry whistled through her teeth. She asked the engine another question just to make sure, but she suspected the truth before she was informed of it. Genevieve Taybury must have been the highborn daughter of a fine family, and the engine had called Valentin a bastard before. There were few good reasons for a grandfather to send a child away, but perhaps, if the child was illegitimate, then Lord Taybury was trying to protect his family from scandal. He might have sent Valentin away when he began to look too much like his mother, or merely when the IPC came knocking, looking for pale, dark-haired boys to take a bullet for the imperial heir.

"What a shit," she muttered, thinking of a small Valentin, torn away from home, unsure of where he was headed. She asked it one final question.

IS LORD TAYBURY ALIVE

NO

She laughed. At least he got what he deserved.

CHAPTER FIFTEEN

Exiles from the Old Country

There has not been a wedding hosted at court since the King himself was married some two decades ago, when he was a dashing young prince. All residents at the court - and many of the common folk in Albonne - are filled with anticipation for the nuptials of the archduke and the scandalous Lady Teneri. — Pherson's Courtly Hearsay

Athalie presented Tanry with a list of invites to the wedding.

"I contacted all of the exiles from the old country that I could find and sent them invitations," she declared.

Tanry, avoiding the twin threats of her father and the impostors, had walked out to the greenhouses only to be caught by Athalie. Purple smoke settled in the humid hothouse air as the princess took another puff from her pipe.

Tanry gazed at the list in her hands, which was

frighteningly long, not in the least because each entry had three or four titles to signify them. "I would not send invites to all of them. They were not all of them friends of the imperials, if you take my meaning."

"I'm afraid that the messengers cannot be called back."

"You already sent them?"

"The wedding is so soon, it hardly seemed prudent to delay."

"Why not push it back? The archduke and I are in no rush," said Tanry.

"Oh, but the rumours say differently. You were spotted out in the musician's folly at midnight. Alone."

"Who could have seen us out there?" Tanry mused. They had watched the doors of the palace for Lord Tresswell and seen no one emerge.

"It's only fair that I help you avoid the scandal. I assumed that your – let's say – lax attitude was because you knew that the wedding was so soon. Unless, of course, you and he are thinking of calling this whole wedding off."

"No, why would we call it off?"

"You are so resistant to my plans. You'd think you did not want to get married at all."

Tanry returned to the imperial suite with a stone in her stomach. Unless she could hire a team of messengers, who were in turn faster than Athalie's messengers, they were going to have a wedding filled with people who had met the imperial family, and Tanry wasn't sure she could convince Valentin to elope with her to Nessa Spa. She had the news on the tip of her tongue when she entered the suite, but it never made it out of her mouth.

"Who the fuck do you think you are?" Bridget filled Tanry's frame of view as soon as she stepped through the door.

"Tanry Teneri, in case you had forgotten." She stepped around Bridget, but was still close enough to get a heady whiff of her perfume, making Tanry cough. Her wig was askew, and a single blonde hair was stuck to her forehead.

Bridget slammed the door shut with such ferocity that Tanry felt a gust move past her. The room was as disordered as it always was. Valentin sat on the couch by the window with the air of a child caught misbehaving by a governess. His shoulders were hunched and his hands were pressed between his knees, which bounced up and down with nervous energy.

"What is happening here?" Tanry asked.

Valentin met her eye but said naught.

"You two schemed together to get Lord Tresswell out of court."

"Saying 'scheme' really makes it sound more complex than it was. It was one small lie that sent him running for the hills."

"You told him that he was required to elope with Matfey."

"One small test to see how well he loved her. It transpired that he did not love her more than his father's esteem." Tanry pointed to Valentin. "Did you tell her all of this?"

"Don't bother with him," said Bridget. "You lied to Lord Tresswell and then had your father rescind the arrangement."

"I think you'll find that my father and Duke Angill did that under their own steam. I would not take it personally. My father is committed to the life of a recluse. Lord Tresswell was a danger to this family. I dispensed with him. All things considered, it's perhaps we keep this among ourselves. Matfey need not know that her dear brother had anything to do with Tresswell's sudden disappearance."

"It is not your business to protect this family," said Bridget. "It is mine. I have been protecting this family for five years. It is *my* job and *I* will protect us, from you if necessary."

"Are you really so saddened to see the back of Lord Tresswell?"

"I was handling matters in my own way."

"You are such a dedicated nanny," said Tanry.

"What does that— what?"

"That is what you are. You are their minder. You were an alchemist, a scientist, but now you just watch over them, and not even that well. I prevented Matfey from marrying a man who chose his father's money over her. You are failing at your task. I am doing it for you."

Bridget took the insult with all the decorum that must have been beaten into her. There was no dam that broke, no fresh emotion that crept forth.

"If you knew what it was to care about someone, to look out for their best interests, then you might understand me. But you have no conception of caring. If you had, you would know that you have not saved Matfey from a loveless marriage, but robbed her of her own choices. If you imagine that love can be measured by a childish test such as yours, then you have revealed just how clueless you are."

Tanry tried to stare her down, but found that she had nothing to throw back at Bridget. "It matters not," she said. "He's gone and the secret is safe. We have a wedding to attend, and it seems that half the damn country are going to be there."

"Our secret would be far safer if you chose this moment to reconsider your hasty plans, and returned home to your beloved estate."

"I will not do that. I cannot do that."

There would be no estate to love or live in unless Tanry wed Valentin. Going home without an archduke for a husband was unthinkable.

"That is such a shame, because I was going to request a private audience with Athalie to warn her about your poor cold feet."

"Athalie is so heartwarmingly behind this marriage. Merely look at all the arrangements she has made," said Tanry, though she knew that her voice was uncertain.

"You cannot be so naive to think that she is taking you seriously. There is nothing you can say to convince her of your sincerity."

"Then—" Tanry spun to Valentin "—you need to say something to her. She believes you love her, that you want to be with her."

"I-I can't do that," said Valentin quietly.

"You have to tell her something, or I will tell her who you really are."

"You don't have the gall, Tanry Teneri," said Bridget.

"You think that I wouldn't? I could tell her that the man she's called Cezsario Boralda-Solkin is a bastard who was handed to the imperial protection corps by an anxious grandfather. Do you really think that she wants to know that? Do you think that her opinion of you can go lower?"

Valentin stared at her, his face red, his fists balled on his lap. "You don't know me," he declared. "But how are you learning these things? How did you know Lord Taybury was my grandfather?"

Tanry thought for a moment. She could not reveal the discernment engine to them, or else they might steal it out of revenge.

"A mere guess," she claimed. "But thank you for confirming my suspicions."

"Her threats aren't real," Tanry declared to Caterina while crouched on the mirrored floor of her dressing room. "Bridget can't tell Athalie anything without revealing too much of herself. She can tell Athalie that I have cold feet, but it won't matter. I do not have cold feet and I *will* be marrying an archduke."

"Well, your dress is ready, if that's important at all. Athalie's tailor has sent a gown over for the ball the night before. I know you're going to hate it, but I think you have to wear it."

Tanry waved her hand to indicate that she didn't care. "Valentin didn't tell her that we were out by the musician's folly, though we know that someone saw us there. My bet is that Bridget got her information from Idonea, as she always does."

"What does that matter? The ghost has not left you alone since all this began."

"For better or worse, I am shackling myself to these people, which means that I am shackling myself to Idonea for evermore. I cannot stand it."

"What choice do you have?"

"There are always choices, terrible though they may be. Idonea can't be touched or threatened, but that does not mean I am trapped by her. She's just an illusion." Tanry looked around at the mirrors underneath them. "I only need to set one trap."

CHAPTER SIXTEEN

As Corporeal As Light

Astral projection, the most severely punished crime on the continent, is more difficult to prevent than murder. Despite the risk it poses to security, little research has been done on astral projection, alchemists generally fearing arrest if the ability is discovered. — The Arcane Arts of Premure

Duke Teneri did not have a great many books on astral projection, but he certainly had a great deal to say about the practice.

"If there was a decent way of preventing the damn thing, we would have implemented it years ago. We wouldn't have the great places of the world covered in mirrors."

"But why are they visible in mirrors?" asked Tanry.

All the velvet curtains in his room were drawn, probably because he had forgotten to have them opened; it made the space hot, dark, and smelly. There were no mirrors through which she could watch for Idonea and it made Tanry antsy, anxious to leave.

"It's a matter of physics. The mirror reflects back light," said her father.

"How can they reflect projections if they are invisible? If they are not really there at all?"

"They're not invisible. That's a common misconception. The projection in its natural state is not invisible. It takes a great deal of will to make oneself invisible to one person, let alone many. It would be nigh impossible to remove oneself from the touch of light."

"But—"

"Why are you bothering me with this drivel? Can you not tell that I am already engaged?" He gestured to a smoking glass bottle on the table behind him. It looked uncomfortably close to exploding.

"I have but one more question. Mirrors usually reflect that which is corporeal. How corporeal is a projection?"

"Not at all. They're only as corporeal as light. That is all they are."

Tanry left her father and began to consider how one would trap light. The answer came, as it always did, while she was doing something else; in this case, it was suffering through a fitting of her new ballgown.

Athalie's tailor poked her no less than thirteen times with pins, despite promising to be more careful each time she complained. She was trussed into a snot-green gown with a tightly cut skirt and a train longer than she was tall. There was a loop fastened to the end so that she might put it over her wrist and carry the train high for the dancing. She was shuffled into a corner of the room with a new triptych of mirrors (the old ones still being on her dressing room floor), so she could see herself from every angle and marvel at how wrong it was for her to be dressed so. She did not know what to do with her hands while wearing such a dress. She wished for pockets.

The tailor brought another set of mirrors and placed them behind her, so she could see every angle of herself in the damned dress. They reflected back and forth in an unending line so that there were a thousand versions of herself trapped in the glass.

She made Caterina empty a wardrobe in the dressing room for her purposes, so she could be certain that she was not observed.

"You have gotten into some strange hobbies, it has to be said," observed Caterina. "What are you doing, exactly?"

"All in good time," promised Tanry.

She pilfered mirrors from the imperial suite and told Bridget that she had broken her own. They were not using them anyway. She stole the glass knife that father used for his alchemy, and pretended that she did not know where it had gone. When she was finished, she picked up all of the mirrors from the floor of the dressing room and had them returned to their proper places.

The trap was set. The next task was to lure Idonea into it. The wedding approached with concerning velocity. Tanry could not cross a corridor without bumping into a servant carrying a floral arrangement. The scent of the orange lilies followed her around the palace, and she choked on it wherever she went.

She saw Idonea only as much as she ordinarily did. The ghost hovered behind Bridget and muttered jests in her ear to make her laugh during a serious conversation. Tanry only caught sight of her because she knew where to look; she could spot the splash of purple in a crowd, or glimpse it in the glass of the orangery window. She knew that Idonea was watching when Bridget turned to thin air and smiled, or made some comment that she pretended was meant for her dog.

She suspected that the game would be up after one attempt. She attended dinner in the imperial suite and attempted to ascertain Idonea's presence. As they were unobserved, Bridget took no precautions in speaking to Idonea while they were alone, though the latter failed to show her face.

They ate in near silence. Matfey sniffled and wiped her nose with a fraying handkerchief. Valentin stared at his bowl and shuffled his food around it. Tanry ate quickly, knowing that she was about to be interrupted.

Caterina, as instructed, pushed her way into the room without being invited. Valentin shot to his feet in surprise.

"Tanry," was all she said.

"Excuse me." Tanry stood up from the table, throwing her napkin onto her plate.

"Where are you going?" asked Bridget.

"Nowhere that concerns you," replied Tanry. She departed the room and hoped dearly that Idonea was intrigued enough to follow.

She and Caterina walked in silence at a pace that indicated urgency. They passed through her suite and to the dressing room, where Caterina held the wardrobe door open. Tanry stepped inside and crouched as Caterina closed the door. She was there, in the dark, wandering if she was being watched, knowing that this was the strangest act that she had ever performed.

She felt around for the alchemic rock on the floor and struck it on the side of her boot. It flared into life with an orange glow. Only when the light was escaping from between her fingers did she look at the mirrors that surrounded her. Tanry was reflected back and forth, like a concertina, or a kinetoscope. Reflected in front of her, like the second half of a cameo set, was Idonea Strader.

"What is this?" she asked.

"Naught that concerns you. Where are you now?"

Idonea frowned. "In a wardrobe."

"Where are you really?" Tanry asked.

She chewed over the thought. "In Veni, in my house."

"I suppose I never considered what you were doing when you weren't spying on me."

"Of course."

"It is in Vania Place, is it not?"

Idonea's face stilled. "How did you know?"

"You can't tell? I thought you would have seen the engine, at least." Tanry smiled. "I asked it a lot of questions about you. I was curious. You live with your sister. She takes good care of you. She feels some great burden for something that happened in your youth. How kind."

"I suppose that this is a poorly veiled threat to keep me from spying on you."

"I do prefer more direct methods myself. I want to be assured that you will not be able to see us until we are safe in Taltois, a place that you will never be able to picture, because I have made it unrecognisable to anyone who may once have seen it."

She grasped the edges of the mirror to her left. She knew that she had to be fast. She felt as if she were on a hunt, ready to pull a trigger and down a stag. She swung the mirror around to face Idonea. The alchemic rock fell to the floor, the light flickering. Tanry could see Idonea's face as Tanry put the mirror between them. The ghost didn't have time to protest.

Tanry looked at the versions of Idonea reflected into oblivion. Idonea began to say something, but Tanry pushed the mirror onto her. For a moment, though it was only by the doubtful light of the rock, Tanry saw the look of fear in her dark eyes. Then she heard the sharp hiss of glass against glass. She held the mirrors tightly together, making a cage of light to trap Idonea's projection inside. Tanry might have feared that Idonea had merely vanished, gone back to her body in Karda Ven, if not for the screaming.

CHAPTER SEVENTEEN

A Fox for Hunting

When an astral projectionist moves their mind from their body, their body is left vulnerable to attack. The most common manner for astral projectionists to be caught is for relatives to find their body, eyes open, but unmoving, possibly speaking as if asleep. — The Arcane Arts of Premure

The day before her wedding, Tanry awoke on the couch, still fully dressed. She crossed uncertainly to the bedroom. It was quiet: both a relief and a concern. The mirrors, bound together with twine, lay on the bed. Tanry leaned down and pressed her ear to the mirror back. There was no screaming anymore, but Tanry could hear the steady whistle of breath between Idonea's teeth. Tanry departed for breakfast, an uneasy feeling making merry in her stomach. It was entirely unreasonable, as she was entirely prepared to marry the archduke Cezsario. There was no need to be nervous about the activity. Idonea was dealt with, and everything was going to plan, but Tanry felt sick with nerves regardless.

It was a breezy morning. Autumn had finally made itself known in Albonne, the late heatwave having fled. She scrunched her eyes shut as she stepped out onto the patio, where breakfast was being served despite the overcast day. She felt hungover, though she hadn't drunk anything the night before. She caught a serving boy and requested a pot of coffee before slouching into her usual chair at the impostors' table.

"Why do I feel as if battle is about to be met?" she asked them.

The impostors shuffled in their seats. From the looks in their eyes, it seemed as if they had not slept much either.

"Retreat is still an option," said Bridget.

Tanry scoffed. "All will be well once we are at home in Taltois."

All through breakfast, Bridget held Idonea-dog on her lap while the creature squirmed. Bridget glanced over her shoulder a few times, but failed to find what she was looking for.

Athalie's ball was set for the evening. The day felt rather useless, as if it was one long held breath. The number of servants in the palace quadrupled, though Tanry could not tell where they had come from. The number of objects needing to be fetched or carried seemed endless. Knowing she was in for an afternoon of listening to a ghost screaming in the other room, Tanry resolved to make use of the parkland beyond the follies and ordered a horse saddled. There was a faux village out there that she hadn't visited. Athalie disdained it, though it had been built by her mother.

Tanry recognised it from the paintings in Pherson's. There were half a dozen quaint buildings with timbers on the outside of the walls and peasant-like designs daubed over the window frames. The path was well-swept and free of the dung that would have caked a real village. There were no pigs lurking behind the stable doors. The troughs were empty. Tanry dismounted and walked her horse through the houses; she felt the quiet to be eerie. She knew well that it was a place for court ladies to sojourn and be free of court attire and etiquette, but she still felt as if children should be gambolling in the street after a dog, or a town crier should wander around the corner ringing his bell.

She turned away from the village, heading for the edge of the ridge, where she thought that she might catch a pleasant view of the palace and Albonne beyond. She fastened the horse's halter to a fence post. Undeterred by her absence, the horse set to eating the long grass around its hooves.

Tanry found a rocky path lined with gorse bushes, each displaying sickly yellow flowers. She climbed over a rocky ledge and the view of the palace was spread out before her, though it did not catch any of her attention, because there was a bench situated on the viewpoint, and Bridget sat there in a white dress with a matching hat, her dark wig braided and coiffed above her shoulders. She had a writing desk open on her lap, and she scribbled with little care for how the ink might stain her lace gloves.

"Should you not be painting?" called Tanry.

Bridget swore quite colourfully and saved her inkpot from being upended by the jolt that ran through her. "What are you doing up here?" she asked, with no pretensions of royalty.

"I did not mean to find you. This was merely a

coincidence."

"Well, undo it. I do not wish to see you."

"Who are you writing to?" Tanry asked, peering over her shoulder.

Bridget covered the page with hand, though the ink was not yet dry. "Must you rifle through every aspect of my existence?" She opened the writing desk and stowed ink pot, pen, and paper inside. Spots of ink fell onto her lap, staining the front of her dress.

Tanry pulled a handkerchief from her pocket and held it out to her. Bridget did not take it. She hid her ink-stained hand behind her back.

"I did not want to impugn your honour," said Tanry, "but Lizseta Boralda-Solkin has no one to whom she writes. She never made any friends at court and everyone she knew in Karda Ven is dead. They cannot wonder why you have ink on your hands."

"It isn't correspondence," insisted Bridget.

"Then it had better be a missive detailing flower arrangements for the wedding."

"The flowers are already decided. Athalie did all of that."

"Then clean your hand."

Bridget tore the handkerchief from Tanry's grip. She cleaned her hand briskly and threw the cloth back. Tanry failed to catch it and it snagged on a nearby gorse bush.

"Why can't Lizseta Boralda-Solkin write a diary?" snapped Bridget. "Why can she not keep a journal of her thoughts?"

"Because she has no thoughts to share. She's dead and she cannot write a journal. When she travels to Taltois, she can keep whatever journal she likes, because the only people watching her will be my servants and I."

"Am I supposed to thank you for that paltry freedom?"

"You easily could. It is far more than you have received here."

"To remain here, I need not sell my brother away. I need not tolerate you."

"My estate is large. I have my own wing. If you never want to see me again, that can be arranged. I am the richest heiress in the country. You can walk for miles and still be on my land. You can hire your own household and tell them what you like, because they will never have heard of Lizseta Boralda-Solkin. Buy any clothing you like. Decorate your home how you want. You will have your freedom."

"What a delightful gilded cage. Before I came here, I had more freedom than you've likely ever had. I was respected for what I could do and what I studied. I didn't need to beg for a carriage to go anywhere."

"Then how did you get about?"

"I had a bicycle. I had my own flat and no one ever asked me when I was going to get married. I didn't need to take a writing desk up a hill to write letters. I had a typewriter and a boy to run messages for me."

"So you were rich?"

"Of course not. I had no money. I had to join the imperial protection corps just to afford my degree. They swore not to take me away, but they sent me out like a fox for hunting. They made me responsible for two children who never had a chance against the people pursuing them. I was left alone, with no recourse, no chance of taking my life back. The only comfort I had was the company of a distant friend. Now she is gone, no matter how often I call out for her."

Tanry's stomach gnawed at her. "She was the weakest link in your facade. She is the reason I figured you out at all."

"She *was*?" Bridget frowned. "How did you know that Idonea was missing?"

"I made an assumption," Tanry lied.

"What assumption can you have made? She has only been gone for the morning."

"Well, then she can hardly be termed as missing."

"What do you know? What have you done?"

"What could I have done? She is a ghost; I cannot touch her."

"I have learned not to underestimate you, Tanry Teneri."

"You should not overestimate me either. There is only so much that a soul can do to an astral projection. That is why this place is covered in mirrors, and even then Idonea hid from the court for five years."

"You have done something. I know that you have."

Tanry shrugged. "You may believe what you will."

Bridget dropped the writing desk. It clattered on the rocks and the lid fell open, letting Bridget's papers fall out and dance in the wind. Tanry watched them, half-entranced, and didn't notice when Bridget grabbed her.

Bridget wasn't a fighter. She was wearing a corset and a long dress and a stifling, heavy wig. She tried to knee Tanry in the stomach but it was an easy dodge. Tanry grabbed both of her wrists and held them tight, even as Bridget tried to get free.

"You had to have known that wouldn't work." Tanry laughed.

Bridget tried to kick her. "Why must you hold my life like this? What right have you to control me? What have you earned? What skills do you possess?" She struggled free from Tanry's grip and stumbled away, the strands of her wig falling around her face.

"You're distracted," said Tanry. "I'll go."

"What have you done with her?" cried Bridget.

"I don't know what you're talking about," lied Tanry. She picked up the writing desk and a handful of the fallen papers. She held them out to Bridget as a pathetic peace offering.

Bridget didn't take them, despite her ownership, no doubt recognising the gesture that they were.

"Fine." Tanry dropped the desk and shoved the papers into her pocket. "See you at the ball," she said.

She strode away, counselling herself not to look back. She went back through the faux village, which felt sickly in its folk tale presentation. When she found her horse again, she reached into her pocket for the papers and smoothed them out. A couple of them were meaningless shopping lists, but also grasped in her hand was the smudged note that Bridget had been writing as Tanry approached. It read:

Alchemical process #345:

Concerning the colouring and lengthening of hair. Colour taken from dark hair and transplanted to light hair. Possibly the reverse process could also work.

CHAPTER EIGHTEEN

A Personal Seamstress

As the mistress of her own household, a lady will have final say on the hiring and firing of servants. She must find trusted, reliable souls, but remember that those in service will never be of an equal class. Friendliness is not required. — Margrit Bellere's Manual for Young Ladies

"She has been screaming all morning," complained Caterina.

Even with the door to the bedroom closed, Tanry could hear Idonea's shouts. Her attention however, was drawn by a foreign object. The golden gown, now finished, was worn by a mannequin. The fuchsia gown, long discarded, had left its own mannequin bare. Now, the snot-coloured gown covered it. Tanry's eyes were hurt just looking at it.

"Gods, it is worse the longer you look at it."

"I'd wager that Athalie is unhappy with you. That is not

your colour at all," said Caterina.

Tanry grimaced. "I cannot be out of here soon enough. I'll wear it, if only to spare myself another of Athalie's petty revenges later on."

"You can escape the ball early, no doubt," said Caterina. She was moving about the room, though Tanry had been too focused on the dress to consider what she was doing.

Now she noticed that Caterina was dressed to go out. She had her coat on, and a hat pinned over her hair, instead of her usual maid's cap.

"Another gentleman to see?" asked Tanry.

"Uh. Not this time. I wanted to warn you, but this has come on rather suddenly."

"What has come on rather suddenly?"

"Princess Athalie was impressed with my work."

"No one can help that." Tanry said this honestly. She had no great love for fashions and fabrics herself, but Caterina had produced more gowns than Tanry thought imaginable in such a short time. She had made a beautiful trousseau for Matfey, though they had no cause to use it. There could not be a soul at court unimpressed by Caterina's abilities.

"She has offered me a position."

"No, she hasn't," said Tanry, instinctively.

"She has."

"What need has Athalie of further maids?"

"She has offered me a position as her personal seamstress."

Tanry's stomach tightened. She didn't want to believe what she was hearing.

"Athalie already has a tailor."

"And you can see his work right there." She pointed at the

green gown, which seemed dull next to Caterina's golden work. She had a point, of course, but it still made no sense. Athalie had not expressed any disparaging comments about her tailor before. This was a ploy, and an effective one.

"Why would Athalie want you, if not to hurt me?"

It was the only reason Tanry could think of. Athalie was a poacher. Mrs Button had warned Tanry about this sort of thing. People were always stealing servants, apparently, though Tanry had never encountered it before. The most ludicrous notion was that Caterina couldn't see the ruse for how transparent it was.

"She was impressed with my work. That is what she said. That is the reason she asked me. I only want to progress my career. I cannot be a maid forever."

Tanry could feel the panic rising in her chest. Caterina needed to listen, to understand. She was so focused on her own ambitions that she couldn't see Athalie's ploy for what it was. She was leaving Tanry for no good reason.

"You cannot be so naive. She seeks to punish me for marrying the man she wants. Once I am away with him, she will have no reason to keep you on."

"I have worked enough to prove my worth to her."

She held her head very high. Tanry had seen her do so before, usually when she had been scolded by Mrs Button or Cole. Caterina had no shortage of pride, which Tanry understood, but she was letting her pride lead her to foolhardiness.

"Are you certain of that?" asked Tanry, feeling rather hollow. She had to convince Caterina that she was being foolish, that her ambitions were futile, or she would leave Tanry. She would not come back to Taltois, and Tanry wouldn't be able to talk to her anymore. She had to tell her that it was a bad idea, that she was better off with Tanry. She had to be better off with Tanry.

"Of course I am," said Caterina in a level voice.

Silence fell over both of them, so deeply that Tanry could hear the ticking of the clock on the mantel. She had been picturing what she and Caterina would do on the trip home. Caterina loved to gossip, and court had provided them with plenty of material. The idea that Caterina simply wouldn't be there was laughable and strange. Caterina had always been there. Whenever Trevor's friends told Tanry she had to leave, she could always find Caterina and complain about them. Caterina had been there when Tanry heard what had happened to Trevor. It was unthinkable that her head had been so quickly turned by one measly offer. She was Tanry's friend, and she was leaving her. Tanry didn't want to believe it, but maybe their friendship had been nothing but a ruse. Maybe Caterina had only wanted to use Tanry to get a better position somewhere else. Maybe she had no regard for her at all.

"I can think of no other reason for a princess to hire a maid as her personal seamstress," said Tanry.

"So I can be nothing more than a maid, then?"

"That is all you have been until now."

Tanry regretted saying it, but her pride kept her from an apology. She had always known Caterina had ambitions of changing her station, but ignoring that idea had been expedient. It had allowed her to pretend they could continue to be friends.

Tanry had thought, and never really examined the idea, that Caterina would always be around, and that Tanry would never truly be lonely.

Caterina stepped back from her. She picked up her carpet bag. "I have rooms prepared already," she said. "I will send someone back for the rest of my things."

"If you leave, it won't be easy to come back," Tanry warned her. When she said it, she was sure that Athalie's offer was nothing but empty air, yet right after the words left her mouth, a seed of doubt sprouted in her stomach. Athalie had been determined thus far, and she had not backed away, even when her schemes didn't work. She, Tanry presumed, had wanted to scare Tanry away with an elaborate wedding, and now they were having that elaborate wedding, and Athalie had not cancelled a single item. Perhaps her offer to Caterina was a scheme, but also genuine, and there was a real chance that Caterina would not come back.

"I'm well assured of that," declared Caterina. She left.

Tanry was alone with the revolting gown and the cries of a ghost in the other room.

CHAPTER NINETEEN

Battle Must Be Met

Princess Athalie is the most splendid and gracious host, though often she attends her own balls with reticence. This can only be viewed as a virtue, as she possesses too much humility to revel in her achievements. — Pherson's Courtly Hearsay

The green gown made it impossible to march. The skirt was too narrow, intended for ladies who glided, rather than walked. Tanry, as a lady who had never come out in society or attended social events for most of her life, hadn't mastered the art of gliding around. She held up her skirts as high as she could, and marched towards the grand ballroom. Dressing had taken longer without Caterina's help. Her hair remained in its most basic chignon, and Tanry only had her signet ring in terms of jewellery. She knew that she didn't look like the fine lady she was supposed to be.

She moved towards the door, ready to elbow her way into the ball, when a voice called her name.

Valentin was seated on a gilt chair by the doors to the ballroom. He'd been cleaned up. He wore a white suit with a high collar and a blue sash, like she'd seen in paintings of the imperial family. He looked far better, she thought, than she did. No one would think that they belonged together.

"What were you waiting for?" she asked him.

"You, obviously." He stood and held his arm out for her.

"You'll have to hold me up. Athalie sent me this awful dress as punishment."

"You look lovely."

"Don't lie."

"You don't look like yourself."

"That's better. Let's go. Battle must be met." Tanry hooked her arm into Valentin's. She steeled herself as two footmen grasped the doorhandles and opened the doors.

"Wait until we've been announced," cautioned Valentin. They hovered in the doorway as a herald blew on a rudimentary horn and cried out:

"Archduke Cezsario Concerto Dalibor Boralda-Solkin and Lady Tanry Teneri."

Valentin guided her over the threshold into the glittering ballroom. They stood on a raised platform with a grand staircase that promoted no purpose except to display the people who stood upon it.

They were met by raucous applause. The musicians stopped playing to stand for them, and half of the attendees bowed. Tanry guessed that it was some etiquette rule based on social standing that kept half of them upright. Tanry paid no mind. She was looking for Athalie.

The princess stood in the centre of the crowd, as was appropriate for the leader of the court. She wore a lilac gown that Tanry had seen her wear before. She took off her glasses to clean them, but Tanry thought it was her means of refusing to see what was in front of her.

"We should stay for as little time as possible," she told Valentin. "We have a big day tomorrow, and I would rather not be here."

"Me neither, but we have to do one thing first."

He steered her towards the dance floor. Tanry tried to dig her heels in, but she wore the flimsy slippers Caterina had packed.

"Only one dance," Tanry insisted.

"Just for appearances."

"Make it an easy one. No one ever taught me how to dance."

"Why not?"

They were in the middle of a crowd that had parted around them. The musicians rested their bows against their strings and the conductor raised his baton in greedy anticipation.

"I did not have a dancing master as you did," she said. No one had thought to teach Tanry correct courtly dances, though she suspected that she wouldn't have had the patience to follow them. Trevor hated to dance too, and his dancing master abandoned them after Trevor went hunting during their lessons. Tanry would have followed him, hunting and gambling, and never wandering how to dance a quadrille. Duke Teneri, a constant academic, never imagined that his children might have required the skill.

"Follow my lead, then," said Valentin, and Tanry found herself briefly comforted by his presence at her side.

With one discordant note, the music began. It was an overly romantic piece with long, drawn out notes, and Tanry found herself gripping tightly to Valentin's arms as he led her about the dance floor. Her face was hot from embarrassment. She kept her eyes trained on Valentin's face, so he could give her an indication of which way they were to move next. He didn't try anything adventurous. Tanry tripped on her second step and Valentin had to catch her. He did not attempt to spin her around the floor, or lift her up. To her relief, other couples joined in, and their more expert dancing moved attention away from her. They stopped before the song ended.

"I think that's all we have to do," Valentin declared.

Tanry stayed close to his side, nodding at people who tried to greet them. Valentin found a waiter and collected two crystal glasses of champagne from his tray and handed one to Tanry.

"Sustenance," he said. "The princess is coming to speak to us."

She was approaching them like a bespectacled predator.

"You look resplendent this evening, Lady Teneri," said Athalie, ignoring Valentin.

"Don't lie."

Athalie snorted. "I do appreciate your frankness, Lady Teneri."

"I'd wager that's the only thing you appreciate about me."

Athalie perhaps found that too frank, because she frowned at the remark. "Why are you leaving the dance floor so quickly? You are being wed tomorrow – you should scarcely stand to be apart."

"Dancing is hardly my best skill."

"Who would care? You are the bride. Go on, dance." She ushered them back to the dance floor, where a much faster tune was playing.

"She's good at punishment," muttered Tanry.

"You'll be fine," Valentin tried to assure her. "You need to hop from foot to foot with this one." He tried to demonstrate.

Tanry attempted to copy him, but she couldn't do it in time with the music.

Valentin laughed. "You look like a marionette, you know," he said.

"How am I supposed to prevent that?"

"Have you never tried to move more gracefully?"

"You may as well ask a dog to ignore a rabbit."

He took Tanry by the waist. "Copy me again," he instructed her.

"It's much harder with this song," she complained, gathering the train of her skirt into one hand. "Why do people enjoy this torment?"

"Because it is fun when you know how." He laughed again.

It was hopeless. Tanry couldn't pick up the skill in the middle of the song. They could only giggle their way around the dance floor until the song ended.

They stumbled out of the throng of dancers and towards another footman with a drinks tray. Tanry took two.

"What are you going to do tomorrow?" asked Valentin. "The day is mostly dedicated to dancing."

"How awful. I've never attended a wedding. I barely know what to expect."

"Even I have attended several weddings and *I* am in exile."

"Do people get married at court often?"

"No. You are unusual in all senses of the word. No, when Athalie takes a progress, the court goes with her. More weddings happen then. They like to have the princess in attendance."

Tanry hadn't appreciated that before. It would have taken a lot of work for the impostors to stay ahead of all the people they were likely to meet on a progress, and whether they had ever encountered the imperials.

Tanry spotted Matfey alone, trying to pretend that she was focused on the contents of her drink.

"I must speak to your sister. Go and make nice with whoever you need to make nice with."

"I'm unlikely to see any of them for quite some time, so I suppose I shall start my farewells."

Tanry had no intention of making nice with the denizens of the court. She made her way towards Matfey, but she was caught by Miss Annabilla Katydid, who gasped in excitement.

"Lady Teneri, how gorgeous you look."

"You must not pay me false compliments, Miss Katydid."

"Of course not. We have been discussing what kind of dress you would wear since you became engaged. We were certain that you would surprise us. Your choice tonight is certainly proof of that."

"I must speak to Laurina now."

"Soon you will steal her away to your remote estate. You can spend a night with us." Miss Katydid steered her towards Lord and Lady Bayard.

Lady Bayard was wearing the same dress that she had worn to the last ball with a new lace trim attempting to disguise that fact.

"You danced wonderfully, Lady Teneri," said Lady Bayard.

Tanry snorted. "This place is intolerable. I don't know how Athalie stands it."

"Whatever can you mean?"

"I have never been taught to dance, Lady Bayard. That would have been apparent, I'm sure. I am desperate to return to a world that I understand. Pigs, I understand. Forestry. Hunting. You won't see me at court again."

"I hope then that we can call on you at Taltois. I have so wanted to see that part of the country."

"We shall see. I need to speak to Laurina." She picked up her skirt again and strode away.

She caught Matfey by the arm and began to steer her around the perimeter of the dance floor.

"Where are we going?" Matfey asked, dizzied by the sudden movement.

"I needed a word with you, with a reduced chance of someone overhearing."

"Oh. I suppose that makes sense. That dress does look awful on you."

"Thank you. But anyhow, when you go on progress, how do you stay ahead of the other nobles?" asked Tanry.

"What do you mean?"

"If there's anyone from Karda Ven, how do you know whether they would recognise you?"

"Idonea tells us."

"She does?"

"She is in Karda Ven. She was a part of the protection corps. They recruited us and trained us. She knows all of these things. She was preparing for tomorrow. If Athalie makes good on her threat to invite every exile from the home country, then we will need her to dodge any accusations."

That was going to be difficult, as Idonea was trapped inside a mirror in Tanry's bedroom.

She had no time to dwell on the matter, because she spotted Athalie and Valentin across the dance floor. They were leaving the room together.

"I must go," Tanry told Matfey. "You are supposed to be rebellious. Cause some mayhem and people might really believe that Laurina Boralda-Solkin is here."

She left before Matfey could mumble a reply. She could not have Athalie and Valentin cause a scandal the night before her wedding. Not when she was so close to victory. She marched through the people, ignoring their attempts to garner her attention. She escaped into one of the heavily mirrored corridors, but could not see Athalie and Valentin. There were only the wigged footmen who stood like ornaments stood at intervals. She grabbed the nearest one by the collar.

"I will pay you three guineas to tell me which way the archduke and the princess went."

Silently, he pointed to a corridor to their left.

"Thank you. You can bill my father for the expense."

She crept towards the corridor, feeling pleased to be wearing slippers for the first time. She was quiet by instinct, rather than design. She had no real intentions of eavesdropping: she just wanted Valentin back. He was the perfect shield. He would make conversation with just about anybody and Tanry need not participate. Yet when she heard their voices, she knew that she could not interrupt.

The door to the library hung open. She could see only one

alchemic light on a table, casting an orange glow over Athalie's face and turning her glasses opaque. Tanry pressed her back to the wall so she could not be seen.

"It's hardly a marriage of convenience when it is this inconvenient," said Athalie.

"You know full well that you have made it more of an inconvenience than it ever needed to be." Valentin sat at one of the window seats. He had picked up a book and he flicked through it idly, though it was too dark in that corner for him to actually read.

"What can she offer you? What does Tanry Teneri have that no other lady at court possesses?"

"You addressed her as she prefers just there," he said.

"You did not answer me."

"I have said that it is a matter of convenience. I have no money and Lady Teneri needed an archduke."

"Now *you* are not addressing her as she prefers."

Tanry peered through the gap between the door and the wall. Valentin stared ahead, refusing to look Athalie in the face. She, in turn, pored over the books she had selected.

"Some habits cannot be relinquished," admitted Valentin. "Tanry has sworn to find dowries for Lizseta and Laurina. If you can't see how advantageous that is, then I do not know what else I can do to explain."

"You know that I could have provided dowries for your sisters. I have promised it thrice over."

"I did not ask it from you, Athalie. I would never ask it from you."

"But you would ask it of Tanry Teneri."

"She... It is different with her."

"How is it different?" Athalie asked.

"It scarcely matters. My sisters will be protected and I will have a living to rely on, at least. I will no longer have to beg you for anything."

"I will give you anything gladly. It's no hardship, Cezsario. I do not understand why you hold this pride, and especially not when it comes to Tanry Teneri."

Valentin did not respond. There was naught that he could say.

"Your silence cannot protect you," said Athalie after a moment. "I cannot stand it when you lie to me. I cannot stand lies at all."

"My princess..."

"I am not yours, as you have taken great pains to remind me."

"Your Highness."

"I could have been yours, but I seem to lack something that Tanry Teneri has in abundance."

"You have – there is nothing that she has over you. She is not – she could never be better than you are."

Tanry might have been offended, if she hadn't thought that Valentin's opinions were entirely fair. She had not expected friendship from him, not really. She didn't understand why there was a sinking feeling in her belly, so she elected to ignore it.

"Why are you marrying her instead of me?" Athalie asked.

Tanry nearly burst through the door, such was her surprise. She'd known they had regard for each other, but it was nonsensical to believe that marriage had been proposed.

"It's not because of that," said Valentin quickly.

"Then why *are* you marrying her? Why, when I can offer you everything that she has offered you and more? I don't understand. I asked you once and I thought I must have surprised you. I thought I would just wait, then when I asked again, I believed you must think too little of yourself. I spent so long telling you I didn't care and I needed no status from you. When I asked you the third time and you said no, I thought that you must not be ready to marry, or perhaps you didn't want to wed at all. I thought I could make my peace with that because I would still always have you nearby, and you could be my friend. But now you're going to marry her for no other reason than it's convenient to you."

"It isn't like that, I swear," insisted Valentin.

"Then do you love her?"

"What?"

"Do you love her?"

"Athalie, you cannot ask such a thing. You and I both know that it is more complicated than that."

"Then do you love me?"

"Why do you ask?"

"There is no practical reason for you to marry her over me, unless you love her."

"I don't..." Valentin's voice trailed off as he ran out of things to say.

"If you don't love her and you only respect her as someone who can help you, then it doesn't make sense that you accepted her proposal in a matter of weeks. Unless there is something else that I do not know about. Unless there is something that Lady Teneri has over you. Unless she has forced your hand in some way."

There was a pause. Tanry was certain that Valentin was about to throw himself at Athalie's feet and beg for her forgiveness. He loved her. He would tell her everything. He would tell her that his name was Valentin and that his sisters were called Bridget and Matfey and one of them was an alchemist. He was a bastard and his grandfather had given him away to protect his mother's honour. He had been the decoy for the real archduke, who was now dead, probably.

"There is nothing," said Valentin.

"I do not understand."

"I have affection for her – for Tanry."

"Is affection enough?"

"I love her, then."

They paused again.

"More than me?" asked Athalie.

"More than you," he said with a sigh.

"Really?" Athalie asked, her voice breaking.

"What other reason could I possibly have for marrying her instead of you?"

Tanry backed away from the door. His voice had been so soft and sad that she couldn't stand to hear it. She rushed into the ballroom, where a waltz was being drawn out.

Matfey caught Tanry's eye from across the floor and waved. Tanry cut through the dancers to get to her.

"I am champing at the bit," Tanry announced.

"What do you mean?"

"Champing at the bit to get out of this place," said Tanry. "My father has it right. I'll go home with a husband and never come back again."

"Do you have many balls at Taltois?" asked Matfey.

"None. My mother may have held some, but I've no idea. No one talks about her."

"Not even your father?"

"No. He only talks about alchemy and who I should be married to."

Matfey stared at her quizzically.

"Why does he never talk of your mother?"

"Who knows? Perhaps he just always preferred alchemy to her. He was never overflowing with love, even for Trevor."

"We speak about them all the time. Mother, Father, our aunts, our uncles. Our eldest sister, though she died when she was a baby."

"But they're not – they're not really yours."

Matfey shrugged.

"We knew them. From when I was a child, I knew them all, and they were not always kind, but when they were taken – their loss was terrible."

"You speak about these distant people more than I have ever spoken about my own mother. What a strange thought." Tanry laughed, though it was more of a bark.

"What was she like, your mother?"

"I scarcely know. She came from a very old, very rich family, like everyone here, I suppose. Her father was an alchemist from Premure. A much better one than my father. I've no idea if she had any talents or interests. I was raised chiefly by my brother. I followed him everywhere. I copied him. I wanted to be exactly like him. I learned to hunt, to drink, to play billiards and cards. No one taught me to be a lady. I was too busy becoming a lord."

"Why do you never talk about him?"

"I— what do you mean?"

"Why do you never mention your brother, if you loved him that much?"

"I— I didn't love him that much. He never had any time for me. He resented my very presence."

She spied Valentin across the ballroom. He went straight to a silver tray and swigged a glass of champagne with little sense of modesty or decorum.

"I have to go," said Tanry. "I'll tell them all that I am too excited for the wedding tomorrow. I have to get out of here."

She tried to move away, but she could not run in her narrow skirt. The alchemic lights felt hotter and more odorous than they had before. Valentin caught her by the waist.

"Another waltz?" he asked.

"I want to leave."

"Aren't you committed now?" He pulled her onto the dance floor. "One last performance," he said. "Before tomorrow."

A moment later, Tanry understood who the performance was for, as Athalie returned to the room. Her head was held high, though her eyes were red.

Valentin pulled Tanry around the dance floor despite how heavy she felt. She could not help thinking of her brother, probably only because Matfey had brought him up. If he had been there, Tanry knew that he would have disapproved of Valentin. Trevor would have thought he was a sop. He would have said Valentin liked poetry too much to be a full-blooded man. He would have told Tanry to marry someone richer.

CHAPTER TWENTY

A Marriage of Inconvenience

Karda Ven once had the richest aristocracy on the continent. The emperor was more generous than any king. The loss of the imperial family was not just the loss of a government, but a way of life. Any Veni nobles that remain are scattered, without funds, and robbed of the esteem they should have possessed. — A Lament for the Old Country: a History of Karda Ven

The golden veil was soft but hung heavily on her head. She clasped a bouquet of marigolds from Athalie's hothouse. Duke Teneri smoked his pipe as if his daughter was not stood there in her wedding dress.

"Is it time to go?" he asked of the room.

"The bridesmaids go first," said Tanry.

"And where are they, then?"

"I don't know."

Just then, the doors to the antechamber were opened. Athalie, Bridget, and Matfey stood there in matching gold dresses with flowers in their hair.

"You're late," said Tanry.

"What does it matter? The bride is always late," said Athalie with a scowl. She fixed the flowers, which she wore with a tiara. "Have you seen the people in there? It's packed, and half of the nobles from Karda Ven were only invited to the reception." She laughed coldly.

Tanry's stomach tightened. Bridget kept her eyes on the floor.

"I don't know why they're here," said Tanry. "I've nothing in the way of friends."

"It's only fair that these poor, exiled nobles get to see their archduke off into married life. Aren't we going in?"

Tanry grasped her father's arm and snatched the pipe from his mouth. "Let's get this over with," she said. "I do hate public displays."

"You and I have an accord there," muttered Athalie. She walked ahead and pushed open the doors.

Orange alchemic lights were hung over the hall, spewing trails of smoke and incense. Athalie, for all that she had done to prevent the wedding, had put together a marvellous display. Every bench was decorated with marigolds and orange lilies with golden silk ribbons. An organ played, and all the lords and ladies craned their necks to look at her. Athalie led the way, but slowly, as if she was eking out every possible moment left where Tanry wasn't married to Valentin.

Only when she was halfway down the aisle did Tanry see Valentin standing there. He was a handsome man, dressed in his imperial regalia. His suit was old-fashioned, but he wore it well; it had the gold embroidery and high collar of which the last emperor had been so fond. He had his eyes trained on Athalie for far too long.

Tanry's heart was racing. She waited for Athalie to step aside, but not to sit down, before she let go of her father and rushed to take Valentin's hand. There were titters in the crowd and giggles as she did so. They probably thought that she was all too eager to be wed. They could think as they wanted. She had her archduke and soon she would be back in Taltois.

Tanry Teneri wed Archduke Cezsario Concerto Dalibor Boralda-Solkin – or so everyone believed - in a ceremony that made more than a dozen ladies hide their yawns behind their fans, and that made the princess weep in despair.

The ballroom was filled with more people than had attended Athalie's two previous balls. Even without Idonea's help, Tanry could identify which of the congregation were exiles from the home country: they wore their old court dress, even though it was threadbare, missing beads, or stained. It was a part of their homeland and therefore a badge of honour.

"Karda Ven seems so ghostly now," said Matfey.

"What does that mean?" asked Tanry.

"I know that I lived there, but it feels like another time. A lost civilisation. Everyone here talks about it with such reverence, yet everyone they knew there is dead. I think of them half still there, residing in the home country, and we are all here, still living among the mortals. Perhaps when I die, I'll go back to the home country."

"You are odd sometimes, when you let yourself speak."

Matfey failed to respond to that.

"Say, can you see my husband anywhere nearby?" asked

Tanry. "That feels strange on the tongue, doesn't it?"

"Oh, he is hiding," said Matfey.

"Why would he be hiding? This is his wedding."

"My darling sister has been trying to summon Idonea all morning but she simply won't come. She is most distressed and it isn't helped by who surrounds us. They are all simply gasping to talk to us."

"Ah."

"Take that woman there." She pointed at a tall woman in the crowd with dark hair and a violet gown. "She is Genevieve Taybury. She's a countess, or she was."

"Oh god," said Tanry, recognising the name.

Matfey gave her a significant look. "I think Idonea would have something to say about it all, were she here."

She moved away. Tanry couldn't stand to ponder the problem at hand. She had already given thanks to every backwater Venian noble whom Athalie had seen fit to invite. It would seem suspicious if she ignored Genevieve Taybury. Perhaps if she spoke to her, the former countess wouldn't feel compelled to meet the groom.

"Excuse me." She sidled into the group where Genevieve Taybury stood. "Tanry Teneri." She held out her hand to the countess. She stared at Tanry quite perplexed.

"I apologise. I am quite unfamiliar with the customs of this land."

"Well, I am the bride and I am introducing myself."

"In my country, brides do not wear gold."

"Yes, they wear white, but that would not suit my complexion nearly so well. Who are you?"

She considered Tanry, then took her hand and shook it.

"Genevieve Taybury."

"No title?"

"You did not give yourself one. It's quite refreshing. I have not known how to introduce myself ever since I left the home country. My compatriots are quite attached to their titles, but without the land I do not imagine I should be called Countess."

"Did you know my husband well when you were in Karda Ven?"

"Not at all. My father was known at court, but I had little to do with the young heir."

"I hope that you will get to meet him soon. I can't quite tell where he has gone off to."

"It would be nice to have a taste of home. My mother, my father – they all died in the war. I have a comfortable existence now. My groom – he was the one to spirit me away here – is the only countryman I have left."

"Look around, there are plenty of your countrymen here."

Taybury laughed. "Back in Karda Ven, I might not have spoken to most of these people. The princess seems to have invited her guests with abandon. My father would not have let most of them shine his shoes."

"They are an odd lot, sure. I would have preferred a smaller affair. Were you ever married?"

"Not myself. My father could never find anyone to his liking."

"My father let me choose."

"Did he now?"

"Well, I know that this is not what he intended, but he should have set some more stipulations."

Tanry left Genevieve Taybury, feeling no less queasy than before. One glance, and she would recognize that the archduke was not the archduke, and was instead her long lost son, and that really would put a damper on the celebrations. Tanry found Bridget hiding behind the seven-tiered cake, her terrier in her arms.

She grabbed Tanry by the arm. "Have you seen Idonea?" she whispered.

"She is in your arms, in case you forgot."

"My brother is hiding. We have no idea whether any of these people knew us."

"Genevieve Taybury implied that most of these people didn't rub shoulders with the imperials."

"You spoke to Genevieve Taybury?"

"I introduced myself."

"Did she suspect anything?"

"No, but she no doubt will if you cannot pull it together."

"We cannot have her here. Not at his wedding. She *knew*."

Tanry signalled to a waiter. He trotted over with two glasses of champagne brandished on a tray.

"Lizseta, drink up."

Bridget shook her head.

Tanry pushed the glass into her hand. "Drink this. Then go over there and drink another. I can have Laurina take you to bed early, owing to your overindulgence."

"Lizseta would never."

"Lizseta never saw her dear younger brother married to a woman she clearly hates."

Bridget, after half a decade of playing pretend, was adept at acting. She drank a few glasses, but mostly she waddled around, letting her dog eat from others' plates and wailing that her brother's virtue was lost.

"Well done, Lady Teneri." Athalie appeared beside Tanry, her pipe in her hand.

"You played well, it has to be said," replied Tanry.

"You understand that I must relinquish my hospitality. Five years is quite enough to host."

"How long do they have to put their affairs in order?"

"Be gone in the morning."

"Understood."

"Don't come back again."

"You could not pay me to, Athalie."

"Good."

"Take care of Caterina, won't you?" asked Tanry.

Athalie walked away without answering.

Tanry found Valentin in the orangery, where he was pretending to nurse a drink.

"I checked the library twice," said Tanry, and Valentin bristled. "I should have guessed that you've been exiled from that domain."

Valentin sat on the edge of the pool and played his hand across the surface of the water. "You saw Lady Taybury?" he asked.

"Yes, I have."

Valentin made a noise with his tongue and stared into the water. "She cannot see me. She cannot even look my way," he insisted.

"It might be early, but we can end this wedding." She

grasped his free hand. "How did they do this in your country?"

"All the men carried the bride to bed."

"We are not doing that. Let's just run." She drew Valentin to his feet; water dripped from his other hand down his trouser leg, and he continued to stare listlessly. "She won't see you," promised Tanry. "We can hide."

The crowd had filtered out of the ballroom and into the mirrored corridor. Tanry picked up her skirts by the hem and ran, holding Valentin by the hand. They drew the eye of all the guests as they flitted by.

"Tanry, stop," gasped Valentin.

"What's the matter?" She turned and he pulled her in by the waist.

"We can't just run off," he whispered in her ear. "We have to give them a show." Feeling his breath on her ear made her want to swat him like a fly, or scratch all her skin away. Valentin leaned his forehead against hers, which felt very strange. It was odd to see him from this angle. It didn't feel like he was looking at her, but like he was staring through her, eyes as close as they possibly could be. Someone nearby whistled and her skin crawled.

"I'm going to spin you," said Valentin. He lifted Tanry's arm above her head and spun her. She was ungainly, so it was more of a shuffle in a clockwise direction.

"Goodnight!" Valentin called to the crowd. There were titters and Valentin laughed. "Goodnight, my bride and I have somewhere to be." There were matching laughs among the watchers.

Tanry turned and saw Athalie in the doorway to the ballroom. She could not describe Athalie's expression, but it bore a hollow feeling. She held tighter to Valentin's hand and led him away.

They went back to the imperial suite, followed by a gathering of busybodies.

"Don't come knocking!" Valentin called at them.

Tanry feared that he might kiss her just to sell the ruse. She couldn't stand that notion, so she pushed open the door and pulled him inside. Shutting the door tightly, she considered propping a chair under the door handle, but thought better of stranding Bridget and Matfey with the nobles from Karda Ven.

"You'd better pack your things," said Tanry. "Athalie wants us gone in the morning."

"I should have expected as much."

"We need to pretend to be having a honeymoon anyway."

The imperial suite was half-dark. No servants had been in or out to clean in five years. As disorderly as it was, Tanry doubted they would be able to pack it all up in a night.

She kindled a fire in the hearth while Valentin took down books from his shelves. They worked in silence, desperately avoiding eye contact with one another. Tanry cracked the alchemical lamps, and replaced the rocks in the ones that had run out of light. She tidied Bridget's paints, which were sheathed in a layer of dust. She collected the papers where Matfey had scrawled sums and figures. She packed Valentin's books of poetry into a small trunk and paused on a journal with an embossed cover. It was so fine that it had to have been a gift from Athalie.

Tanry checked over her shoulder. Valentin had vanished into his bedroom, and she was unobserved. She flicked through the pages of the journal, each marked by Valentin's hand. The journal contained his attempts at verse.

Most pages contained scribbles, crossings out, and whole lines through the work. But then there was a poem, written with no mistakes. 'For Athalie' was scrawled across the top of the page.

When a groom loves his lady,
  There are naught but smiles in the room,
  But there are feelings most uneasy,
  When a lady loves her groom.

Her bloodline, like his mares,
  Was as woven as tapestry.
  It caught the groom quite unawares,
  That she saw him lovingly.

And as his heart did ache,
  He knew she could not wed him,
  Yet even as he knew her sake,
  He indulged her every whim.

His soul was pine,
  Sturdy, fine for chairs.
  Hers was ivory, the most fine.
  They should part, as was fair.

They loved another helplessly,
  And when she bore a child,
  They could not prevent his misery,
  And all were soon exiled.

Tanry didn't know enough about verse to judge its quality. She shut the book and packed it with the rest, attempting not to think about what she had read, but the verse was caught in her mind. It might not have been very complex, but there was a certain truth to be unravelled. Valentin was a bastard, the son of Genevieve Taybury, and he had written a poem about a child fathered by a lady's groom.

She could hear the muffled noises of the celebrations outside.

Valentin returned to the room. His shoulders were slack. He had removed his imperial jacket and stood there in his shirtsleeves. He'd never looked so ruffled.

"Where will you sleep tonight?" he asked.

"In my bed, I expect."

"You're supposed to be sleeping with me tonight."

"No, thank you," she said.

"It means that no one can see you leaving here. You have to sleep here."

"Shit." She rubbed her eyes. "I didn't think about that. I'll take the floor."

"I can sleep on the floor," insisted Valentin.

"Don't be a gentleman, Valentin. I'm the one who blackmailed you."

He put up a cursory argument, if only for the sake of his chivalric ego. Tanry threw down cushions on the floor of his bedroom and laid there, feeling too tired to even shed her wedding dress.

"Do you not want to see her?" she asked.

Valentin rolled over in his bed and grunted in reply.

"She has not met the real archduke," mumbled Tanry.

"He was a better swimmer than I am, and not as skinny."

"Well, if those are the differences, one might not actually be able to tell the difference." She huffed, just so that Valentin would understand her frustration with him.

"When did you last see her?" she said.

She turned her head to see Valentin above her. He was staring very intently at the ceiling.

"I'm your wife now, even if it's in name alone. You could involve me in your secrets, seeing as I am helping to keep them."

"I would rather not," he said with a crack in his voice.

Tanry lay there for some time more. The bed she'd made was hardly a compelling equivalent to a mattress. The words of the poem ran through her head. She wished that they were in her suite, so she could ask the discernment engine questions about Taybury.

The meaning of the poem, she supposed, was that Valentin thought of himself as the groom; too low and too common to marry the lady his heart yearned for. It was too metaphorical for Tanry. Most of the meaning was obscured, so she understood little of the point. Why would Valentin not write about his own life? He was an impostor yearning for a princess – was that not poetic enough?

The poem was stranger than that. Why was this intended for Athalie? What truth did he want to impart? There was some confession in there, she assumed, or why would he write something so close to his own life? His father, she now thought, was Taybury's groom. They had fallen in love, had Valentin in secret, and lost him. Valentin wanted to tell Athalie, even if only in verse, who he really was.

Taybury said that her groom was the only countryman she had left. She left Karda Ven with her groom. There was every possibility that the same groom had travelled with her to Albonne to attend the wedding. Both of Valentin's parents could be there in the court, and was not able to see them.

There was something tragic and haunting about that. They were alive, but separated. Wouldn't Tanry want to see her own mother? Wasn't it unfair that Valentin was denied his family?

She sat up and threw back the blanket, feeling around for her shoes.

"Get up," she told Valentin.

"What?"

"Put your coat on. We can go out of the window."

"I'm not going anywhere."

"I am trying to do something for you. Get up. If anyone sees us, we will just be a happy couple up to drunken antics. Put your coat on."

"They can't see me. We came in here for a reason," he insisted.

"We aren't going back into the ballroom. I'll make sure that no one sees you. Damn, just do this one thing. Your last night in court. Do you really want to spend it in here?"

Valentin probably realised that he wasn't going to be able to talk her out of this plan. He had probably learned a truth of existence: that there was no talking Tanry out of anything.

He put on a pair of trousers and a shirt over his nightclothes. Tanry pushed his window up and hopped out, landing in a neatly tended flowerbed. The imperial suite backed onto the parkland in a quiet area of the court. With some difficulty, owing to her petticoats, Tanry swung one leg over the window frame. She felt the mud seep through the fabric of her slippers. Valentin fussed, putting a plain coat on, shucking off his glittering wedding attire.

Tanry reached inside the window and grabbed his hand. "Hurry up, we don't have long."

"To do what?"

"If I tell you, you won't want to do it."

"Isn't that a sign of how we should not do it?"

"Come on." She pulled on his arm, and he reluctantly climbed out of the window.

"This is a bad idea," he muttered.

"This is your last night here. You've made it to the home stretch. At Taltois, you won't have to pretend as intensely as you did here. No one will remember what you do tonight."

"You always sound so confident."

"Because I am."

"It's dangerous."

"I'm no stranger to risk," said Tanry.

"If I am revealed, you lose your archduke. You will lose your estate."

"Trust me. I am doing something for you. Let's go." She found his hand again and pulled him away.

They kicked up gravel on the paths as they left the soft glow of the palace windows. The way to the stables was not lined with alchemic lights.

"Why are we here?" Valentin asked. He wrinkled his nose as they approached.

Tanry realised she thought of him as an indoor sort of person. He wasn't used to manure.

"I'm looking for the carriages, the ones brought by the guests."

They walked through the stable gates and saw as many carriages as Tanry had ever seen in one place.

"Which one are we looking for?" asked Valentin, his eyes skating over the crests painted on the doors.

"Taybury's."

Valentin became a dead weight on the end of her arm. "You know I can't see her."

"It's a good thing that she's not here, then. We are looking for her carriage."

"I can't think why."

"Oh, it might come to nothing, but I figured I should try."

"We shouldn't be here," he said.

Most of the carriages were empty. With the wedding festivities ongoing, the grooms and the drivers had founded their own party. Tanry could hear the revelries in the barracks beyond the stables. There was one occupied carriage; she could tell by the blue alchemic light on top of the cab. It was plain, but shone in the moonlight. There was no crest on the door, but it was polished so well that Tanry could see her own reflection.

"There," she pointed.

A middle-aged man, a groom in a faded uniform, wiped dirt from the carriage windows.

"That's him, right?"

"I don't know what you mean."

"Hello, sir," Tanry called and the groom looked up. He had familiar dark eyes.

"Are you Taybury's groom?" she asked, holding Valentin's

hand fast so he couldn't bolt.

"I am," said the groom. "What brings you here?" He looked her up and down, taking in her wardrobe, and his brow furrowed. "My lady," he added.

"No one's lady," said Tanry. "Except for his now, I suppose. But you are Lady Taybury's groom, yes? The one who helped her escape Karda Ven?"

"I am." His eyes landed on Valentin and a stillness came over him.

"Tanry, we should go," said Valentin.

"He's just a groom," said Tanry. "What can he do?"

"You are – you are the groom. Not *a* groom. The bridegroom." The groom stumbled over his words.

"I am," said Valentin.

The groom closed the carriage door and turned to face them fully. He stared at Valentin, taking him in with painstaking detail. "Why are you both here, on your wedding night?" he asked.

"I don't rightly know," replied Valentin.

"I merely thought you might know each other from Karda Ven," said Tanry.

"I haven't had much to do with the imperials," said the groom.

"There is no need for pretence here," declared Tanry.

Valentin grasped her upper arm. "We should be going," he said.

"You know him then," said the groom, addressing Tanry.

"I do."

"You know who he is."

"I do. Though I shan't be telling anyone. Nor should you."

"Tanry, we should go back inside," insisted Valentin.

"You should come home," said the groom.

Valentin turned pale.

"Listen to your wife. There's no need for pretence," said the groom.

"I can't do that." Valentin shook his head.

"Val..."

"No," he insisted. "Sir, I appreciate your regard. I have to find my sisters."

The silence between them as they walked back was pained. Valentin, determined as Tanry had never seen him, refused to engage with anything that Tanry said. He waited until they climbed back through the window of the imperial suite before he had a mind to speak.

"Was I supposed to enjoy that?" he asked.

"When did you last speak to your father? Wouldn't you want that?"

"Of course I want that. It doesn't mean that I can have that."

"He clearly understood what was going on."

"If I leave, what happens to Bridget and Matfey? What happens to Athalie?"

"Does it matter?"

"For five years, I've impersonated an archduke. That is a crime worth losing my head over. If any of us reveals ourselves, if the king comes back home, we are all as dead as the imperials surely are."

"Would Athalie do that to you?"

"What hand does she really have in this? Do you think

that any regard she has for me will stand when she learns how intensely I have lied to her? I have used her and her reputation to cement our position at court. We are nothing but criminals, and I do not understand how you can be so cavalier. If I lose my name, you lose your estate."

"It is not even your name."

"I have no other."

"Do you enjoy this? Do you enjoy the title? The esteem? The princess who fawns over you?"

He curled his hands into fists and covered his eyes, like a child preparing a temper tantrum. "I cannot answer that. I cannot believe you would ask me," he said.

"Is that not what you expect others to think of you?"

"If you fell off a horse and died like your brother, I would be a lucky man indeed."

"If you were executed like the parents you pretend to have, I would be even luckier."

It was a very cold night on Valentin's floor.

CHAPTER TWENTY-ONE

All Was Won

The archduke and the archduchesses have been such a common sight at court that it seems likely they will never leave. Our princess has made their life most comfortable these past five years. — Pherson's Courtly Hearsay

Tanry packed her own belongings. She didn't do it very well. She knew all of her fine things would be creased when she arrived back home. It didn't matter. She had her archduke. She didn't need to wear anything in Taltois that wasn't hunting clothes.

Athalie was courteous enough to send footmen to carry her trunk, though Tanry suspected that expediency had more to do with it than kindness. Before long, Tanry was left in her mother's old suite, with only the mirrors on the bed making any noise. She untied the fastenings and eased the mirrors apart by a hair.

"Do not think of following us," she whispered. "I expect you will need to go back to your body, so I think we will get away unnoticed."

Tanry turned the top mirror over, but she saw only her own face doubled there. She knew that Idonea had gone, however, as she heard a hissed insult next to her left ear.

"That's that dealt with," she said to no one in particular. She had no idea why the victory failed to taste sweet. She was going back home, with every assurance that she'd keep her property for years to come. She would no longer have to worry about the spy who had tormented her. All was won.

By the carriages, the mood was dour. Bridget had dressed in a matching fur stole and muff. Her skin was painted like porcelain, though her expression was sourer than any doll's.

"How long will this journey be?" she asked.

"Scarcely a day," replied Tanry. "You will survive."

"We hardly had enough time to pack up the past five years."

"I hope that you left the easel and the pianoforte behind."

Bridget failed to react to that remark. Idonea-dog was yapping inside the carriage.

"It's so strange," Bridget said. "Idonea is being so talkative today, when she has been so quiet of late." She stared at Tanry.

"Are we going to leave, or must we chat here until our ears bleed?" Duke Teneri called to the crowd, sticking his head out of his carriage door.

"He's worried about returning to his books," said Tanry. "But I see no reason to linger."

Silently, Valentin and Matfey climbed inside their carriage. Tanry considered riding with her father for a moment, but she realised that she could not stand the idea. She glanced back at the palace, and the door where Athalie had failed to appear. She climbed inside the carriage after the impostors and closed the door, hopefully never to return.

VOLUME THREE

CHAPTER TWENTY-TWO
The Archduke and his Bride

The archduke Cezsario was not known for good behaviour. At a time when the empire's fate was uncertain, the emperor needed an heir with a good temperament who could learn the mechanics of government quickly, and above all who could present a confident image of an emperor. He was gifted with a son who only wanted to ride horses, swim, and run outdoors. — Gara Thien's Treatise on the Republic of Karda Ven

Despite his better instincts, Zsari stayed for the festival. He'd planned to travel up the road, but now he thought to go to Albonne, and he needed more money for that than he possessed.

The young women of the village made crowns out of autumn flowers. A peddler came through the village with ribbons, and the women deliberated over colours and styles. At the festival, which was on the final day of the harvest, they set up the tables inside one of the larger barns, and lit fires inside metal cans.

Winter's unwelcome breath bothered Zsari wherever he went. He was already wearing all of his clothes. He knew that he looked a mess, but he wanted food, and there was so much of it at the festival.

There were sugared apples with almonds, pies, stews with huge carrot pieces. Zsari ate his fill while the dancing began. Apart from Zsari, every young man in the village was spoken for. They were tied to their partners by brightly coloured ribbons at the wrist. Some of them, married, were comfortable, holding hands as if nothing fixed them together but choice. Others, awkward, forgot they were tied and made jerking movements that pulled their partners about, stumbling.

Zsari knew it was for the best that he hadn't accepted Milla, but confronted with the event, he couldn't help but feel lonelier than before. Milla had asked another farm hand to be her partner, and he'd taken her fancy, as she appeared to laugh at everything he had to say. It would have been nice to tie his hand to someone else's, to feel as if he were not a lonesome soul in the world. But he didn't have nice things, not anymore.

Milla found him as he sat eating alone, dragging her partner behind her.

"I thought you were leaving," she said.

"Your father agreed to pay me until the festival," Zsari explained. "I needed the money."

"Oh, I see," she said with a wry laugh. "I should thank you, anyway."

"What for?"

"Keeping my little secret from Mother. I know you found

it."

He shrugged, trying to pretend the magazine wasn't of any interest to him. Milla didn't appear to believe him, as she laughed again. The band started playing and she pulled her partner away, begging him for a dance.

They played a folk tune that made everyone but Zsari cheer and stamp their feet. Zsari slouched on his bench. Having eaten his fill, he filled his pockets with apples and crusts of bread. He watched the dancers for some time, and then he felt so invisible that he could not stand it, and he swept into the cool night air.

Milla's comment made him think. She'd known that he found her pamphlets, which meant that she'd returned to look at them. That meant that there was a chance of there being a new issue that she'd chosen to hide in the barn.

He rushed over the hill and back there. Lantern in hand, he tore the bag off its hook and laid out the pamphlets.

He was right, because there had been three, and now there were four. The newest one bore a portrait on the front. There was a rich lady, he supposed, in an extravagant dress, with curly hair and dark eyes. A veil covered the back of her head, and she held hands with a young man in imperial dress.

Zsari didn't need to read the caption to know that that was supposed to be the Archduke Cezsario Concerto Dalibor Boralda-Solkin. The most disquieting thing was that the headline of the issue was 'The Wedding of the Year." Checking the caption, he read:

Archduke Cezsario and his bride, Lady Tanry Teneri.

Zsari swore aloud as he flipped through the pages. They were all about the wedding. The author detailed all the illustrious guests, which included the two archduchesses, and Teneri's wealthy father, and the Lyalian princess, Athalie. There were drawings of the wedding cake, a monstrosity with seven tiers; the breakfast, which possessed seven courses; and the canapes on which the court gorged themselves. There were details about the clothes worn, with particular attention paid to how smart the archduke looked, and how fine his gold braid was. Then there was his new wife. She was an heiress, the richest in Lyalia, and would inherit an estate with over a thousand acres. It was a whirlwind romance, the magazine claimed. Zsari thought that the haste might well have involved Lady Teneri's money, and how badly Valentin wanted it.

A hot, itchy jealousy picked at him.

He wanted to find them as quickly as he could, but he was only on foot, and many days from Albonne.

There was a saving grace in the last few paragraphs of the issue. The author noted that the archduke and Lady Teneri were departing for her estate, Taltois.

If Zsari remembered his geography lessons correctly, Taltois was closer to Calness than Karda Ven, but it was substantially closer to Rindan than Albonne. He could get to Taltois before the winter was out, though he wasn't likely to find work once he arrived. That part of the country was too rural for inns, and the harvest work would be done on all the farms. Still, it was a risk worth taking. He could go, find Valentin, and then...

Well, then everything would change. Then he wouldn't be alone. If Valentin had taken his life from him, he would take it back.

Zsari didn't wait to bid the folk of Rindan goodbye. His coins were in his pocket, and he had as much food for the journey as he was likely to get. He expected they would all wake late, owing to the exertions of the night before. He set off alone on the north road, his belongings in a sack that he slung over his shoulder.

As he walked over the hills, passing men on horseback who called him names, and farms where the mothers called their children indoors as soon as they saw him, snowflakes began to fall from the sky. They started wet and mild at first, but before the day was out, drifts were forming around his feet.

He continued on. He would get to Taltois, or die trying.

CHAPTER TWENTY-THREE

An Extension of His Self

It is paramount to raise young gentlemen to understand the livings they will one day acquire, and young ladies to support their husbands. As such, it is only fair to educate both groups separately, each for the needs of their future. — Margrit Bellere's Manual for Young Ladies

Winter brought snows that made riding, walking, and any sort of escape impossible. The house, which had been draughty before, had suffered in Tanry's absence. Servants had to be set to work airing and preparing new rooms. It had been Tanry's plan to keep her wing for herself, placing the impostors elsewhere, so they might not encounter one another at all. A fortnight into their return, though, the only habitable rooms were still in Tanry's wing, damp having been discovered in several unmanaged rooms across the house. She had to see all three of her new family members everyday. Despite the inclement weather, Tanry took to spending time – nights even – in the painted caravan that had belonged to her mother.

She built up the little fire, boiled tea for herself, and slept under her warmest woollen blankets. It might have been a pleasant time, if it hadn't been for the interloper.

Tanry was familiar with vagrants. They weren't entirely common, as Taltois was far from the highways of Lyalia. This vagrant must have had something keeping him from the roads and cities. No doubt there was some crime he was fleeing from. If that was the case, then he was not afraid of adding more to the list, as trespassing on her estate was his favourite pastime.

She'd first noticed him before the snow fell. She'd caught some movement at the treeline, just beyond the sculpted lawn, and assumed that it was her groundskeeper, but soon found him in the walled garden. She saw him next when she went to sleep in her caravan. She watched the flakes fall past the window and spotted a figure by the temple folly on the shores of Taltois' lake. Between the pillars there was a man, stocky and dressed in clothes so ragged that he would have been turned out of the seediest tavern. Not a moment after he was spotted, he slunk away like a fox. She resolved to find his den.

When she was forced to spend time in the house, though, she found her home had become a storm of unwanted rivalry.

Beck Cotterall, her brother's dearest friend, had failed to leave since Trevor's funeral. He had taken over Baroness Vetera's parlour for an art studio. The tile work was stained with oil paints because the fool had never thought to lay down sheets.

Cotterall was already a staunch enemy of Bridget's. That day, he made the mistake of asking her if she wanted to join him to work in his studio, to which she raised her chin and said:

"Are you an accomplished artist, sir?"

"I should like to think so."

"Have you had your work purchased by a gallery? Do you have a patron or an academy to sponsor you?"

"No, nothing like that."

"A hobbyist," sneered Bridget. "I think I shall continue to paint on my own, as I have no need for your expertise."

After that, Bridget retired to her parlour, which was really Tanry's parlour, and Tanry followed. Bridget had allowed her dog to scratch at every piece of furniture, and Tanry was already overcome with repairs.

"You could just have told him that you no longer paint," said Tanry.

"He would only have asked again." Bridget sat at her tea table, drawing Idonea-dog onto her lap. The dog squirmed and attempted to gnaw on Bridget's hand.

"I'll get rid of him. My brother is gone. There is no further reason for him to be here."

Tanry went to the window and looked out. There was a set of tracks in the snow across the west lawn that had no obvious owner. They led back to the lake. She scanned the view for the trespasser, but saw no other sign of him.

"You told us that there would be privacy here," said Bridget.

"I did not think that my brother's hanger-on would still be in residence."

Cotterall's presence was an obstacle Tanry could not have predicted. He still behaved as if Trevor were alive and he were a semi-permanent resident of the household.

Bridget seemed to lose her train of thought. She tapped a notebook in front of her with her forefinger, chewing on the inside of her cheek. Idonea-dog leapt from her lap and started running in circles around the tea table.

"Where is your father's laboratory?" asked Bridget.

"Don't even think of it," Tanry warned. Her father worked in his library, and Tanry had been banned from entering without an invitation from a young age. She couldn't imagine the disaster that would come if Bridget entered that space.

"I thought I was safe here against being revealed. I thought I could study alchemy."

"It is not safe against my father's moods. He should be left alone. Give a maid a list of materials you require, and we can turn another room into a lab for you."

Bridget seemed satisfied by that plan. She opened the notebook in front of her and began writing a list. She was so eager that she flicked ink over the tabletop. She stopped, and looked up at Tanry.

"I want a typewriter," she said.

Tanry snorted. Of course she had the gall to request such an expensive item. "You might want to think a little smaller first."

"I want a typewriter. I used to have a bike, a university place, and my own typewriter. I want my typewriter back."

"Gods above, I'll put an order in. Busy yourself with something else until it arrives. I don't have spare typewriters to hand."

The expression on Bridget's face was tooth-achingly smug. "Idonea!" she called.

Tanry winced. Idonea-dog rushed up to her and jumped, standing on her hind feet, her tail wagging so fast that it blurred.

"She's on the floor. Why are you calling her?"

"I haven't seen her for too long. She should have helped us with the wedding."

"She can't just appear here. She's never seen this place. She has no idea what it looks like." Taltois wasn't pictured in any gossip magazines like the court at Albonne was. Idonea would have no way to picture any of the rooms she was projecting into. It allowed Tanry to feel safe, knowing that Idonea could never project herself from Karda Ven into Tanry's parlour.

"She should have followed us from court. We should have made sure she was following us."

"Clearly she was busy that day."

"Clearly."

Bridget stared at Tanry, whose palms turned clammy. There was no way that she could know what Tanry had done. She hadn't known at the wedding, so there was no way for her to know now.

Tanry left the room without allowing Bridget to say anything more.

She retrieved her boots, intending to track the trespasser from the folly, but paused in the grand hallway. In pride of place above the mantel was the painting of her brother on his horse, with Taltois painted behind him. It was a huge thing, taller than Tanry, with Trevor's eyes painted so that they followed you around the room.

She'd never studied art, but she knew the language of the

painting. The big house was painted behind him and his horse reared, triumphant, like he was about to march into war.

Trevor was painted with the estate because he was meant to wield it as an extension of his own self. But he would never own Taltois. It was *her* estate by right and by merit. She had worked for it, and now, by marrying an archduke, she had won it.

As she stood there, she thought of a use for Beck Cotterall.

CHAPTER TWENTY-FOUR

A Trespasser

In the rich houses of Lyalia, married couples traditionally commission a new portrait to celebrate the union of the families. Such a painting should be hung in the new family home: with the relatives of the groom. — Tradition and Etiquette in Lyalia

"I am not painting over Trevor's portrait," Cotterall insisted. "It would be insulting to his memory, and it was done by a master."

Tanry took the opportunity to assess Cotterall's other paintings, displayed in his studio. He wasn't a master, she could have guessed that, but she supposed that he had potential. He'd done a number of studies of the grounds of Taltois, which was good, as she wanted it in the portrait. Like Trevor's portrait, she wanted the grounds behind them. She would do better than Trevor. She would have an archduke in her portrait. If he was the piece that sealed her power, then Cotterall could paint him as well.

"You have new canvases, don't you? And materials? I can have some ordered, seeing as I also have to order a typewriter."

Cotterall had made a pile of canvases next to the glass doors. Many of them were half-done, as if Cotterall had just given up on his vision part way through. Elsewhere, there were jars filled with well-used paintbrushes. Each of them was missing bristles, or boasted dried paint. Cotterall was in dire need of fresh supplies, she reasoned. He could be bought.

"You do? Why?"

"People in this house keep getting ideas. I want the archduke and both his sisters in the painting too."

"And your father?" Cotterall always gestured with his hands when he spoke. When he said the word 'father', he pressed both palms together and pointed his hands down at Tanry, rather as if he were in prayer, but also in a manner she could only think of as patronising.

"There's no reason to bother him. We can start tomorrow. You can take that painting of my brother home with you."

"I— I don't think that I could do that," he said, stuttering.

"Then I will have to find a storage room for it."

"Why would you do that, Tanry?"

"I'm in charge of this estate. I don't need people thinking of my brother when they walk through the door."

News of the portrait did not go down well with its subjects.

"Tell me that you are not going to have people look at it," said Bridget in the weariest voice one could fathom.

"No, I'm going to save it for my private boudoir. Of course

people are going to see it."

"I need to be seated in it," declared Valentin. "I'm too tall – someone will notice."

"No one will notice that you're too tall. Whatever that means."

"You will have to have him paint my chin narrower. Lizseta's chin was always much slimmer than mine," said Bridget, pinching her own round cheeks.

"You know that this is not the first likeness of you since you left Karda Ven. There have been sketches in Pherson's for ever ball Athalie held," Tanry complained.

"We knew the man who did the sketches for Pherson's," explained Bridget.

Despite Tanry's protests, she had turned Tanry's parlour into a laboratory. Thus far, she had mixed white powders to form a paste that hardened and stuck to the tabletop where she had concocted it. She'd apologised, but Tanry knew that the table couldn't be salvaged. Instead, Tanry had taken to removing the best and most expensive pieces of furniture from the room while Bridget wasn't looking. She was using this conversation to move two slender end tables, which she was hiding behind her legs.

"He did a terrible likeness," said Matfey, rather meekly. "He would alter your appearance for nothing at all. He just wanted to have favour at court, so he would do anything."

"The portrait is a poor idea. Call it off and send the painter home," demanded Bridget. "And why are you standing like that?"

"You've grown a spine since we moved to the country and I don't like it," said Tanry, trying to stand as if it was natural to hold her coattails out to hide a pair of tables.

"Is he a very good artist?" asked Matfey before Bridget could respond.

"He's here, and that is far more important. Matfey, you should keep an eye on him. Ask him if he needs anything, make some comments on his work. Every portrait artist worth his salt can be persuaded into producing a more flattering likeness."

"Why are you not monitoring him, if the portrait was your idea?" asked Bridget.

"I have an estate to run. Matfey can make nice with the painter." She tried to back away, pushing the tables across the floor, but Bridget was staring at her too intently.

"Why are you taking two tables with you?" she asked.

"I'm moving them to my sitting room," Tanry explained. "In future, please make use of tablecloths. They are a wonderful invention."

Bridget rolled her eyes, but pulled the edge of a rough cloth over her work station regardless.

Tanry went straight from their meeting in the parlour to Acrelane Farm, where the roof needed mending, and offered her assistance to the young tenant family. She met with her land agent, Liam Russeau, at his home. A chill was keeping him indoors, and Tanry wanted to catch up on all she had missed while at court, despite the inclement weather. She needed to set aside funds to pay Cotterall and purchase a typewriter, after all.

Then she needed to mark funds for her new family members. Valentin had a modest allowance. He had no expensive hobbies to satisfy, and had already declared he had no need for his own house. Bridget and Matfey, as Tanry had promised, had respectable dowries set aside, and a budget for new gowns.

"They can do a season, but only one. They weren't wed at court, so I think we need to set our sights lower. A settled country lord might be more interested in them than the social climbers at court," Tanry said. Russeau's wife, a curious soul, leaned her head around the kitchen door to listen to their conversation.

Russeau nodded knowingly. "And the typewriter?" he asked.

"Take it out of Lizseta's gown budget. She scarcely cares about dress as it is."

"Yes, but what is it for?" he asked.

"For typing, I imagine."

Mrs Russeau stopped pretending she wasn't eavesdropping, and looked right at Tanry.

"What does one need a typewriter for, if one already has a pen and paper?" she asked.

Tanry gaped, not quite sure how she was to explain this latest eccentricity in the archduchess' character, then the notion came to her.

"These imperial types are quite eccentric. I think that in their home country, no request was denied, no matter how odd. It's worth our while to humour them, just for a little. Just until they remember that their country is a republic. Lizseta doesn't care for new clothes these days. She can have the typewriter."

Tanry trudged back to the hall as more snow fell. She hadn't been able to find enough funds to secure renovations for the other wings of Taltois, so she would have to live with alchemic experiments in her parlour for the time being. At the very least, she had her caravan to escape to.

It was to her dismay that she saw a trail of smoke leaving the chimney of her hideaway. Someone else had laid claim to her refuge, and she could not have that. It was her land, her caravan. No one else had a right to it.

She burst in without knocking.

"Get out," she announced, without checking to see who was inside. It hardly mattered. She had half expected to find Valentin, but crouched by the wood burner was someone else. It was the trespasser, which felt obvious.

The first thing she noticed was the smell.

He smelled like the inside of a stable on a hot day. He was wearing the clothes of a tramp. They were so muddied and ragged that there was no way to identify one garment from another.

At Tanry's voice, he looked up. To her surprise, he was young. It was a belief that she'd never examined: her idea that no tramps could be young and handsome. Handsome, maybe, but not at all well-groomed. He had a patchy beard that he had attempted to cut, so it was uneven on all sides, and dark hair that might have been wavy, but was too matted to tell and his very dark eyes stared at Tanry with such utter judgement that one might have assumed that she was trespassing on him.

"How long have you been here?" asked Tanry.

The interloper shrugged, unmoved by her presence.

"You can't be here," she said.

"Why not?"

"Because I live here."

"Don't you live in that huge house?" he asked.

"Yes. All of this is mine."

"Then you probably don't need this caravan as well."

"Look, I'm not unreasonable. It's awful out and you can't sleep under a tree. There's a tavern in the village. I'll give you some money to stay there a night." She dug in her pocket and produced some coins for him.

The trespasser inspected her hand as if she was handing him a bug. He took the coins, counted them, and tucked them away.

"I suppose that's fair," he said. "Good day."

He left the caravan without another word. Tanry was left to wonder at the odd interaction.

CHAPTER TWENTY-FIVE

Living Apart

Should a young lady sit for a portrait, she would do well to remember her dancing lessons. Poise and patience are key virtues. She must remain still and silent, so as to not disturb the artist. — Margrit Bellere's Manual for Young Ladies

Tanry received an unexpected letter from Lady Bayard, which she read during their first portrait sitting.

'Sitting' was a strange word to describe the ritual she had entered into. Bridget had spent the morning washing and styling her wig. It was a fairly neat solution, Tanry thought, to compensate for the lack of a maid; Bridget could style her hair, and only after it was done, fix it to her head. She had applied a strange layer of cosmetics that Tanry supposed were to make her look like poor Lizseta, but Bridget was so unhappy with the effect that she kept making adjustments using a tiny mirror she kept in her sleeve.

Valentin, who had become morose, had to be cajoled into wearing his wedding suit for the occasion. Since their arrival, he spent all of his time indoors, pretending to read poetry while he stared at blank walls and taking long, cold baths.

At the very least, during the sitting he sat still in his armchair and didn't fuss. Tanry just hoped that Cotterall could transform his blank stare into something thoughtful.

The letter, such that it was, dripped with Lady Bayard's fawning tone. Tanry's absence in Albonne had not dampened her attempts to gain a richer friend.

"There's murmuring of peace treaties, though no one quite believes it," Tanry told the family.

Matfey was trying to position herself behind Valentin's chair, though Cotterall kept telling her to step to her right. She shuffled, but not enough, and Cotterall had to ask her again.

"The king might come home, so I suppose it's a good thing that you left court," said Tanry.

"Why is that?" asked Cotterall.

Bridget shot a furious look at Tanry. "She only means that we prefer it quiet. If the king returned, we would be bothered by every visitor to court who thought that we were a curiosity," said Bridget. She wrestled with Idonea-dog, who she insisted be in the portrait. "Tanry, swap places with me. You can stand and I can sit with Idonea-dog on my lap."

"That would make it look like you've married Cezsario and not me," replied Tanry.

"What does that matter?"

"It's a wedding portrait. You two are only here because I've decided it's worthwhile."

"Of course, nothing can happen unless you deem it worthwhile."

"I can paint the dog in later," offered Cotterall. "If you decide that's what you still want."

Bridget reluctantly agreed to this, and let Idonea-dog scamper away to ruin more of Tanry's antique rugs.

"What else does Lady Bayard write?" asked Matfey, seemingly to steer the conversation back to comfortable topics.

"She wants to come visit us, but I shan't be inviting her. Athalie is holding balls again. There's talk that she wants to be wed. It all sounds terribly dull."

"She wants to get married?" asked Valentin, and Tanry's stomach overturned at the heartbroken tone of his voice.

"It's what Lady Bayard said. I'm sure you won't be invited to the ceremony."

He sank back into his chair, his expression more dejected than it had been before.

"She's probably just trying to get us back to court," said Tanry. "Athalie has never attempted to marry anyone. Her father will come home with some prince for her to marry. Isn't that how it goes? Heirs are not free to marry as they please."

Matfey put a hand on Valentin's shoulder, though it failed to comfort him. They lapsed into silence as Cotterall started his work.

"You have to be still," he said, "but you don't have to be so silent."

"We spend too much time together," said Tanry. "We've nothing left to talk about."

An hour or so passed, then Cotterall announced that he wanted to take a break and a walk. Tanry leapt to her feet and went to look at the painting. It was still a sketch, and only Matfey had any eyes. Bridget appeared behind Tanry.

"I should be skinnier," she said.

"You're older. It doesn't matter," said Tanry. "No one stays the same."

"Laurina, you should go with him," ordered Bridget, ignoring Tanry and nodding after Cotterall.

"Why?"

"Get to know him. You need a good rapport if we are to pull this off."

Matfey sighed, but followed Cotterall out of the glass doors regardless.

"I'll be back," announced Tanry. "I need my father to put his signature to some papers." She waited a moment, but neither Bridget nor Valentin made a protest. Tanry didn't know why she expected them to. They had no reason to like her, but she found herself disappointed that they cared so little about her presence. She departed, having spotted Matfey standing in the snow with Cotterall, her arms folded tightly to her chest. Cotterall shrugged out of his coat and draped it around her shoulders. Matfey didn't move away, or freeze under the coat's weight, but turned to thank him.

Tanry could not afford to give too much weight to that interaction without her thoughts spiralling away from her. She marched up the grand staircase and to her father's library.

Somehow it had become muggy, like the inside of Trevor's smoking club, though the library lacked the cabal of young men puffing on cigars. Tanry coughed as she entered the room, if only to illustrate her distaste at the fog that covered the painted ceiling.

"Is this really wise?" she asked. "Should we not station you in a less flammable room?"

"I might have already moved, if you hadn't been letting a young lady play at alchemy in my house." Her father was stood over a workbench that was so cluttered that it could hardly be called scientific.

"She is doing alchemy in my parlour. I hardly see how that is inconvenient to you."

"I am writing papers! Imagine the laughing stock I would be at the Society if they learned that a girl is playing at experiments in my house."

"Why are the Society so troubled by a girl?"

"What is she even creating?"

"I don't know, but it's keeping her distracted. You can still move rooms. Or, at the very least, open a window. No one needs to smell your experiments."

He didn't listen to that, but picked up a glass beaker and tipped two fingers of green liquid into it. It foamed immediately and spilled over the rim, covering his hands with a sticky substance.

"What is she doing? What is her project?"

"Father, I don't much care. Don't bother her. I can't have disagreements."

"I thought she was a painter. I thought that was why Cotterall was keen to meet her."

"She scarcely paints anymore."

"Is that not odd?"

"Young ladies pick up skills merely for ornamentation. We can hardly blame them when they lose interest."

"I would prefer that she was embarrassing Cotterall and not me." He wiped his hand on his shirt front, leaving a green stain, trying to pretend that he hadn't just made a mess.

"She is not embarrassing anyone. She has merely requested space for her hobby. Is this the reason for your new fervour? You feel threatened?"

"A duke need not feel threatened by the work of a girl."

Tanry laughed.

"She's an archduchess. She outranks you, Father."

He threw down the beaker. It didn't spill; the strange foam stuck to its sides even as the beaker rolled across the worktop.

"Not in the academic community!" he declared.

Tanry, unmoved, clicked her tongue. "Well, I'm freeing up funds for whatever she wants. Consider it her dowry. I promised her that."

"If she was wed, her husband would not let her do any of this," he complained.

"Good thing I'm no one's husband."

She went back downstairs, but Valentin and Bridget were nowhere in sight. Through the glass doors, Tanry could see that Matfey and Cotterall were deep in conversation despite the falling snow. Matfey raised her hand and touched him lightly on his arm, where he must have felt it through his shirtsleeve.

It had nothing to do with Tanry, she knew. They were lost in their own world, and they didn't know she was watching them. Yet she felt terrible, as if a line had been drawn and she was on the other side of it. Her house had more residents than it ever had, and she still did not have a single person to speak to. It would have been fine had Caterina been there. That was another thing to blame Athalie for.

It seemed like Matfey and Cotterall would not return to the sitting, and Tanry had no will to wait around like a duck for them to come indoors. She found her long boots in the hall and stepped out into the cold. She made a little plan for the afternoon in her head. She would build up a fire and roast chestnuts. She could be happy with her privacy.

Bridget would have her typewriter and she wouldn't bother Tanry for anything else. Valentin already wanted nothing to do with her. That was all as it should be. She could move them out of her wing and then they could live apart. She wouldn't need to hide in her mother's old caravan.

That was a fine thing, because there was another trail of smoke coming from the chimney.

She ran through the last drifts of snow and flew up the caravan steps in one leap. She threw open the door, but the trespasser could not even muster surprise at her arrival. It looked as if he had never left.

"Why are you back here?" she asked. "I thought you were moving on."

"Yes, then I moved back."

"Well, get out again."

He stared at her, head cocked to one side, and held out his hand, palm up.

"You can't be serious," she said.

He knelt down in front of the burner, warming his hands and pretending she were not there.

"You have to leave. This isn't your property," she said.

"Is it yours?"

"Yes."

"Are you the Duke Teneri?"

"No, but I will be."

"Should I warn the man?"

"Just get out."

He held out his hand again.

Tanry sighed. She could spare a few coins just to get her caravan back. She paid him and he let himself out.

She roasted her chestnuts, but still felt terribly low. She considered writing to Caterina, but had no notion of what she would say. She didn't dare mention anything real about Valentin, Bridget, or Matfey in a letter. She couldn't tell Caterina anything true or meaningful, so there was no point in writing at all.

CHAPTER TWENTY-SIX

Only Through My Own Misfortune

It is vital that the virtue of young ladies be protected. They should not find themselves alone with an unmarried man, which is scandal enough. Young ladies should not be included in the audiences for active sports, especially where men participate in states of undress. — Margrit Bellere's Manual for Young Ladies

They had three more sittings with Cotterall, and the estate settled into a sort of routine. They didn't eat meals together. Her father ate in his library, Bridget in her laboratory. Valentin did not leave his bedroom unless he had to. Matfey took her duty to be nice to Cotterall in stride and began taking tea with him, with only a maid as a chaperone.

Tanry had no hunts to partake in. Her tenants needed her help, but with nothing enjoyable. They only needed firewood and hot food, rather than company and good cheer.

The snow had been so sudden after the muggy autumn, few of them were as prepared as they could have been. She held a soup kitchen in one of her unused barns, mostly for something to do. Cook made four vats of soup and had the stable boys totter down the hill and to the barn with the heavy saucepans, where Tanry lit candles and laid folding tables. She sent invitations to every one of her farms and promised food and cheer. Dozens of her tenants turned up, most with their children in tow. Tanry helped serve, and tried to ask them all for the names of their newborn children.

"This is nice," said a voice. Tanry ignored it at first. She was talking to Russeau, making an assessment of whose roofs needed mending and whose windows needed new shutters. Only when she turned away was she perturbed to see her trespasser blowing on a spoonful of soup.

"Didn't I send you away twice?" she asked.

He was sitting at the table nearest to her, with a pile of crumbs around him. "And then you invited me back for soup."

"My tenants I invited, not you."

"How could you turn away someone so poor and needy?" he asked. He tried to bat his eyelids, a movement that he hadn't quite perfected, but he had very dark eyes and Tanry couldn't help but think they were pretty.

"I've paid you twice," she insisted.

"That money is gone. You'll have to pay me again."

"I will have you escorted off my property."

"Will you?"

"I can, and I shall."

"You had better hurry up then, because I might finish this soup soon, and you know, I have places to be." Slowly, he put the soup spoon in his mouth.

"Yes, you seem overwhelmed with opportunities. Get off my estate."

"How is your new husband treating you?" he asked.

Tanry scoffed, then remembered that was a reasonable question to people not in the know.

"He's fine. He's not a local. He wouldn't be interested in helping here."

"I know that he's from Karda Ven, yes."

"How thrilling. I didn't come here to gossip," she said.

"What has he told you about his childhood?"

Tanry squinted at him. "What interest does a trespasser have in the childhood of an archduke?"

At that afternoon's portrait sitting, Valentin was more despondent than ever. He'd failed to shave, and though it made little difference to Cotterall, Tanry couldn't help but feel disquieted. Bridget, who had by now received her typewriter and thrown herself into alchemic experimentation, nursed a small burn on her index finger.

"How did that occur?" Tanry asked.

Bridget folded her other hand over the injury. "It hardly concerns you."

"Maybe so, but forgive me for being concerned. I am only interested in what experiments keep you busy."

"Has your father demanded you ask me?"

"No. I never do anything in his interest. If I did, none of you would be here."

This made Bridget snort.

"And you would have no capacity to study alchemy," Tanry

reminded her.

"If you could all remain still, it would be appreciated," said Cotterall, sticking his head out from behind the canvas.

"I only mean to show curiosity," said Tanry. "We all live under the same roof. What harm is there in showing a little interest in one another?"

"I didn't think you knew how to be friendly, Tanry," said Bridget.

"Perhaps you do not know me."

"Perhaps not. But I think that I am right."

"Stillness, please," said Cotterall.

"We should save this conversation until after the sitting, so Mr Cotterall can concentrate," said Matfey.

"My lord – archduke – could you sit as you were before?" asked Cotterall.

Valentin was slouched in his chair. Tanry tapped his knee and he flinched.

"Mr Cotterall needs you upright," she said.

Valentin turned his head and blinked at her, as if he wasn't sure what she'd said. He sat up a little, but not enough to make a difference.

"How long will this take?" he asked.

"Longer if you slouch," said Tanry.

"It really shouldn't be too much longer," Cotterall told them. "At least, your part won't be, archduke."

"I didn't want to be in this portrait. I shouldn't be in this portrait," muttered Valentin.

"You're my husband, so you are meant to be here," replied Tanry.

"Only through my own misfortune," he said.

Tanry got to her feet, ignoring Cotterall's dramatic sigh. "Cotterall, can you give us a minute?"

"Why? I'm almost done."

"We are going to have this out now, and then this will go a lot smoother. Go and change your paint water, or whatever artists do."

"I did prefer it when Trevor was in charge around here," said Cotterall as he stood.

Tanry had no idea why that smarted. Trevor had never organised anything. Cotterall was just saying that he preferred disorder to the alternative. It was not her concern that he was wrong.

She turned to the impostors. "Can we not get through one more sitting? Can we not finish one portrait?" she asked.

"We should not be doing a portrait at all," said Bridget. "It's still too dangerous."

"Is it your intention to delay the work so it never gets finished?"

Bridget shrugged. "Maybe you should simply refuse to pay Mr Cotterall, and he will leave with the work unfinished," she said.

"No," Matfey interrupted. "He has worked so hard, and he needs to prove himself to his father."

"What does that matter to us?" asked Bridget.

"It's cruel to hire him and then tell him that he can't finish the work."

"He will finish the portrait and it will hang in the hall," declared Tanry. "It would be more suspicious to drop the thing now, Bridget, you should know that. Please would you all plaster on a pleasant expression and get this done?"

Valentin, for no reason at all, got to his feet.

"Valentin, you are keeping Cotterall waiting."

"I am always going to be getting something done, waiting something out. There will never be any respite, will there?" he said, with the weary tone of someone who had been continually punished by malevolent gods.

"Valentin, just sit down."

"Bridget, will there be any respite? I thought here – I thought we would have to pretend less, but there are servants and Mr Cotterall and the Duke. Will they not ask questions about why the archduchess has gained an interest in alchemy with no schooling? Must we always do this?"

"Sit down, Zsari," said Bridget in her most imperious voice.

"Do not call me his name!" Valentin shouted, so suddenly that Tanry jolted. "I have taken his whole life, I cannot stand to hear his name as well."

"Do you have another choice?" asked Bridget quietly.

"I know that I do not, but I cannot stand it," replied Valentin.

"Do you think that I can?"

"You are freer here than you were at court," said Tanry. "There is no fear that the king will arrive here. There is no one writing a gossip magazine. You need not hide in front of Athalie."

She realised as soon as her mouth formed the word that it had been foolish to mention Athalie's name. Valentin turned on her, angrier than she'd seen him, even on their wedding night. He had been distraught, hopeless, but never truly furious.

"Why do you feel the need to be kind to me?" he asked in a sour tone quite at odds with his words.

"Why should I not be kind to you?" Tanry asked, because she did not understand.

"You have blackmailed me. You have dragged me here against my will. You have turned the princess – our only friend in this country – against me. I have been pulled from my home, with no recourse for return, for the third time in a relatively short life. I hate you so much, Tanry. Do me the grace of hating me back."

His words stunned the thought out of Tanry. She was reminded, in a manner that confounded her, of a day on which Trevor had stolen her coin purse to use at his card table. She had never known how to be angry until that moment. Upon the discovery, she had run to the billiards room and upended the card table so no one could play. The cards, once she'd gathered a handful, crackled nicely in the hearth. She was beyond such childish manoeuvres now, but the same lump rose in her throat.

"If you do feel that way, than you should make your own way in the world. You need not stay," Tanry told him.

"How will you keep hold of your entailed estate without a husband? How far will I get before you remember that you need me? What can I do, without my own name and my own fortune? What will Bridget and Matfey do without me? How will they explain my absence? I am caught here like a fly in a web."

"There's no need to speak so, Valentin," said Bridget. "Little has changed here."

"Everything has changed. Athalie is not here, and she will never speak to me again."

Bridget sighed, rather in the manner of a parent about to chastise their child. "You shall survive that," she said.

Valentin, for all his proper demeanour, could not stand to hear that. He turned on his heel and left the room without a word of explanation.

"Matfey?" Tanry asked.

"Yes?"

"Please apologise to Cotterall, and assure him he will be paid."

She couldn't stand to be in the house. She couldn't speak to Bridget, or Valentin, or even Matfey, who fretted over Cotterall for no apparent reason. She had one good option, and she did not even care to check for a trail of blue smoke before she fled to the caravan.

There was hardly a reason to be surprised when she found him already there. He had taken it upon himself to try and wash his clothes using the caravan's tin washtub. They were hung up above Tanry. They smelled terribly and each item was riddled with holes. Fortunately, he had kept his stained trousers on, though they were a thin barrier between them and decorum.

"I hoped you'd be busy," he said with a shrug.

"Why must you still be here?" She tried to address his face and not look, even glance, at his bare chest.

"If you want to pay me to leave again, please could you wait until my clothes have dried? It's foul weather out there."

He did have her there. She could not send him out without so much as a coat on a winter's day. For the moment, she would not have her caravan back. Tanry sank onto the floor next to the wood burner. She ran a hand along the floor there, but found no grit or ash.

"Did you clean in here?" she asked.

"I also fixed the hinge on the door. Thank you for noticing. And I mended the harness." He pointed to where the horse's harness was hung on the ceiling. Tanry tried to find something interesting to look at on the blank wall of the caravan.

"There's no need for that," she said. "This caravan hasn't moved in years."

"Well, now it could," he said. "Where's your husband?"

"What interest do you possess in my husband? Why have you come here? This is hardly a city centre. If you're looking for a better life, go to Albonne. Don't freeze to death out here."

"I've avoided cities as a rule." He adjusted the shirt hung on the line above him.

"You are only fraying my nerves by staying here."

"Why is it only you who leaves the house?" he asked. "You and the staff."

"Cotterall and Laurina keep taking walks in my mother's rose garden. Laurina is a proper girl though, and she won't go too far alone with him."

"I didn't think that the archduchess Laurina was a proper girl." He was strangely informed on palace gossip for a tramp.

"Perhaps she has grown into one. What does it matter to you?"

"You have no notion of my life, or what might matter in it."

"I suppose that's true," said Tanry. "But I suspect that you know as much about mine."

"I know who you are."

"You know who I am from gossip rags, no doubt. From experience, there's a lot they don't see."

She didn't stay for much longer after that, but she didn't order him to leave either. He had no clothes, after all. She went to her own bedroom, where she could see the caravan nestled under its tree. Smoke continued to rise from the chimney.

CHAPTER TWENTY-SEVEN

A Folly by the Lake

It is vital that young ladies remain indoors during inclement weather. They are well-known to have poor constitution and will take ill if they are stood outside for any amount of time. — Margrit Bellere's Manual for Young Ladies

The first alchemic explosion occurred over breakfast. When it happened, Tanry found that she was hardly surprised. Matfey, however, was startled out of her chair.

"Who did that?" she asked, crouched on the ground, ready to dive under the table.

Tanry finished her mouthful before replying. "There's an equal chance that either of them did it."

"Are you going to find out?"

"That will only encourage them."

There was a second explosion. Sighing, Tanry stood to

leave.

"Are you checking?" asked Matfey.

"Yes, yes. We aren't going to burn to death today."

She climbed up to her old parlour. Even before she arrived, she smelled the sulphur. She slunk into the room, and leaned on one of the elegant columns.

"Was that you?" she asked.

Bridget looked up from her work table. She wore a pair of goggles, giving her the appearance of a bug. Her wig, which she had unsuccessfully tried to bind back, fell in strands around her face.

"Only one of them," she admitted. "The second, I think."

"Must we exist with the fire buckets at the ready?" asked Tanry in a drawling voice.

"Your fire buckets are downstairs and they are not ready."

"I'm thinking of moving them."

Bridget cursed as she tried to adjust her hair, strands falling out of an ineffectual plait. "Long hair is no good for alchemy," she said. She had produced (or, more likely, stolen) a burner that glowed blue, and her bench displayed a neat row of empty beakers and a pile of typed notes stacked on one end. She was evidently a different sort of alchemist to Duke Teneri.

"You should cut your hair," said Tanry.

"I can't do that. It's her most famous attribute." She tried to tuck the strands away, but they stuck to her damp fingers.

"Why do we want that anymore?" It seemed to Tanry that they were far from Albonne, and even further from the imperial court of Veni. What did it matter if the archduchess had shorter hair?

"Alone, we are no one. Together, we pass as the lost

children of Karda Ven."

"Is that so?"

"Human nature. The more of us there are, the harder it is for folk to find our flaws." She indicated her hairline, where the lace front was just visible.

"What do you intend, Bridget? How will you publish your research as Archduchess Lizseta Caela Loreatha Boralda-Solkin?"

"The joy is in the doing, not in the recognition," declared Bridget.

"Then could I suggest that we preserve that joy by presenting fewer explosions?"

"It was only a mild one. No windows were even broken." She gestured around at the windows, all intact.

Tanry's eyes fell instead on a china cabinet which had a fresh crack in one of its panes. She stared at it until Bridget turned around and noticed it.

"I'm going to fix that. I meant to fix it already."

She had an energy in her that Tanry hadn't seen before. This was the first conversation they had probably had where Bridget's face wasn't frozen in a scowl. She picked up a page of her notes and read through them, her eyes greedy. Tanry saw that next to the pile was a familiar silver-backed hairbrush.

"Did you take that from my room?" she asked.

"I thought you were not using it."

"It was my mother's. Please give it back."

Bridget went very still. She picked it up and held it out to Tanry without question. "I apologise. I thought it was just another thing. This house is full of so many things."

"They are important, a lot of those things." The brush was

cool against her hand. "I can get you another brush. Caterina left some behind."

"It's not for my hair. Not exactly. I am making an alchemic brush to change one's hair colour for a period."

"Is it working?"

"The chemicals are unstable. That's how best to explain it to a lay person."

"Please make them more stable, if you can."

She did not bother to pay a visit to her father. He was too attached to his explosions to be stopped. If he knew that Bridget's experiments were cosmetic in nature, he might not feel so threatened by her, but Tanry didn't want to give him that satisfaction. Bridget had already had more success with her limited capacity than Duke Teneri had with all of his funds behind him. He deserved to stew in his insecurities.

She returned to her room to stow the hairbrush. Glancing out of the window, she saw that snowflakes were sticking to the glass. The caravan was barely visible through the driving snow. She couldn't see a flickering fire through the window and wondered where her new friend was, and whether he was risking his life in the snow.

He was not her concern. He was not her tenant. He was not her family. They had merely shared a few half-friendly interactions. She had other problems to attend to.

Though Valentin might hate her, she was responsible for him. She had to watch out for him, whether he liked it or not. She instructed Mrs Button to have food taken to his room, as he hadn't eaten breakfast. When the food was sent back untouched, she had a footman take up firewood. If he wouldn't be full, at least he could be warm. After that, she sent a newspaper. She went to the library, ignoring its occupant, and found poetry books that she didn't understand, leaving them outside Valentin's door.

Outside, the snowstorm grew in ferocity. Before long, she could only see a blank, white stretch outside of the windows. She hoped, against her better instincts, that her caravan was occupied.

She couldn't find Matfey, but ran into Cotterall outside of Matfey's bedroom door. He was bent down, fingers on the carpet, in the manner of a man who had slipped something under her door.

"You all right there, Cotterall?" she asked.

"Oh yes. It's good carpet that you have here. High quality." He patted it.

"I paid a lot of money for it."

"Hmm, yes. Very good."

"Have you seen the archduke today?"

"Oh, no. I suspect that I'll have to finish the painting from memory." He stood up and shrugged.

"He will come around. I will make sure that he does," Tanry tried to assure him.

"You have a strange relationship, if you don't mind me saying."

"I do mind, Cotterall."

"I know that Trevor is gone, but I did think that we could still be honest with each other, like we used to."

"Go on then. I do appreciate bluntness, as you well know."

"You do not seem to be in love with the archduke."

"Who is in love, Cotterall? It's hardly common."

He blushed and stared at the ground. "Your brother never

would have married against his will, you know," he said.

"Trevor never had to fight against the law to inherit his own property. I will make sure that painting gets finished."

She glanced to the window. The snow was fierce, but she could make out the shape of the folly by the lake. Between the pillars, there was a figure with his arms held tight to his side. The fool was outdoors during a snowstorm.

"Cotterall, we'll speak later." She dashed away.

She found a cloak that he had slung over a marble statue and swung it around her shoulders, then forced herself outside. The wind scraped against her face as soon as she was out of doors. She ran as fast as the snow drifts would allow, towards the folly. True enough, there he was, dressed in his rags again.

"What are you doing?" she demanded.

He was shaking. "I thought you wanted me gone," he complained.

"I've no need to find your body the next time I go hunting."

"I ran out of wood for the fire," he admitted. "I went looking for more and only made it here."

"How have you survived this long? How did you live through other winters?"

"I wasn't always living out of doors." He pulled his wet coat tighter about his shoulders. Snowflakes dotted it like pearls, but they were quickly melting.

"Why are you here? There is still no good reason for you to be in Taltois."

"Are you going to make me leave again?" he asked.

"You know that there is nowhere for you to go in this weather." She could imagine him walking the miles to the road and collapsing there, frozen to death in a minute.

"Then why insist that you want me gone?"

"I hardly want you here."

"I don't know why you continue to speak to me, or why you have not had me removed. You have plenty of people who could have done it."

"I am not so cruel."

"Who else knows that I am here?"

She thought for a moment. She should have warned her staff about the interloper on the estate, but it had entirely slipped her mind. She could have requested two of the stable hands carry him off of Taltois by force. She could have sent a hand to fetch the sheriff and had the trespasser arrested. But that, she reasoned, would not have solved the mystery of the man.

"Who are you?" she asked. "It doesn't matter if I don't understand. Tell me anyway."

"My name is Zsari," he said.

"Good, thank you." She shivered.

His eyes drifted to the lake, where snowflakes landed and melted on the water.

"Where did you come from?" Tanry asked.

"Why do you care to know?" he snapped.

"I thought we were turning a corner, Zsari. Do you think that you are more interesting as a mystery? Is your life so boring that you must keep it hidden so that people will wonder about you?"

"Oh, don't do that." He rolled his eyes, which she thought was a bold move for someone of his station.

"What?"

"Make assumptions."

"Why shouldn't I? There's certainly no proof of who you are. I only work with what information I have."

"You can't see past the end of your nose." He was standing very close to her, regardless of how improper it was.

"I can see out of my own window, or I wouldn't have known to come help you."

"Have you helped me? I think that you've only come here to berate me and to avoid your husband."

"He is avoiding me well enough on his own."

"Is that it? Are you so terribly bored that you have to come out here and bother me?"

It was rich of him to say. She had an estate and a hall with hundreds of rooms. He was well below her notice – or he should have been – so what right did he have to capture her attention? What right did he have to think of himself as equal company to her husband?

"What do you mean? Do you think you are the same as him?"

"How are we so very different?"

Their voices were raised, though Tanry couldn't remember when she started shouting.

"You are a nightmare. I can't help you. Good luck," she said.

"You were already not helping me."

"There is firewood outside the stables. If you run, you shouldn't get too cold."

"Why come here to tell me that? I could have guessed that."

"Shouldn't you be on your way?"

"I came here over the mountains. I slept in ditches and under bushes. I risked my life in ways you can't even conceive of. I am not leaving here until I finish what I came here to do."

"And what did you come here to do?"

He couldn't respond. He started a sentence a few times but lost momentum. He ran his hands through his damp hair and paced across the folly.

"So there's nothing? There's no reason that you came here?" Tanry asked.

"I knew that you wouldn't understand," he complained.

"Make me understand."

"I don't think that anyone can make you do anything," he said.

"Fuck you for not trying."

She could barely breathe and she didn't know why. It was cold but she couldn't feel it. She should go inside and abandon him, but she didn't want to, for reasons that she couldn't explain.

He was no one. He was a tramp who regularly trespassed on her property. She should consider him naught more than a bug, or another unwelcome pest. Tragically, he seemed a welcome pest. She didn't want him to leave. She wanted him to be as far from her as possible. She should throw him in the lake.

He was stood close, though in all his pacing she hadn't noticed when he approached again. He was so close that she could see flecks of gold in his eyes.

"You would never believe me. No one ever has, for what it is worth."

"You must be such an individual in all the world," she said, sarcastically.

"Maybe I am!"

"Like hell you are."

She grabbed him by the collar. For a moment, it was to pull him in, but a moment later she pushed him away. He stumbled, his arms flailing, and fell backwards. She thought for a moment that he would catch himself, but he failed and fell into the lake's black water.

Tanry swore. She had no idea whether he could swim, but with her luck he probably couldn't. She rushed to the edge of the folly, but found that he had righted himself and was swimming with confident strokes back to her. She reached down and grasped him by both wrists, pulling him out of the water and back into the folly. It was an inelegant journey. He nearly fell twice.

When he was free of the water, he lay shivering violently on the floor of the folly.

Tanry pulled off her cloak and put it around his shoulders. "That was foolish. I didn't think," she said, still holding him.

"You never think, do you?" he barked.

"Fuck you." She could hardly help herself. She kissed him, her grip tight on his neck. His clothes and skin were freezing, but his mouth was searingly hot. They broke apart. Tanry stumbled backwards, reeling.

Zsari swore. "God above," he said. "Why are we doing this?"

"You're hardly the first," she scoffed.

"You shouldn't feel special yourself," he said.

He stood, and they both halted for a moment, breathing heavily. Water dripped from Zsari's hair down his forehead.

Then he reached for her again, his cold hands on her neck. She pushed back, pinning him against a column as she kissed him. He made a noise in the back of his throat and she smiled against his lips. She scraped her teeth against his bottom lip as he moved his hands over her hips. They broke apart for a moment, and Zsari moved to her neck, where she felt his teeth against her skin. She needed to get her hands underneath his clothes. She needed him indoors and not shivering. Her fingers were going numb. She pushed back from him and Zsari made a slight huff of disappointment.

"We can't do this," she said.

"I don't mind."

"I'd rather you weren't dripping wet."

"So would I."

"I'm taking you in." She made to move, but Zsari caught her by the wrist.

"There is something I ought to tell you. About my name."

"It's Zsari. You said."

"It's short for something."

"What?"

"Cezsario."

"That's a bit grand."

"It's short for Archduke Cezsario Concerto Dalibor Boralda-Solkin."

CHAPTER TWENTY-EIGHT

A Missing Brother

Mothers should prepare young ladies for the task of child-rearing. They should not shy away from descriptions of the act itself, lest young ladies be shocked on their wedding nights. Performing this duty for their husbands will be a young lady's highest accomplishment. — Margrit Bellere's Manual for Young Ladies

Tanry went indoors alone, opened a window in the billiards room, then beckoned to Zsari, who was hiding behind a bush. She had taken all her other dalliances in the stables or abandoned farmhouses so she had no reason to worry about servants' wandering eyes. This was far more awkward.

She peered into the grand hall and, seeing no servants or family members, up the staircase and into her wing ran with Zsari's hand in her own. She pushed him into her suite, and towards the bedroom, and he raised his eyebrows.

"Don't get excited," she said. "I'm going to have a bath drawn so you don't freeze to death."

"Whatever you say."

"Just hide in the wardrobe. I'll find you some clothes too."

Zsari did as he was bidden, though he felt the need to wink at her as he closed the wardrobe doors.

She reached for her bell, ringing sharply until Uma, Caterina's replacement, bolted through the servants' door.

"It's freezing," Tanry said, shaking snowflakes out of her hair. "Can you have someone build up a fire, and draw a hot bath?"

"Of course, my lady."

"I'll be back," Tanry finished, feeling no need to explain further. She needed to find clothes, and doubted that her own would fit Zsari. She went to Trevor's room.

It had been a long time since her last visit. It held little of him anymore.

Trevor had never tidied and he'd never allowed anyone else to do it for him. On all her previous visits, she'd found his bed messy, its sheets recently vacated. There were usually clothes strewn about the floor, some belonging to the young women Trevor dallied with. Now, his sheets were drawn tightly across his bed. All of his drawers were closed with no shirtsleeves or cravats spilling over the sides. The curtains were tied back, rather than shut to allow Trevor to sleep through most of the morning.

There was no use in dwelling on any of that. She needn't think about how Trevor was never going to sleep in that bed again and that he would never again look at himself in that mirror.

She crossed the room and threw open the wardrobe, but was perturbed to see only an empty rail and a single spider inside. She didn't allow herself to stay and wonder who had tidied away Trevor's things; instead she spotted a leather case on the edge of the washbasin and took it. There was another place in the house to find a young man's clothes.

Unfortunately, Matfey was leaving her bedroom as Tanry returned to her wing.

"Why are you so wet?" asked Matfey. She was dressed in a fur-lined coat and matching muff, but she had put flowers in her hair.

"It's snowing. Where are you going?" Tanry asked in reply.

"Oh, uh." She tried to hide a piece of paper inside the muff.

Tanry sighed. "If you insist on consorting with Cotterall, could you at least be a little more subtle about it?"

"I don't know what you mean." Matfey refused to make eye contact with her.

"I'm sure. He's downstairs."

Matfey fought back a smile and hurried past Tanry.

Tanry rushed on, going to Valentin's room and creeping in without knocking. She had some luck, because he was not there. He'd abandoned a set of clothes on a chair, and Tanry grabbed a shirt, trousers, and a pair of older shoes that she hoped she could replace.

"Is there someone there?" called Valentin.

Tanry's heart stilled as she looked towards the door to his study, which was ajar. She might have called out in reply, but thought perhaps there was no reason to. Valentin wanted to hate her; there was no reason to ask for his good will on anything. She held her jaw shut and slipped out of the room.

There was no sound in the halls. The servants were away, busy with their work, and all of them too well-trained to make a noise. Tanry missed Caterina. She had a family now, but they were hidden in crevices, unwilling to speak to one another. She very nearly missed the bustle of court life.

She went back to her room. Uma stood over the copper tub, her sleeves rolled back, settling a pair of black alchemic warmers in the water.

"It's ready, my lady," she said.

"My thanks." Steam rose in gentle spirals from the tub. Once Uma had left, Tanry set down the leather case and opened it, laying out her brother's shaving kit.

"Zsari?"

From inside the wardrobe, he made a small sound.

"Bath's ready," she said.

"Your house is quiet," said Zsari. He opened the doors and gave her a strange, soft look.

"Here's a shaving kit. Wash. Warm up."

"Are you not staying?" he asked.

"Presumptuous."

He shivered violently again.

"Get in the bath before you catch your death."

Whatever excitement she might have felt was dissipating. In the warmth, her head felt clearer. She could be kind to Zsari, but it was lunacy to bring him inside and sleep with him. He was confused. He claimed he was an archduke. He claimed he was *Valentin*. He was a fool who was trying to fib his way into a warm bed and a full stomach.

"Tanry?" said Valentin's voice.

She dashed into the corridor, slamming her door shut so that no one might see Zsari shedding his stinking clothes.

Valentin was there, but he was not quite himself. A shadow marked his chin and creases covered his clothes as if he'd slept in them.

"Were you in my room just now?" he asked.

"No, it was probably a servant."

"I know it was you. I was doing you a courtesy by allowing you to admit it."

"How do you know?"

"Because I saw you leaving with my clothes."

She could feel her cheeks burning. "What do you want, Valentin?" she asked, in her most demanding voice, hoping to scare him away.

"Why must you call me that? Do you know who might be listening?" he hissed.

"I do not have anything of yours," she said.

"You are not a good liar, Tanry."

"I will buy you more clothes if you want them."

"Don't buy me anything. I don't want to be dependent on you." He bristled with barely contained pride.

It irked her. So much about him irked her. "You have no choice."

"I do not have to take anything from you."

"You were content to eat out of Athalie's hand, but you cannot accept a single thing from me when I have offered it."

"What choice did I have but to accept you?"

"You made the right choice for yourself and your sisters. No one from Karda Ven is ever coming back for you. You're alone here. Figure out how to survive."

"And where does that leave us?"

"What do you mean?"

"We are married, Tanry. Only in name for now, but I wonder what will happen when you need a child to inherit your estate."

"I will figure it out."

"Will you? Or will you want to come to my bed? What part of our agreement does that fall under?"

"That will not happen," she said, decisively. "I have to go now."

"Can I have my clothes back? Can I go in there and check?"

She put her hand up, blocking the doorway. "You cannot go in my room," she said.

"Ah, we are such a loving and companionable pairing. Fuck you, Tanry. Do not go in my room again. Offer me the same courtesy that you demand for yourself." He stormed away.

Tanry waited by her bedroom door for a full minute, her fists clenched tightly. She was being stupid. There was no need to feel upset because of what Valentin had said. She had no reason to care about his opinions. She would figure out what to do about children. It had never been a concern of Trevor's. She certainly didn't need Valentin's children. They would probably be weepy and moon over poetry that Tanry thought was trite.

She didn't need him. She didn't want him. He was a morose sod. She didn't need Matfey either. She was sappy and driven to distraction by any man who so much as glanced her way. Bridget cared for naught but her meaningless experiments. Caterina had been a fine companion, but she had chosen to leave. The only person Tanry had was a fantasist who was taking his first bath of the season.

She went back into her sitting room and pulled the covering from the discernment engine. She need not wonder. Zsari could refuse to answer her questions, but she had a device that could reveal all.

She lined up the cogs and asked her first question:

WHY IS ZSARI HERE

The machine spun and mulled over this for several moments before the central dial turned. She didn't need to take down the letters, as the reply was only one word:

VALENTIN

That made little sense. He had asked after Valentin more than she liked, but there was no reason for Zsari to come to Taltois to see him. Perhaps Zsari had known Valentin in Karda Ven, but that made little sense. No one, as far as she understood, knew that the decoy family existed. No one except Idonea Strader, the terror that she was, and it was unlikely that she had sent Zsari. Still, there was always a chance.

DID IDONEA SEND ZSARI

The engine didn't take long to answer.

NO

Tanry considered that she might have made a poor assumption. Zsari might labour under the illusion that Valentin was the Archduke Cezsario Concerto Dalibor Boralda-Solkin. It was possible that he was hoping for a touch of celebrity to elevate his humdrum life.

DOES ZSARI KNOW VALENTINS SECRET

YES

Tanry frowned. It didn't make any sense. Zsari knew

somehow that she was not married to an archduke. That made him dangerous, though she couldn't say how. The impostors had kept their secret from Athalie and every servant in Albonne. She pondered over the possibility of Zsari being a relative of Lady Taybury, but there was an obvious thing to ask, if only to rule it out.

DID ZSARI LIE ABOUT HIS NAME

NO

Shit.

CHAPTER TWENTY-NINE

Their Lost Country

The imperial state of Karda Ven has, since its demise, become the preferred subject for romantic artists. Karda Ven is pictured as a state of elegant opulence, cheer, and tradition. Most artists fail to recall the widespread poverty and political unrest that led to the birth of the republic. — A Lament for the Old Country: A Response

The discernment engine was the pride of Premure and a marvel of craftmanship. It did not lie. It might obfuscate, but it was never inaccurate.

The tramp who had crawled onto her estate was the real archduke. He had grown up in the finest palaces on the continent and cut his teeth on the world's most famous diamonds. He was the only person in the world who could undo the lie that Tanry had bought into. The last member of a family lost in songs and the romantic recollections of a lost age. And he was having a bath in Tanry's room. He had come for Valentin because he knew that Valentin was a fraud. He was a problem to be dealt with now. There was no need to bring this problem to the family. Tanry could dispense with Zsari on her own.

The sun was setting. The emotions of the past hour or so had wrung her dry. Any brief excitement she'd felt at kissing Zsari had floated away.

She slunk back into her bedroom, which was hot from a freshly roaring fire. Steam had misted her gilt mirror and the glass in her picture frames. She closed the door and locked it, then dragged a chair in front of the servants' door.

Zsari's eyes followed her around the room. He was in the bathtub still. The water had turned grey and suds floated across the surface. He'd shaved.

She had to admit that it was a marked improvement. Now that she knew, she couldn't help but notice the differences between Zsari and Valentin. Zsari had a rounder face, but it was gaunt, trimmed by years without excess food. He might have been stocky where Valentin was lean, but now his collarbones stretched against his skin and she could see his ribs just below the rim of the tub. They might have been alike when they were children, but time had run its course.

Zsari set both arms on the edge of the tub and leaned his chin on his hands. "I didn't think you were coming back," he said.

"This is my room."

"There are a lot of rooms in this place. I thought you might go to one of them."

Tanry could hear the crackle of the fire and the soft

lapping of the water in the tub. "How did you find out where Valentin was?" she asked, sitting down on the floor just across from him.

Zsari sighed so heavily that she saw his shoulders move. "I thought he was dead like everyone else, then a girl in the village I was in bought a copy of Pherson's. It was all about some society wedding. I saw my own name on the cover."

"That must have been disconcerting."

"I didn't realise that I'd married the richest heiress in the country, but you learn something new everyday."

"And now you want a piece? You want to be paid your dues?"

"I only want to no longer be alone. Can you understand that?"

Tanry ignored him and shed her coat and jacket, throwing them over the back of a chair. She knew Zsari was watching her, and she was determined for the moment not to acknowledge that fact.

"I mean you no harm," said Zsari. "Nor Valentin, or Bridget, or Matfey."

"Your name causes harm anyway. I needed to marry an archduke. If people knew that I did not, then I would lose everything that I care about."

"What do you intend to do with me?"

"I don't yet know." The room was sweltering. She unbuttoned the front of her waistcoat and rolled up the sleeves of her shirt. "I'm sure that if I paid you to leave, you would merely come back for more."

Zsari shrugged. "I suppose I would. I came a very long way to get here, and I will see Valentin. I have paid too much in time and pain to get here."

Tanry leaned on the rim of the tub. "If you were to see Valentin, what would you do to him?"

"I don't quite know. I only want my life to change."

"I suppose you want the palaces and the horses and the jewels back."

He snorted. "I'm no fool. There isn't a way back. The home country isn't out there anymore. The home country is some place inhabited only by the dead." He shifted in the bathtub, and Tanry leaned on the edge too. His head was close to hers.

"The home country is the place whence no travellers return," said Tanry.

"I shan't go back. That place won me so much misery."

"Do you not miss it, the life you had with your family?" asked Tanry.

"What do you know of family?"

"Very little, I suppose," said Tanry. "I only have a father now, and I think that he cares very little for my health and happiness."

"Still, he is alive."

"I scarcely know him. Did you know yours?"

Zsari shook his head. Droplets of water ran down his shoulders and Tanry was fixated for a moment watching them.

"I guess not," he replied. "We would have been closer, I always thought, had I been older. I think he just didn't have a lot of interest in children, but he did in young people."

"Sounds like more of a general than a father."

"I had my mother. I had my sisters. Whatever he could have provided, I was not short on. Now I just mourn them all."

Never before had Tanry been called to examine her life so. She'd never imagined herself as being someone in want of companionship. She had always found it in Caterina mostly, or, she supposed, in Trevor.

"Are you not angry with them?" she asked.

"What should I be angry with them for?"

Her explanation died on her tongue. Zsari could not be angry at his family for leaving him because they were taken away. Tanry was angry at Trevor for his carelessness. He could have, and should have, been there. If he had not been so drunk, he would not have died. It would have been so easy for him to survive, and then Tanry would not have had to blackmail Valentin, or marry at all.

"Sorry, I should have thought before I asked that," she said.

"You haven't spoken to anyone about this, have you?"

"Have you?"

"I have not revealed a single true thing about myself in five years," said Zsari, with an attempt at a laugh, though Tanry could tell that it was forced, and the notion weighed on him.

"I knew that, I suppose."

"Mourning is a quiet thing. You can't do it as a group activity, though perhaps I'm drawing too much from my own experience."

"My brother died. It is the first and only time I've lost someone, and he was the only person I truly had to lose. I followed him around when I was a child. I admired him. I wanted to be exactly like him. I didn't realise how foolish he was. Maybe I didn't appreciate what sort of person he was. I think if he weren't my brother, I wouldn't have liked him."

They sat like that for a few silent moments, hearing only

the logs fall in the fire.

"Sorry," said Tanry. "I don't think I realised how much I loved him. I think I was just angry instead."

"I'll never be angry with them," declared Zsari. "That was a privilege for when they were alive. It's not something you do to people who are lost. Not in their lost country."

"You have your lost country. I have my own home standing around us. No one works to keep it together but me. There is no vanished Taltois. There is only Taltois as it is, and I will keep it. I will keep its people fed."

"I'm sure my father said something similar," he said with a small laugh. "Have you considered how odd it is that we are having this conversation while I am entirely naked?"

"An hour ago I had my tongue in your mouth, I wouldn't think too much of it."

"What would you say to doing that again?" he asked.

Tanry considered. "Finish your bath. Dry off. Then we'll talk."

He eagerly grabbed a bar of soap and lathered his arms. He spotted her watching him and laughed. "Taking a peek before the show?"

"Don't compliment yourself."

"And why shouldn't I?" He grinned.

"I don't know who you think you are."

"I think that I am an archduke and therefore of interest to you."

"I see."

"You already pushed me in a lake. I know that you're interested in me."

"That was a mistake and I'm trying to make up for it."

"I'm still upset. You need to make it up to me more." He dropped the soap and leaned towards Tanry. "I'm afraid that I might have caught a cold. You will have to warm me up, or I will simply pass away."

"All right. I've taken the hint." She ran her thumb across his bottom lip.

"God above," he whispered. "When the paper said I was married, I didn't think that it would be someone like you."

"Meaning?"

"I made the right call marrying you."

"You didn't have much say in it."

"I wouldn't have cared."

She pulled him in by the chin and pressed her lips to his. She was slower than the last time, more exploratory. She wound her hands into Zsari's hair and they came away wet. She broke away.

"Get dry," she ordered him. Zsari didn't waste time, pulling himself out of the tub and reaching for a towel. Tanry took a moment to admire him, silhouetted by the fire, before he wrapped the fabric around his waist. She shrugged out of her waistcoat and dumped it on the floor.

She shouldn't, she knew, but who was to stop her? Not her husband, and not her father. She could sleep with an archduke if she wanted.

"You better not pay me for this next part," said Zsari.

"It depends on how quickly I want to get rid of you."

He was much more handsome now that he was clean shaven and no longer smelled odd.

He leaned on the edge of her bed. "Are you coming over here, or are you having second thoughts?"

"God, no."

She pushed him down by the shoulders and crawled on top of him. His arms, hot to the touch, pulled her close.

CHAPTER THIRTY

Family in all but Blood

For young ladies intending to impress suitors, breakfast is a key time. Gentlemen remember what happens at the beginning of the day most keenly. — Margrit Bellere's Manual for Young Ladies

Tanry half-woke and stretched her arm across the bed, but found it cold. She sat up, letting the covers fall back. The water in the bathtub had cooled, the warming rocks having failed. Zsari was nowhere in evidence.

Tanry swore once, very loudly. The fool had clearly decided to explore, with little thought as to who might have seen him leaving Tanry's bedroom.

She threw on a set of her pyjamas and a velvet dressing gown, and crept into the hallway, which was deserted.

"Zsari?" she called in a soft voice. She thought better of it and called loudly, "Cezsario!"

Behind her, a door opened. Matfey, dressed but with her hair loose, stuck her head out.

"Why are you looking for him this early?" she asked.

"He was just here," said Tanry.

Matfey's eyes raked over her, and Tanry realised her mistake.

"I know there was someone in your room last night," said Matfey.

"Don't pry. It's none of your concern."

"Was Valentin in your room last night?"

"Mind your own concerns, Laurina."

Tanry walked away, even as she knew Matfey was giggling. She could be dealt with. It was more important to find Zsari before anyone saw him. She padded down the grand staircase but saw no sign of him.

"Cezsario!" she called again.

There was no reply.

And then she heard a scream.

It was a man's scream, one of shock rather than fear. Still, it was a sedate morning and no one should have been screaming.

She ran to the dining room and was met with an unwelcome tableau.

Valentin stood in the bay window with all the colour drained from his face. He didn't notice Tanry entering, because his eyes were fixed on Zsari at the head of the table.

"So I see we are getting acquainted," said Tanry. "But there are other people in this house, so can we keep it down?"

"Tanry, that's..." started Valentin, his shaking hand raised to point.

"I know who he is," she interrupted him.

"You're looking well, Val," said Zsari, though his tone wasn't kind.

"You— Uh—"

"Now, I know I don't look well, but it seems like you've been well fed these past five years."

"Well— I— Where— where have you been?" Valentin asked. Tanry would have described his manner as 'aghast' but it didn't seem strong enough a word.

"Oh, you know. About." A strange look had contorted Zsari's face. Tanry had never seen someone look both deeply amused, livid, and smug all at the same time. It was a mix of emotions that Tanry could only describe as dangerous.

"How did you find us?" asked Valentin.

"It was in the paper that you married Tanry," explained Zsari.

"Tanry? Tanry, you should leave us."

"You're ordering me out of my own dining room?" she asked, offended. "I already know who he is."

"How long have you been here?" shouted Valentin at Zsari. "And are you wearing my clothes?"

"Yes."

"Oh, I don't like that." Valentin adjusted his shirt collar as if it was tightening. "Why are you here?" he asked.

"Weren't you waiting for me? Wasn't that what you were told to do?"

"We thought you were dead!"

"You must have enjoyed living my life while I was left for dead," said Zsari.

"If I'd known—" Valentin started with an imploring tone, but Zsari spoke over him.

"You'd have given it all up? You'd have told the princess that you were an impostor?"

Valentin shuffled his feet.

"You would have kept my life for yourself," said Zsari. "You always wanted it. You lived at court with Princess Athalie in comfort while I was starving and nearly freezing to death and mourning my entire family. And you were fine." Zsari's voice cracked.

"I thought you were dead," begged Valentin.

"Am I supposed to be grateful for that?"

Just then, there were footsteps and both of them fell silent. Tanry had a moment to admire how alike they actually were. Valentin had grown longer and leaner, while Zsari was of a height with Tanry, but they had the same pale complexion and dark hair. If she hadn't known better, she would have called them brothers.

Tanry was interrupted from this reverie by the arrival of Bridget and Matfey. Bridget was attempting to adjust her wig at the hairline and no doubt this was the reason for their delay.

"Shit," said Bridget, her facade gone as soon as she saw Zsari. "Shit. How are you here? When did you get here?"

"Oh, some weeks past," said Zsari.

Bridget's jaw fell open. "You have been at Taltois for weeks? Who knew about this?"

"Just Tanry." Zsari smiled at Tanry and she scowled back.

"You knew he was here and you didn't tell us?" Bridget asked Tanry, though it had the tone of an accusation.

"I didn't know he was an archduke. I thought he was a tramp trying to wring me for money."

"In her defence, I *was* a tramp trying to wring her for

money."

"How did you get here?" Bridget asked.

Zsari had no chance to reply, because Cole appeared in the doorway with a tray and a silver cloche. He took in the scene before him, taking a moment to note Zsari's bare feet.

"Eggs for the archduke," he said. "Did anyone else have requests?"

For a moment, they stared at one another silently.

"I want eggs," said Zsari, his eyes drawn to the sideboard loaded with breakfast food. "I want three."

Cole looked to Tanry for her approval of the newcomer.

"Get the man some eggs," she said.

He set the tray down at the head of the table and waited for Valentin to sit. Valentin, who stared at Zsari with the wariness of someone being hunted, sat down and let Cole finish the ceremony of lifting the cloche. A pile of perfectly scrambled yellow eggs steamed there, though Valentin seemed far from hungry. Zsari rushed to the sideboard, where he piled handfuls of bacon and bread rolls and sausages onto a plate.

Cole left and they were alone again. Zsari sat himself at the other end of the table, where he had a full view of Valentin.

"It feels like you were enjoying your time with Princess Athalie. She kept you well fed, entertained, got you a rich wife."

"Athalie had nothing to with that," said Valentin, as quick as a whip.

"So you found a wife off your own back? How enterprising, Valentin. I didn't realise you had it in you." Zsari shoved bacon into his mouth, barely stopping to chew.

"I was the one who made the arrangement," said Tanry.

"Athalie really had nothing to do with it."

"I never met her, but she was on my list," said Zsari through his food.

"Your list?" asked Valentin, who was not eating.

"They made a list of potential brides for me, as heir to the country. It could only be princesses. Political matches. Athalie wasn't at the top of the list, but she was up there. A reliable match. Of course if we had met, then your charade wouldn't have panned out."

"Zsari, none of us chose this. None of us planned this. The IPC sent us away to protect you, and we never wanted to stay," said Bridget.

"I don't think that Valentin feels that way. I think that he always wanted what I had." Zsari gestured at Valentin with his fork, a piece of bacon falling from the end and landing on the tablecloth.

"You can't be bringing up this childish feud again," said Bridget. "Do we not have bigger concerns now?"

"I don't know. I just wonder whether Valentin will allow me to have my life back. I think he's gotten comfortable as an archduke. And my, look how tall he's gotten. And he's so defensive of the princess. Who can guess why."

"Don't talk about her," snapped Valentin.

"I'll talk about who I like."

"There is someone coming," warned Matfey, who was stood next to the door. They fell silent and a moment later she said: "It's just Beck."

Beck Cotterall, all smiles, stepped into the room. His face fell when he took in the mood of the scene.

"What do you mean, 'it's just Beck'?" asked Bridget.

"Only that it's Beck and we can trust him." Matfey shrugged and sat down at the breakfast table.

Hesitantly, Cotterall moved to her side.

"What are we trusting him with?" asked Bridget.

"Nothing he doesn't already know," said Matfey.

She might have elaborated, only Zsari chose that moment to tear off a piece of bread and throw it at Valentin, who yelped.

"Stop it," ordered Bridget. "Not again."

"Was this a regular event when they were younger?" Tanry asked of Matfey.

"They were always together. I never spent much time with Laurina, but Valentin had to taste Zsari's food for him."

"Ah, I see." Tanry's stomach dropped to her feet as she registered what Matfey had just said.

"This is Valentin," she told Cotterall hurriedly, pointing at Zsari. "He's a friend from Karda Ven." That was a start, but she couldn't explain Matfey's mention of Laurina when that was supposed to be her own name.

"Tanry, I know which one Valentin is," said Cotterall. "The tall one, who you married. Though I am not sure where this other one came from."

Zsari saluted him and continued eating.

"Ah, shit," said Tanry.

"You told him?" Bridget gasped. She cuffed Matfey across the back of the head. "How could you tell him?"

"If you must know, Beck and I have an announcement to make," said Matfey as she took Cotterall's hand.

"I don't care," Bridget interrupted her. "This is so irresponsible. This endangers all of us."

"This is just like Tresswell again," groaned Valentin. He was hit in the face by another piece of bread and made such a startled look that Tanry stifled a giggle.

"I am not like Tresswell," insisted Cotterall. "I am not after any money. I am in love with Matfey."

"Gods, you should not even know her name," said Bridget. "Matfey, you have doomed us all."

"One more person who knows the secret is one more person who can reveal it. If anyone finds out, then I will lose the estate. None of us will have anywhere to live."

"It's not a concern, Tanry," said Cotterall. "I wouldn't do anything to hurt Matfey."

"We didn't get rid of Tresswell for you to reveal everything to the next man who was kind to you," said Valentin.

Matfey turned to Valentin very slowly. "You 'got rid' of Tresswell?" she asked.

They did not get to hear whatever outrage this revelation conjured, because Duke Teneri chose that moment to attend breakfast. He headed straight for his usual seat at the head of the table, but soon found that Zsari was seated there. Rather than be surprised at the hungry stranger in his house, Duke Teneri turned to Cotterall.

"One of the old crowd, is he?"

Cotterall stared quizzically at the Duke, so Tanry cut in.

"Yes, Father. He's one of Trevor's old pals. He's visiting Cotterall."

"We used to get a lot of that." He sat down on the side of the table.

On cue, two footmen appeared with a plate of fried eggs and an ironed newspaper. Duke Teneri, unaware of the tension around him, opened his newspaper and vanished behind it. Zsari used this opportunity to throw two more pieces of bread at Valentin, who could not help but throw them back. The first one hit Zsari on the shoulder. Tanry shot her hand out and caught the second. She stuffed the bread into her mouth as her father looked up from his paper.

"What is everyone standing around for? Do you people take all day to eat breakfast?" he asked.

Cowed, the party sat. Matfey shuffled her chair as close to Cotterall's seat as she could. Tanry sat next to Zsari, who happily tucked into his eggs. He had no table manners. It was as if he had never been trained at the imperial court. Tanry found that she approved.

Bridget didn't eat. She cut her food into many small pieces while staring at Matfey and Cotterall. Valentin, whose eggs had gone cold, did nothing but stare red-eyed at Zsari. Tanry herself could barely eat. There was too much waiting to happen.

Of course her father did not notice. He had his own preoccupations to consider.

"My experiments are proving successful," he told the table proudly. He was met with silence, until Tanry said:

"Father, I don't think that anyone knows or cares what experiments you are performing."

"I am going back to the true root of alchemy, if you must know. Other materials can be turned to gold, but no one has perfected the process yet. I think that the key is fire. Heat changes all states."

"I'm sure no one has ever thought of that," said Tanry, though she was certain that her father would ignore the sarcasm.

"It's all going terribly well, if you must know. I do hope that your experiments are going as well, Lizseta."

"Father, there's no need for that." Tanry cut in.

"I am just making conversation."

"Then make another."

"I only want to know how her experiments are going. I plan to invite some members from the alchemists' Society here soon, and it wouldn't do to have her experiments unexplained."

"Would the Society speak to someone who wasn't a member?" asked Bridget, which almost made Tanry's heart stop.

Duke Teneri laughed. "They wouldn't consider the work of a woman. Especially not one who engages in such frivolous work as hair brushes and face powders."

Bridget's mouth was pressed tightly closed, though it seemed she was exerting all her will to do so. "I have made great strides," she said. "I have completed a prototype. I am sure that whatever my work might lack in academic interest, it makes up for in commercial potential. If this were Karda Ven, I would have applied for a license of patent already."

"I had no idea that archduchesses in Karda Ven whittled their time away with business proposals," the duke said, his tone acidic. "I thought you were a painter, and meek-minded. Now that you are here, it hardly feels that you are a young lady at all. I have no idea what you were taught in Karda Ven, but that is not how we do things at Taltois."

Bridget's face went quite pink. She sat for a moment, her mouth open, searching for the right thing to say. Tanry wondered if her pride would win above her will to stay disguised, but before that battle was fought, Tanry considered what her father had said.

"How *do* we do things at Taltois?" she asked. Her father didn't seem to hear, so she had to ask again: "How do we do things?"

"Tanry, why do you ask? I am trying to eat my breakfast."

"No, you are trying to start a competition with Lizseta and you are telling lies."

"I don't expect you to understand," he said.

"God, you're such a hypocrite."

Zsari, who had shovelled a whole piece of bacon into his mouth, choked.

"Tanry, do not speak to me in such a way. I cannot believe you." The duke put down his newspaper, which was how Tanry knew he was serious.

"You can't believe me? You don't even know me. You have never cared to know me. I have hunted and smoked and got drunk with Trevor's friends and you never cared. And now, Lizseta does something unladylike, and you cast aspersions because it inconveniences you personally. No one must be a fine lady at Taltois until Duke Teneri bids it, because we all must live by his word, though he has not visited his tenants in over ten years."

"Quiet now, or I shall punish you for your insolence."

"Would you even know how? You had no need of me until your heir died and you thought you could sell me to your nearest friend. That doesn't matter anymore. I have my own husband. I found him myself and I made his family my own. You will not give them any orders, instructions, or insults. They are my family and you will not treat them in such a way."

"Or what will you do?"

"I will close the gates and make sure that the alchemists' Society cannot visit."

Quite abruptly, her father stood up. "I never should have listened to your brother. I should have sent you away to be schooled." He left without finishing his eggs.

"Could you actually do that?" asked Bridget.

"I don't know. I need to make sure that he doesn't just disown me. He could do a lot more to me than I could ever do to him. The law is on his side."

If Tanry thought that Bridget might have thanked her for coming to her defence, that idea was dispelled when Bridget turned to Matfey.

"How could you tell him everything? Our situation is far from secure, as you can tell."

"Our situation would be far simpler if you didn't insist on experimenting. You know well that Lizseta would never have dreamed of doing alchemy," Matfey snapped back.

"And Laurina never would have done something so conventional as marry an artist with no money."

"I have some money," said Cotterall, rather bashfully. "My father doesn't support my ambitions as an artist, but he hasn't disowned me."

Matfey put her hand on his wrist and he stopped talking.

"I think that we have been brushing over what Valentin said earlier," she said. "You 'got rid' of Tresswell?"

Valentin's face was as white as the tablecloth. "It was Tanry's plan," he said.

"We work together for one plan and he chooses to blame it all on me," Tanry said. "Matfey, we knew we couldn't trust Tresswell, so we told him that you wouldn't have a dowry. He couldn't marry you without any money. I doubt that he would have stuck around had he known that you were really an orphan from the streets of Veni."

"You don't know that, Tanry."

"You've found someone better. It all turned out. I think if Valentin and I played the same trick on Cotterall, then he would marry you even with no dowry."

"Well, Tanry..." Cotterall started.

"Do not ruin this for yourself, Cotterall."

"My father might not have cut me off, but that doesn't mean I can afford all the supplies I really need. Matfey, well, she told me about your agreement."

"Cotterall, if you stop talking right now, I will double the dowry."

None of this, of course, calmed Matfey. She stood up, not caring for how her chair scraped unpleasantly against the floor.

"It has been five years since we left Karda Ven. We have been a family in all but blood for five years, and you decide to sneak behind my back to end my engagement."

"Matfey..." Cotterall clutched at her sleeve. She pushed his hand away.

"This doesn't concern you. This concerns Valentin," she said.

"And Tanry," said Valentin weakly.

"Tanry blackmailed you into marrying her."

At this statement from Matfey, Zsari stopped eating altogether and stared, frozen, at Tanry.

Matfey continued: "I more or less expected this from her, but Valentin should have known better. He should have behaved as a brother should."

"As someone with a real brother – or who once had one – it doesn't always go that way," said Tanry.

"I have brothers," snapped Matfey. "I have three of them, and two sisters. I think I know much more about family and loyalty, Tanry, than you ever could."

Valentin stood. "Matfey, I did what I thought was best for our family. I did the only thing we've done since leaving Karda Ven: keep the secret. Idonea told us to, so we did it. We refused servants, company, friends. We pretended to be other people for five years. You wanted to tell Lord Tresswell who you really were when you knew that it would endanger Bridget and I. I didn't tell Athalie anything. I turned down all her proposals. I betrayed her in the worst ways I could have, all to protect the three of us. Do not criticise me for doing what I was supposed to."

Cotterall tried to take Matfey's hand again, but she didn't let him.

"God, I don't know if I can bear hearing you complain anymore." Zsari was slouched in his chair, tapping his fingers against the tabletop. "You couldn't have servants? What hardship. You had to keep a secret from Athalie. God."

"I don't mean to compare hardships, Zsari. I cannot imagine what you have gone through," said Valentin.

"I nearly died more times than I can count. Even just to escape, I nearly drowned and froze to death. I wanted to be good when I came here. I wanted to find you and get a little comfort and maybe remember old times. But I saw you living my life and I had to be jealous. You had comfort and the favour of a princess and a beautiful wife. It feels like you barely care about me. I'm here, and I'm breaking your secret, the one that you've worked so hard to protect. Here you are, arguing over it, and it is as if I'm not here to contest it. It is as if I died."

"What do you want, Zsari? I can't give you anything. I can't bear you tormenting me either. What is it?" Valentin asked him.

"You can't pay him to get rid of him," said Tanry. "I don't think that he actually wants to go."

"You can't," said Valentin.

"I'm staying." The words came out of Zsari's mouth very fast. "I can join the charade until we work out how to resolve this. I can pretend to be one of the old crowd if I have to."

"Zsari, it worked once," said Bridget in a soft voice, "but Duke Teneri might ask more questions. He's already suspicious. He would ask who your parents were, or he would wonder why you never go home. We couldn't keep it up."

"You can't send me away," said Zsari, trying to keep his voice from breaking. "You are the only people left from home. I will have this."

"Zsari, you have to go," Valentin insisted.

Zsari let out a long breath and the tension left his shoulders. He rubbed his nose with the back of his hand. Putting both palms on the table, he pushed himself to his feet. "Well, I suppose I'm not wanted at family breakfast. But Val, you should really know that, while I didn't marry your princess, I did fuck your wife."

Tanry had thought she was more or less safe in this conversation, but of course that was a misguided notion. All eyes in the room were drawn to her.

"I think that we're done here," she said.

"Oh, not even slightly," replied Bridget. "When did this happen? How did this happen?"

"Bridget, it really is not your concern," said Tanry.

"If you are sleeping with an archduke, then I will find out about it."

"What does it matter?"

She did not get time to answer, because Valentin decided it was not worth staying. He marched from the room, everyone's eyes upon him.

CHAPTER THIRTY-ONE

A Poetic Streak

The discernment engine was the pride of Premure: a device capable of telling absolute truth. Do not be deceived, it is no longer held at the university. Generations ago, the engine went missing. Many believe that it was taken into the care of the Dean, and held in secret, the purported theft having been spread as a rumour to keep its true location secret. — The Arcane Arts of Premure

Contrary to the mood of the residents of Taltois, the day turned out to be bright and clear: a herald of the coming spring.

Zsari, who had been divested of his terrible boots and who couldn't fit Valentin's shoes, was confined to the house. Tanry followed him at a distance. He walked down the halls of Tanry's wing, stopping to admire the art on the walls.

"I can see you behind me," he said. "Are you going to scold

me for the way I behaved?"

"I don't think I behaved much better, I admit." She went to stand by him. He was looking at a painting of the landscape around Taltois. In the time of Tanry's grandfather, a famous painter had lived at Taltois and did studies of the landscape, before he'd gone back to the city and gotten addicted to opiates. The paintings themselves were worth a fortune.

"You don't want me to leave, do you?" he asked.

"I don't know what to do, Zsari. I thought being back here would fix everything, but it's much the same. I don't know if I can let you stay."

There was an alternative that she briefly considered. The ideal scenario, if one could be imagined, would see Zsari take Valentin's place. He could pretend to be her husband, pretend that he had been in Albonne for the past five years, and Valentin could leave at his will. That would be a neat solution to the whole ordeal, if only Duke Teneri could be relied upon to keep the ruse. He knew what Valentin looked like, and he'd already been lied to about who Zsari was. Revealing the truth to him would backfire, she feared. Valentin and Zsari were no longer children, and time had wrought its differences on them. She feared that one could no longer be easily passed for another.

"I don't know where I'll go," he murmured.

"Go north. Go to Nessa Spa. You can start again. I'll send you off with something valuable."

"I'd rather not go at all. I don't even have any shoes."

"I will get you some shoes."

"And until then?"

"You can't possibly go anywhere."

He smirked. "At least someone is happy to have me, even for a little while."

"I need to do some damage control," said Tanry. "Don't get into any trouble and don't talk to my father."

"Noted. Can I go to the kitchens?"

"You can, but only if you tell the staff that you're Cotterall's friend and that your name is Lewis."

"I can do that," he assured her.

"The trick to a good lie is not adding too much detail. Don't stay long enough to start a proper conversation."

"Can we talk later? Properly."

"And by talk you mean..?" She left the end of her sentence hanging, leaving a pointed silence for Zsari to pick up on.

"There could be other activities if we found the time." He grinned.

"Good," she said. "We wouldn't want to waste any time."

Tanry was good at running things. She knew how to keep the estate in order so that it turned a profit every year, and when it didn't she made sure everyone got fed regardless.

She couldn't smooth things over with *people,* though. She didn't know how. But making sure that the impostors were happy was now part and parcel of running Taltois. Matfey was the easiest place to start. Her wants were simple.

Tanry found her and Cotterall in the latter's studio, where the latter had returned to working on the portrait.

"Can I come in?" asked Tanry as she was entering anyway.

Matfey was pacing in front of the doors. "I don't care to speak to you," she said.

"Have you considered that I might have something useful

to say?" Tanry sat down on one of the armchairs they'd used for the portrait, winding the sash of her dressing gown around her hand. "Cotterall, am I right in thinking that your father would give you a house on his estate when you are wed?"

Cotterall shrugged. "Yes, but it comes with a living. I would need to become a parson and the life of a country clergyman wouldn't suit my ambitions."

"I'll make sure you get a studio in Albonne. Call it a part of Matfey's dowry. I want you and Matfey to be set, with whatever life you might choose."

"That's very kind of you, Tanry," said Cotterall.

Matfey stopped her pacing. "Don't agree to anything. With her, nothing is a gift."

"Come on, Matfey. What will it take?" asked Tanry.

"For me to forgive you?"

"And Valentin, if you would be so kind."

"What does he have to do with it?" She sneered at the thought.

"I'm his wife. I'm speaking on his behalf."

"Definitely not with his will, though."

"Matfey, what is it that you want? Ignore Valentin and Bridget. What do you want that you never dared to ask for?"

She stared at Tanry, her round eyes glassy. She chewed on her bottom lip. "I want my brothers and my sisters. I want to go to Karda Ven and get them back."

As she said this, Cotterall put down his paintbrush and opened his mouth, but Tanry did not let him get a word in.

"Done," she said.

"Tanry, it can't be that simple," said Cotterall.

"It can't be that hard. I'll hire an investigator and get them to Taltois. Or, I'll give you the money to do the same thing. It might endanger the secret somewhat, but not if we were suitably discreet – and if Matfey thinks that it's worth the risk."

Matfey thought on this prospect for several seconds, her arms folded decisively over her front. "Idonea would caution against it," she said.

"Idonea isn't here."

"We haven't heard from her since before the wedding."

"Yes, clearly she no longer cares enough to participate. When you are married, we can find the best investigator. But, only after the wedding. We need to introduce this to Bridget slowly, or she will have a conniption."

"Do you think she will forgive me for it?" asked Matfey.

"No."

Her face fell.

"You'll have to start by apologising to her for telling Cotterall, then proving in some way that you can be discreet. Use my father as an example. He's easy to pretend in front of because he's usually barely listening."

Tanry left the studio feeling rather satisfied. Matfey and Cotterall would wed as soon as the banns could be read. He was Trevor's old friend and a trustworthy sort. Tanry could sponsor his art career and he'd never be tempted to throw them to the wolves. It was beginning to come into place.

Next, she had to calm Bridget's fire. Her whims were harder to solve than Matfey's, but Tanry couldn't back down from a challenge. Bridget was easy to find. When she was frustrated, she went to work. The smell of sulphur filtered down through the corridor and into the grand hall.

"Should I ready the fire buckets?" asked Tanry.

"Nothing is on fire," said Bridget in a low voice. "Though I'm beginning to wish that I was going up in flames." She was stood by her workbench, looking with dejection at a collection of hairbrushes.

"They aren't going to alchemise themselves, you know," jested Tanry.

"Oh, that's not a problem." Bridget picked up a brush and plucked a lock of hair loose from her wig. She ran the brush through the dark curls and as the brush passed through, the hair turned a buttery blonde.

Bridget held it for a moment so that Tanry could inspect it, then ran the brush through it again, returning the hair to its original colour.

"It's only that your father has a point," said Bridget.

"I wouldn't give him that much credit."

"I can make the most effective alchemic device, but it won't matter because the Society here will not listen to me."

"And they would in Karda Ven?"

"It would have been hard in Karda Ven, but not impossible. My friend, Aven, he got better marks, even though he did not work nearly as hard as I did. He had job offers and I had to work for the IPC just to get by. But back there, at least women were allowed to attend university. There isn't a single woman with a university place in Lyalia."

"I could help you, if you like."

Bridget tutted. "I know that you are just trying to buy me off. I assume you promised Matfey a greater dowry," she said.

"Only so she would agree to apologise to you. She and

Cotterall will be married as soon as possible and I will make sure that Cotterall is so indebted to me that he will never think of betraying us."

"That does not protect us from idiocy." Bridget organised the hairbrushes on the table in front of her, pushing each slightly one way then the other, though they seemed perfectly organised to Tanry.

"Nothing will." Tanry sat down in an armchair and crossed her legs. "But it's one step closer to an accord, is it not?"

"That depends on what you want," said Bridget.

"I only want everyone to be happy at Taltois."

"Bullshit. You want Zsari to stay."

"I'm not so foolish, Bridget. I hardly know him," Tanry lied.

"Maybe so, but you will want something or other and I won't want to give it to you."

"What if I got the Society members to view your work?"

Bridget laughed and shook her head. "Your father would combust," she said, revealing that she had a full picture of his character.

"He wants them here. He can deal with the consequences. If they like your work, would they buy a patent?"

"They might." Her eyes flicked to the mirror behind Tanry. "But it doesn't matter. Lizseta cannot join the Society of Alchemists. It would be too suspicious."

Tanry stood. She walked to the window, lost in thought, and admired the view of the lake and the folly, which was laden with snow.

"What if we made it more plausible? Lizseta can learn new skills outside of Karda Ven. What if we told the Society that you are my father's apprentice and he taught you everything that you know?"

"Because then he would take all the credit, and that rather defeats the purpose."

"So there is no way to make you happy?"

Bridget shrugged. "There is no way for me to be content at Taltois. If your father throws a fit at my work, then there is nothing for me to do. If I continue with my work, your father may realise that we are impostors and disinherit you. It is all very well that Matfey has found that she wanted, but I cannot do the same."

Obviously Bridget felt that she was done with the conversation, because she fixed her goggles over her eyes and picked up a glass container from her bench.

"What are you doing now, if the hairbrush is done?" asked Tanry.

"A tincture to change eye colour," Bridget replied.

"How does it work?"

"I know that you've no understanding of alchemy."

"I can learn. How does it work?" Tanry approached her work bench, looking at the small glass dishes with brightly coloured droplets in them.

"Speaking in lay terms, it's not like paint where the colour is covered over with another. It is more like dye, where I am trying to change the colour on a chemical level."

"Will the person be able to see when you are done with them?"

"Hopefully."

"How will you test them? I don't think we can find any willing participants." Tanry's mind conjured an unbidden image of Bridget chasing her down and holding her eyelids open.

"I need to make it first. You're getting a bit ahead of me."

"Can I help in any way?"

Bridget considered. "I need someone to measure out all this, but you have to be precise."

"I can be precise," Tanry insisted.

"You are a hunter and a groundskeeper. Precision is far from your area of expertise." It was Bridget's attempt at an insult, she knew, but she found that she enjoyed being described in such a way. She'd always resented 'Lady Teneri', feeling that the name was not descriptive enough, but thinking of herself as a hunter and a groundskeeper was compelling. It felt purposeful.

"Show me how," Tanry requested.

Bridget rolled her eyes but held up the glass flask. She tapped one of the lines inscribed on the outside with her fingernail.

"Fill it to here, but be aware that the surface of the liquid isn't even."

"What? Is this water?" She sniffed it and coughed.

"No, it isn't. Don't drink it. The surface of the liquid is raised where it touches the side of the glass."

"And I measure it to there?"

"No, measure it to the other part."

Tanry tried to follow her instructions, though she was a very exacting tutor, and she tipped out the measurements Tanry made and did them again. Eventually, Bridget laid out a series of fresh glass dishes and told Tanry that her help was not required.

"I can't pretend that I have any influence with the Society of Alchemists," said Tanry as she moved towards the door. "But if I could get you a career, would you be happier here?"

Bridget pressed both of her hands to the worktop and sighed. "Truth be told, Tanry, there is so much standing in the way of my happiness that I doubt anyone can fix it."

"Then tell me your guiltiest want. You can fear no judgement from me."

Bridget pushed her goggles up her forehead. The action made her wig slip and a lock of blonde hair escaped. She stared at Tanry, and Tanry couldn't imagine what she was thinking. "I want to no longer be responsible for anyone. Matfey and Valentin are grown and I don't want to have to worry about them anymore."

"You can trust me with them."

"Then prove to me that you are about their well-being. Prove that you can keep them safe."

It was easy to care about Matfey. Her wishes were already known, and already easy to fulfill. Tanry summoned Russeau and set out plans to read the marriage banns and hire a private investigator.

The real hurdle was Valentin. She knew that he had a poetic streak, but it was confirmed when she found him in the folly by the lake, despite the falling snow.

"Are you trying to catch your death?" she called.

She had dressed properly to come outdoors, but Valentin wore only a light jacket and his trouser legs were caked with snow. He only turned his head slightly to acknowledge her arrival.

"I knew you had a romantic spirit, but I didn't think you were this given to drama." She realised as she said it that it sounded more insult than jest. "I— You should come inside before you catch your death."

He ignored her.

"I would rather not bury you, Valentin," she said, more harshly than she intended.

"I will go indoors when I choose to go indoors. Not all in my life has to be done by your decree," he said. "Why will you not leave me alone?"

"I need to prove that I care about you. I need to do something to make your life here easier."

"Hold up the skies, cut them down and use them as curtains. You are far more likely to achieve that than to make me happy living in your house." He stared at his hands and Tanry saw the glint of something gold that he held there.

"What have you got there?" she asked. Valentin did not own much in the way of jewellery.

At her question, Valentin pushed his hand into his pocket, concealing the item. "It's none of your concern, though apparently I can have no privacy where you are concerned."

"Forgive me for asking."

"Don't be insincere. You have never wanted to be forgiven for anything."

"Gods, what else can I do but be polite?"

He laughed coldly. "Why did you keep Zsari from me?" he asked. "It would not have endangered me to know that he was here."

"I really didn't think it was him. I thought he was certainly dead." This complaint made no sense to her. Valentin would not have paid attention to her if Tanry had told him there was a trespasser living in her caravan.

"Then how did you learn this morning who he really was?"

"Ah, no, that was before."

"How? How could you have known?"

"I can't tell you that."

"Why not?"

"I have secrets, Valentin." Her aunt had charged her with keeping the engine safe. She'd told Caterina, and every other servant who had helped her move it, but who could an aristocrat trust if not their servants? Tanry thought that even her father didn't have a notion of what the discernment engine was.

"Ah, I see. My privacy means nothing but yours is paramount."

Tanry shuffled on her feet. She'd used the discernment engine to pry open his life and take all of his secrets. The baroness had given her the engine because she was family, but Valentin was her husband now.

"Fine. You can have the secret, but you have to come indoors."

"This is a ploy."

"No, it's not. You should know by now that I'm not so subtle a schemer."

She took him to her sitting room – she saw him stiffen as he crossed the threshold – and she uncovered the discernment engine.

"What am I supposed to be looking at?" he asked.

"My mother left it to me. Well, she left it to Trevor but..."

She cleared her throat and carried on. "It came from Premure. It's alchemic, though I've no idea how it works. Whatever you ask it, it tells you the truth."

"Oh."

"What? You don't want to know more?"

"No. It all makes sense. I don't know how else you figured out our secret, and how you figured out Zsari. There wasn't a single solution in my head, so it may as well have been an arcane device that I have no understanding of."

Tanry felt as if she could taste the bitterness in the air. "Is there anything you want to ask it?"

Valentin shook his head.

"Really?" Tanry asked. "You can ask it all the secrets of the universe if you want. Or if there's anyone you really hate, you can find out their most embarrassing secret. Anything you want."

"I don't dare ask."

"Why not? It's all there. You can know anything."

"Can you ask it where my mother lives?" he asked in a small voice.

"I knew she was at the wedding. I knew it was her."

He nodded.

Tanry duly laid out the question in the dials. The engine whirred, then spat out a village on the border near Calness, certainly nowhere auspicious.

"She's within visiting distance. Well – not a short visit. But it wouldn't look amiss if we invited some faces from the old country to come and stay."

"I don't even know if she would come."

"If she knew her son was here, wouldn't she come

325

running?"

"She never acknowledged me, Tanry. What reason do I have to believe that her intentions have changed?"

Tanry didn't know an awful lot about mothers, but as a child she'd created an imaginary one. She had been told that mothers loved their children more than anyone ever could. Her father never showed anything like that, so she had to believe that love was stored in mothers. Trevor's stories made her believe the same. In his tales, their mother was the most beautiful woman to ever exist. Her hands were soft and she sang in a way that wasn't practised, but was sweeter than honey.

Lady Taybury had seemed reasonable enough. She would come looking for her son.

Tanry turned the dials on the machine again.

DOES TAYBURY WANT HER SON BACK

"Why are you asking that? You can't ask that." He reached for the machine, but Tanry grabbed his arm and pulled him back.

"You have to ask the machine everything you're too afraid to ask."

"Why?"

"When else will you get to? Or will you always wonder if your mother ever loved you? It's not a comfortable feeling, Valentin."

The engine's output dial turned. Tanry didn't need to look at it to know what the answer was. It stopped at three letters instead of two. She was staring at Valentin, whose eyes flicked to the engine as if he felt too guilty to look at it.

"It doesn't matter. I'm supposed to be an archduke. She

can't acknowledge me."

"But don't you want to know?"

"I last saw her when I was ten years old and I've never had the option to see her since."

"You can see her again."

"You can't tempt me with my old life, Tanry. I can't go back. It's not fair."

"I can't figure you out. Do you enjoy denying yourself the things you want?"

"Do you ever get tired of taking everything without thinking what the consequences might be?" he snapped. Strangely, Tanry felt a stab of shame at his remark. She should not have cared, but perhaps he had a point. Perhaps he was right to be angry at her.

"When was the last time that you did something for yourself? If they took you from your mother when you were ten, then you — where did you go then?"

"The Imperial Protection Corps. I used to test food for Zsari, and then I was his double. They sent me out instead of him whenever they were worried for his safety. Then when I was fifteen, we crossed the border and the real charade began."

"Oh, so you had no time for yourself, your entire life." She turned the dials of the engine again.

DOES TAYBURY MISS VALENTIN

The answer was three letters long again. Silently, Valentin approached the engine. It was not a victory yet, but Tanry felt some small satisfaction. That was – until she saw his question.

DOES ATHALIE MISS VALENTIN

Any speech Tanry might have been about to make died in her mouth. The discernment engine whirred. It didn't come to this conclusion quickly, but spun for what seemed to be an age before giving an answer.

NO

Valentin left the room without another word.

Tanry reached for the engine again. From her use of the machine, Tanry had learned that the truth was never as simple as it appeared. She turned the dials, changing the question ever so slightly.

DOES ATHALIE MISS CEZSARIO

The engine answered quickly.

YES

CHAPTER THIRTY-TWO

An Education in Alchemy

Membership to the Society of Alchemists is as exclusive as one would expect from an organisation of its esteem. Applicants must give a demonstration to certified society members, who will judge its intellectual value. Only after a demonstration is completed will the Society consider funding research. — Manual for the Society of Alchemists

No one took meals together that day, presumably owing to unresolved trauma from breakfast.

Tanry ate with Zsari in Trevor's old study, which in its disuse was covered in dust sheets. Their choice of room was made in the hopes that they would be undisturbed, even by servants. No one was likely to come looking for them in a dead man's room.

Zsari still ate like he was preparing for a long winter. He

had finished half a loaf of bread and nearly a whole wheel of cheese. They sat together in the middle of the rug, not caring much how many crumbs they dropped.

"You never met his mother?" Tanry asked.

"No," said Zsari through a mouthful of bread. "I barely knew who she was."

"He's got a complex about it. He hid from her at the wedding."

"A little bit of that is my fault," Zsari admitted.

"What could you have done to make him strange about his mother?"

"Remind him everyday that he was a bastard and therefore worth less than I."

"God."

"You wouldn't have liked me back then," he said.

"You told him that?"

"Yeah, I hated him."

"But why? He hates me more than anything and he still manages to be polite about it."

"Oh, he was just better at being me than I ever was. He was better at etiquette. My tutors liked him more. He was a better dancer. He was never angry. And he was so good at following protocol. I was trying to sneak out of the palace with the serving girls and he was reading notes on debates in parliament. He would have made a better emperor than I would have."

Tanry was amused for a moment by an image of young Valentin, reading dry political texts by candlelight.

"Do you miss that?"

"What?"

"Being an archduke. Waiting to be an emperor."

"I miss my family and having a reliable roof over my head. Nothing else held any romance. You had it better. You got to run outside whenever you wanted. You didn't need a body double to go outdoors so the gunmen tried to shoot him instead of you."

Tanry choked on her bread. "That happened?"

"Oh, not to Valentin. But not for the want of trying. They got Idonea once."

For a moment, Tanry chewed on a crust, lost in thought.

"You've had an odd life," she said. "You should speak to Valentin. Figure out all this shit."

"I can't do that if I'm being sent away," he complained.

"I will try and keep you here. I will convince them to let you stay."

He laid back on the floor. "I think you are chasing a lost cause there," he said. "I think I'll head north from here. I've never travelled to Calness alone."

"Stay with me," said Tanry. She set the crust aside and laid down on the floor beside him.

"It was only one night, Tanry. You will have other nights with other people."

"I want you to stay. Why can't you stay?"

"Wanting something is not enough."

She buried her face into his neck.

"You get used to losing things after a while," he continued. He shifted and put his arm around her.

Tanry sent a personal messenger to the Society of Alchemists in Martois, which she reasoned was faster than waiting for a post carriage. She invited them to witness a demonstration on her father's behalf. The rest would follow.

For the next day, Zsari stayed in Tanry's bedroom, half-dressed and half-asleep.

Taltois descended into uneasy silence, as if no one really lived there. Tanry walked past rooms where Matfey and Cotterall giggled with their heads close together; Bridget was hard at work on her projects. Tanry couldn't help but feel that there was something she was missing.

The Society members gladly accepted her invitation for the end of the week. They were all old friends of Duke Teneri and were curious about his work. She planned a dinner and chose the wine, though she had no idea how to get them interested in Bridget's work.

The banns were read for Matfey and Cotterall, and Tanry told Russeau to find them a townhouse in Albonne.

Everything should have been falling into place, but Tanry could feel the melancholy chilling in her bones.

On the day that the Society members were due to arrive, Tanry woke to find that Zsari was already dressed.

"Where are you going?" she asked.

"Your guests are coming. I am going to hide in the caravan and not invite any unwanted questions." There was something odd and tight in his voice.

"Are you all right?" she asked.

"Fine. I will just stay out of the way."

"You aren't thinking of leaving, are you?"

"No one else wants me here. I don't know what else to do."

"I'll see you later. I'll deal with the Society and I'll come find you in the caravan before it gets dark."

He leaned in to kiss her lightly. "Good luck," he said.

She felt it was necessary to have luck. She met with Bridget in the grand hall as the carriages drew up.

"Are they a favourable lot?" Bridget asked.

"No idea. I'm going to tell them that my husband is unwell. Do you know where he is?"

"In his room," said Bridget. "Sulking."

They heard voices outdoors and both fell silent. Tanry straightened her cuffs, but noticed as she did that there were flecks of mud on her sleeves. There was nothing to be done, as Cole was opening the door and showing the Society members inside.

There were three of them, and upon first sight they looked to be identical old men with bushy moustaches. There were some small differences, though, mostly in the number of gold badges they wore on their lapels. The old man with the most badges looked around the hall, eyes lingering on the murals, and sniffed.

"We might have expected a proper greeting," he said. "Fetch your master. Tell him that we've arrived."

Bridget let out a short laugh. The eyes of the men were drawn to her.

"What would a proper greeting entail?" asked Tanry quickly. The Society members stared at her with a puzzlement usually reserved for small children.

"All of the staff awaiting our arrival on the steps, and your master greeting us himself."

"Ah," said Tanry.

Bridget struggled to hold a giggle in, and it was infectious.

Tanry couldn't keep from smiling. "Well, Princess Athalie does not stand on such ceremony, so I don't see why I should. As for my father, he is expecting to meet you in his library."

There was a moment of dull, painful silence, interrupted only by Bridget's giggling.

"I apologise, my lady. I didn't recognise you."

"We have never met; how should you?"

"I am Lord Deshaney, and these are my colleagues Lord Berulam and Lord Shaw."

"Very good. This is my sister-in-law, the Archduchess Lizseta Caela Loremarie Boralda-Solkin."

"Oh. An archduchess?"

"My husband, the archduke, is indisposed, I'm afraid."

"Oh."

Bridget laughed again.

"I'll show you to the library, Lord Deshaney. My father is waiting there with his demonstration."

If Bridget possessed any respect for the Society of Alchemists, their arrival had dispelled it. Tanry led the delegation up the grand staircase. Lord Shaw offered his arm to Bridget, but she declined it, and faked offence in a way that made Tanry laugh again.

"Lady Teneri, I did not realise that you would still be at Taltois once you were wed," said Lord Deshaney, presumably in an attempt to excuse his behaviour.

"Were you expecting me to move to my husband's house?"

"Why should I not?"

"You may have a word with the republic of Karda Ven then. I'm sure that they will be amenable to returning his property."

"Your father made out that you were going to marry Duke Archibald. He's an old friend."

"Perhaps you should take my father's word with a grain of salt, when I am the authority on my own affairs."

Upstairs, the hallway smelled suspiciously of smoke. Choosing not to comment, Tanry showed the lords into the library. Her father had dressed in his best day suit and stood ready behind his workbench. His eyes were narrowed and focused on Bridget as they entered the room.

"Tanry, why is the archduchess here?" he asked.

"Father, Lords Deshaney, Berulam, and Shaw are here for your demonstration," Tanry replied, ignoring the question. Deshaney grasped Duke Teneri's hand and shook it.

"We've missed you in the Society. Terrible business with your son, terrible terrible business."

"We were surprised to hear from you, truth be told," said Lord Shaw. "We thought you were done with alchemy after your recent tragedy. You intimated as much at our last meeting."

"My priorities changed," said Duke Teneri, avoiding Tanry's eye. "And I had a breakthrough in my research."

"Yes, your letter indicated that you were working on pure alchemy. Lead into gold."

"My daughter's letter," muttered Duke Teneri.

"Your daughter?" Deshaney looked at Tanry.

"I sent the message," she said. "I guessed you would realise that, since I was the one who signed it."

"You did not take your husband's name?"

"Must you continue to ask about my husband? I thought

we were here to witness some alchemy."

The room fell rather silent, then her father clapped his hands together.

"Alchemy! If you will sit down with a view of the bench." He had prepared three chairs, so Tanry and Bridget moved to stand at the back of the room.

"Will this be impressive, do you think?" whispered Bridget.

"I am more likely to turn into a rabbit before your very eyes."

Her father seemed not to notice their conversation, because he raised his hands like a magician attempting to perform with flair.

"I believe that in my research, I have made great strides towards the achievement of pure alchemy. My work, despite being isolated from the work of the Society, is therefore unfiltered by the conceptions of pure alchemy. I am alone here with no other alchemists nearby to confuse my thoughts."

He breathed out, leaving an awkward pause, then picked up his alchemic spark, kindling a small fire in the dish in front of him. "I believe that heat is the secret to pure alchemy, and that we have been ignoring this simple solution thus far."

He turned a dial on the side of the bowl. The flame flickered blue and then stopped moving. Even from the back of the room, Tanry felt the wave of heat that came from it.

"Are you going to melt lead, Teneri?" asked Deshaney with a laugh.

"It's a bit more complex than that," replied the Duke. "Melting implies a relatively low heat to what I am attempting to achieve."

"That's nothing you couldn't achieve in a kiln, of course," said Deshaney. "Your average potter can't turn lead into gold."

Disdainfully, Duke Teneri replied, "Your average potter does not have the education in alchemy that I do."

"Then by all means, go ahead."

Duke Teneri puffed again, trying to steady himself. He picked up pieces of metal from the bench.

"Of course, I have to prepare the substances." This involved breaking parts off with a small hammer and bathing them in a series of chemical concoctions that Tanry thought didn't change the metal at all. As he announced every new chemical, Bridget made an audible reaction, usually a wry laugh.

"Now the heating process begins," Duke Teneri announced, fixing a pair of dark goggles over his eyes.

Lord Berulam was deep in a whispered conversation with Lord Shaw. The duke picked up a ceramic cup with a pair of iron tongs, which he held over the flame. If he had meant for this to be exciting to watch, then he was woefully mistaken. Watching a pot be heated had all the visual interest of watching paint dry.

Deshaney sighed quite audibly. "Is this going to continue for much longer?"

"I've not yet shown you the fruits of my research," complained Duke Teneri.

"You've shown me the fruits of Duke Archibald's research from twenty-five years ago."

"I have made some innovations."

"Doing it with updated heating methods is hardly innovative."

"It is nearly done."

"Set it down, then, but I sincerely doubt that there will be any gold inside that capsule."

Feeling that the conversation was about to take a rough turn with a fire still kindled, Tanry stepped forward.

"You've had a long journey. I'm sure I can convince Cook to provide you with some refreshments," she said in her best approximation of a hostess.

Deshaney stood and nodded at her. "I think that is a sound idea. Perhaps you and the archduchess could show us around the grounds." He turned his sneer to Duke Teneri. "While His Grace tidies up."

While she knew next to nothing about the art of alchemy, Tanry was an expert in the art of Taltois.

"The landscaping here was done by Competency Green. He worked on the palace in Albonne too." She gestured to the man-made creek and ridge that was meant to obscure the view of the village from the house.

Lord Deshaney nodded approvingly but made no comment. He looked around at the frosted ground and the patches of slowly melting snow.

"Why did you write to us, Lady Teneri, if your father had little to show us?" he asked.

"I know little of alchemy. For all I knew, there could have been something marvellous planned."

"He is far from ready for presentation. I don't know why he would recommend such a thing to you."

"I suspect it was something to do with the archduchess."

"What would she have to do with anything?"

Tanry thought quickly. There was no good way to explain Bridget's ambitions, given Lizseta's demure role in society. There could only be a bad explanation, but it was not impossible to get something out of this situation. Bridget could get a little of something from these people, even if it was not all she desired.

"The archduchess is quite the hobbyist, and Princess Athalie is such an intellectual. She encourages research and that sort of thing."

"Even among women?"

"Women read quite widely, I think you'll find."

"But the archduchess..."

"She has such an interest in alchemy. She's nothing of my father's education, as you'd expect, but she has an innate aptitude."

"For alchemy?"

"And why shouldn't she?"

"I simply never thought that an archduchess would take up alchemy," said Deshaney.

"They take up all sorts of things when they no longer have a country to govern," replied Tanry with a shrug.

"I do suppose that's true, but it is most unusual."

"That's beyond me to say. As I said, I truly know nothing about alchemy."

The notion of a female alchemist was intriguing enough for Deshaney to drop back and walk next to Bridget.

Tanry could not claim any satisfaction from the interaction. Bridget's concerns would not be alleviated. At the bottom of the lawn, she could see the caravan with a trail of smoke rising from the chimney. Little had been solved.

She gathered the staff to pull off an early supper for the visiting lords. Duke Teneri chose not to make an appearance, but it went unremarked upon. Matfey and Cotterall arrived and announced their engagement to the strangers. Lord Deshaney gave a toast in their honour, then asked that the carriages be drawn up. Tanry offered rooms for the night, should they prefer, but Deshaney said that the society had rented a house in Martois.

"I think we have seen enough here," he said. "But thank you for your hospitality."

The sun was going down and Tanry watched the carriages depart down the winding drive. Beside her, Bridget watched them go and itched her wig.

"What did he say to you?" Tanry asked her.

"He thought I was a hobbyist and looking for a husband." She snorted. "He was impressed with the theory behind the hairbrush, at least. Then he proposed that I would be a good third wife for him."

"You could play up the husband angle. It might get you into the Society."

"My dignity is worth more than that, Tanry."

"At least he was not suspicious. He thought you were an archduchess and never considered otherwise."

"I should accept my crumbs."

The Society had come and gone and nothing had changed.

Bridget stuffed both hands into her hair. "I need to wash this," she announced and strode away.

Alone again, Tanry looked out at the empty lawn, unable to even see the lights of the village.

She went to the caravan, expecting to find Zsari there, yet when she approached, she heard a pair of voices. Unprepared to entertain a crowd, Tanry waited outside. Stood under the window, she couldn't help but overhear that conversation happening inside. Of course, she was trying to eavesdrop, but she thought that it was inevitable regardless.

"We haven't sold a single gem." She heard Valentin's voice.

"You haven't needed to, with the princess paying for your every whim," replied Zsari.

"Zsari, please—"

"You cannot pay me off with my mother's jewellery, Val. I will not vanish into the night because you have given me some funds."

"I have to make this better, Zsari. I have to try," Valentin begged.

"I was so naive to come here. I should have known that it would go like this."

"You should have known that you would sleep with my wife?"

"Your wife? The absolute cheek of that statement," Zsari laughed coldly. "You know she's not your wife because you married her under *my* name. No, I should have expected you to turn me out. I don't know why I expected any familiarity from you."

"It is not as simple as that."

"I just don't want to be alone again. I am the last one left. We are the last ones."

There was silence for a few moments. It was broken by Valentin.

"Why did you run after the carriage?" he asked.

"What?"

"On the last day. We left the Kendana palace and you ran after the carriage. Idonea tried to stop you."

"I thought you were going to die. I knew they were sending you out to die. They dressed you up in our clothes and put you in our carriage. I knew they were going to fake our deaths."

"I didn't know that at the time," said Valentin.

"You really should have. The signs were all there."

"I realised when I was crawling over the mountains after being shot."

"You got shot? And survived?"

"Obviously. I'm tougher than I may appear."

"That's a fine thing, because you don't look tough at all. How did you get away?"

"Idonea appeared. She warned us just in time. She led us across the mountains into Lyalia. Wasn't she with you, at the Kendana palace?"

"No. She vanished. The rebels attacked shortly after that," said Zsari.

Tanry grew tired, and guilty, of listening to them. She walked up the steps to the caravan door and knocked. Valentin and Zsari fell silent, as is the habit of people accustomed to keeping secrets.

"It's only me," she said. "The alchemists are gone. You don't have to hide anymore."

Valentin opened the door. "I'm going indoors then," he declared. "Don't leave without seeing me again, Zsari."

After he was gone, Tanry climbed inside and fell face first onto the bed.

"That good, huh?" said Zsari.

"I don't know how to fix things."

"Why do you want to so badly?"

"I don't know how to live near the misery of others," she said.

"Then why did you create so much of it?"

She had nothing to say to that, so she lay there in silence. Zsari laid down next to her and together they watched the sky go dark through the little caravan windows.

Tanry dozed off. When she woke again, she wasn't sure of how much time had passed. The sky was lighter than she expected. Thinking that she'd accidentally slept until morning, she bolted upright. She reached out and shook Zsari, who blinked awake slowly.

"Is it morning?" she asked.

"I don't know," said Tanry. She shuffled off the bed and went to the window. The sky was touched with orange, though it did not look like an exceptionally red dawn.

"Fire," she said.

CHAPTER THIRTY-THREE
The Heart of the Blaze

It is good sense to keep an eye on all open flames in a household. Servants are particularly prone to leaving candles unattended next to curtains. In the event of a fire, the lady of a household should make sure to question all of her staff. — Margrit Bellere's Manual for Young Ladies

Zsari made a confused noise and Tanry shook him again.

"There's a fire," she told him, though he barely seemed to hear her.

Tanry burst out of the caravan and felt faint. The roof of her house was on fire. From the windows of an upper floor room, flames danced and crawled up the walls. Without thinking to stop for her jacket, Tanry flew across the lawn. She was not the first to arrive. There was a collection of her tenants and staff gathered.

"It's coming from the fucking library!" she shouted. "It's spread to my goddamn wing."

Cole appeared, dressed in his nightshirt and a greatcoat. "We don't know when it happened," he said. "We thought you were inside."

"We need to get a human chain down to the lake with the buckets," Tanry ordered.

"Already done." He pointed behind him, where the staff were forming an uncertain line down to the lake.

"More folk are coming," said Cole. "We sent Uma to rouse them in the village."

"Tanry!"

She heard a voice calling to her. She wanted to rush to the lake and join the chain, but Cotterall was pushing through the crowd to find her.

"I can't find your father," he said. "Mat – Laurina is with me."

Tanry's stomach dropped. She hadn't considered that. From behind her, Zsari arrived and swore.

"Where's Cezsario?" he asked.

Matfey was wearing Cotterall's coat over her nightgown. She was crying. "I can't find either of them." She sobbed and covered her face with her hands.

At that moment, the front doors opened and a figure staggered out. He turned towards them, and Tanry saw that it was Duke Teneri. He held his hands up and Tanry saw peeling skin and angry red burns.

"You fucking idiot!" she yelled. "Look what you've done."

He stopped. "It was that trollop. She's untrained."

"She's making hairbrushes, you fool. Where is she?"

"She wasn't in her bed," cried Matfey. Cotterall put his arm around her.

"And Cezsario? You checked his room?" Tanry asked.

"He wasn't there. I worry that he might have gone to speak to Lizseta in your parlour."

That room, if the library was the heart of the blaze, was close to the centre.

If there was a single thought in Tanry's head, she could not have recognised it. Instead, all her energy translated directly into action. Before she knew it, she was running, ignoring the shouts of the people around her, and diving through the front doors. Nothing in the front hall was on fire, but the ceiling was marred by a cloud of grey smoke. Tanry covered her mouth with her sleeve, regretting the haste of her actions. Wasting time was not an option. She pulled her handkerchief from her pocket and held it over her mouth, then ran up the stairs. She turned to her right and saw the flames leaping from the library door.

"Valentin! Bridget!" There had to be a reason they weren't outside with the rest of the household. She didn't dare dwell on such a notion. Even stood in the corridor the heat was scalding. She coughed, and then could not stop coughing.

She couldn't run straight past the flames, but there was a servants' door that would lead the same way. She struggled to open the door and staggered through. The air was marginally clearer and she ran as fast as she was able, counting the doors until she found the one to her own parlour. She threw the door open and was hit by a wave of heat. It made her gasp, though she couldn't get a full breath.

The damask curtains she'd ordered from Calness were aflame. She dropped to the ground and crawled, but could see neither Bridget nor Valentin. She tried to call their names but couldn't get enough breath into her lungs.

It occurred to her how stupid she had been to rush inside. She had no real idea where Bridget and Valentin were, if they were still living. Not a moment after she had this thought, she saw a spool of dark hair on the floor. It was half-burned. Tanry looked past it and saw Bridget crouched there with no wig to cover her blonde curls.

"Valentin?" Tanry asked in a croak.

Bridget's eyes travelled to a shape on the carpet beside her. Tanry crawled to him. His eyes were shut and his mouth hung open. He was still in his day clothes, though now covered in soot. Tanry shook him by the shoulders but he didn't wake.

"Sorry," she muttered, before she raised her palm and slapped him across the face. His eyes opened as he jolted awake. Tanry grabbed him by the arm and pulled him up with as much force as she could muster.

"Go now." She indicated the servants' door.

Bridget understood and they crawled, Tanry pulling Valentin along.

The passageway was now as full of smoke as the parlour and Tanry saw the light of the flames at the end of the corridor. She heard a creaking in the ceiling that made her afraid, and knew there wasn't enough time to crawl down the corridor and go down the grand staircase. They needed to get out faster than that. At the other end of the servants' passage there was a dumbwaiter that served Tanry's parlour. She pulled Valentin in that direction, despite his protestations. She felt around in the wall for the opening and pulled the door open. Each small movement felt like an ache.

"Get inside," she instructed Valentin.

His eyes were bright in his soot stained face. Tanry pushed him towards the hole and he understood, crouching inside. Bridget was on all fours, coughing her lungs out, so Tanry pulled herself to the mechanism alone. She grabbed the pulley and lowered Valentin down a floor, then waited a moment, hoping that he was alert enough to crawl out of the contraption. Then she pointed at Bridget.

There was a crash and they both froze. It was too near. Tanry pulled on the rope as hard as she could and the dumbwaiter shuddered into place. Bridget crawled inside. It was uncomfortably hot. Tanry's eyes watered so much that she could barely see. She lowered Bridget to the ground floor, then collapsed against the wall. Only then did she realise that she had trapped herself upstairs. Without anyone else operating the pulley, she couldn't get downstairs.

It was to her surprise that the dumbwaiter rose back into place beside her. It was being operated from the ground floor.

Tanry crawled inside and once situated, knocked on the floor twice, hoping that was signal enough. It felt like an era passed, but then she descended into the clearer air in the kitchen. She crawled out of the dumbwaiter. The alchemic lights had failed and Tanry could only see Bridget and Valentin by the dim light of the banked hearth. Both of them were sootier than chimney sweeps. Any vestiges of imperial grandeur were lost. Valentin's shirt was torn, while Bridget's petticoats were singed. Tanry's chest hurt.

"What happened?" she asked.

"My skirt caught fire," said Bridget. "Val saved me."

Valentin was leaning against a wall, his legs shaking visibly. He stared at his hands, which were blistered and burned.

"We need to get out of here," Tanry said.

Tanry made for the door to the kitchen gardens, but Bridget caught her by the elbow.

"I can't go out there," she said. "They can't see me like this."

"This building is on fire. We can't hide here."

"I don't have a disguise. There is no Lizseta anymore."

"It doesn't matter – we still need to leave."

"No, it does," said Valentin. "If they know that we are frauds, you lose the estate. Matfey loses her dowry. We lose everything."

This made Tanry pause. She grabbed them both by the arms. "We will continue this outside. The kitchen garden is nowhere near where everyone is gathered."

They stumbled into the cool air, though none of them could stop coughing. Tanry led them into the corner of the walled garden.

"If Lizseta is gone, then she has to be gone," said Tanry.

"What are you suggesting?"

"I can hide you. Then you can go home, I suppose."

"To Karda Ven?" asked Bridget in a hesitant voice.

"If you hide now in my caravan, no one will see you," Tanry told her.

"And then I can go home?"

"I'd be in charge of Matfey and Valentin. You could go home. Be an alchemist. Lizseta died in a fire."

They stood in silence, listening to the crackle of the flames and the distant discussions of the fire fighters.

Tanry held out her hand. Bridget took it and they hurried around the far side of the house, out of sight, until they reached the caravan.

By this point, Valentin's adrenaline had failed him. He threw up in the grass and then he needed Tanry's help to walk. When they reached the caravan, Tanry helped him inside and closed the curtains. She tore strips of fabric from the bed sheets and found cold water left in the kettle.

"You stay here with Bridget," she told Valentin. "I'll tell them that I couldn't find you." She knelt down and examined his burned hands. She didn't envy him the blisters he was about to have.

"No, I need to prove I'm alive," he said. "The archduke can't die."

"The archduke is by the lake. If he wants to, Valentin Taybury can walk away."

The archduke was out there, waiting for them. He could love Tanry, maybe. He could even marry her, if she asked. But – she couldn't do this to him. She couldn't do it again. Valentin had to be free to go where he would, and Zsari had to be too.

"I don't know how to do that," muttered Valentin.

"Easy. You know where your mother is. You go find her. Then you do what you want," Tanry said.

"What of you?"

"I married an archduke. I think I was always meant to be a rich widow. I've fulfilled the terms of my father's agreement. He lit my house on fire."

"You are serious?"

Carefully, Tanry began to wrap his hands with the torn fabric. "You hate it here. Go somewhere else."

Bridget knelt down beside Tanry, taking the bandages away. "I'll take care of him. You have to get back before they think you're dead too."

Tanry stood back, finding the doorknob.

"Stay out of sight," she warned them.

She went back to the kitchen garden, then stumbled towards the lake. Ladders had been erected and people passed the crested water buckets up them to pour through the library windows. Tanry was too tired to judge whether the fire was under control. Her lungs hurt and she wanted to throw up. She had to steel herself for what was about to come next.

She wandered back into the crowd, where mothers now gathered with their young children under their coats. Someone gasped.

"She's there!" they cried. Before she knew it, Zsari and Matfey were in front of her. Matfey stared at her hungrily, raking every part of her for a clue.

"Where are they?" she asked.

"I couldn't find them," said Tanry.

Matfey's scream was enough to rend the heart.

CHAPTER THIRTY-FOUR
The Next Life Begins

Few vestiges of the empire remain. Many nobles fled, others were executed. Many more were sent to debtor's prison, where their fate was uncertain. Even the servants of the imperials didn't escape notice. The emperor's personal guards (the imperial protection corps) vanished almost entirely after their leader was publicly executed. There is little doubt in this writer's mind that they were killed because of their supposed loyalty to the emperor. — A Lament for the Old Country: A Response

The fire claimed the library and part of its roof. Half of the west wing was ruined. Tanry's bedroom escaped the worst of it, sparing the discernment engine from destruction. All of this seemed incidental, because the archduke Cezsario Concerto Dalibor Boralda-Solkin and his sister Archduchess Lizseta Caela Loreatha Boralda-Solkin were declared dead. No bodies could be found, but the roof had collapsed in the parlour, and the fire had burned hot enough to warp the iron grate from the hearth. No one expected any bodies to be found.

Tanry was given lease to stay in Russeau's house. She wandered about, silent, covered in ash. It was presumed that she was in shock. Perhaps she really was, but not in the way that everyone thought.

Deep in the grounds of Taltois, there was a caravan. In the chaos after the fire, it was overlooked. No one saw Zsari walking there with food, clothes and with a small chest that had the imperial crest stamped on the lid.

The evening after the fire, when the air still smelled of smoke, Tanry escaped the notice of her carers to return to her mother's sanctuary. Crammed inside were Valentin, Bridget, Matfey, and Zsari, sitting on the floor around the chest. Valentin's hands were bandaged. His breathing was not quite right, but he claimed to be fine. Bridget had a nasty burn on her right calf where her dress had caught alight.

"Thanks for waiting," said Tanry as she stepped inside.

"We weren't really waiting," said Matfey, "but welcome."

Tanry knelt beside Zsari, who put his hand on her knee. He leaned forward and flicked open the latch of the chest. Inside, there was a piece of red velvet, which Zsari removed. Underneath lay a bandit's darkest dream: strings of pearls, rubies, sapphires, diamond brooches, and a tall silver tiara.

"This belonged to my mother," said Zsari. "I think the spies wanted you all to get caught by the rebels with them. If you had the imperial jewels with you, anyone would assume that you were the imperial family."

"I hid it in my skirts," said Bridget, "and carried it across the mountains."

They set out all the pieces on the rug and then all looked to Zsari.

"I can't take it all," he said. "It's more of a liability for me to sell all of this than it is a help. The buyer will think that I stole it."

"You'll take this, though." Carefully, owing to his burns, Valentin picked up a gold bracelet. The links, Tanry saw, were individual portraits. The miniatures, preserved perfectly behind glass, were of four young children with dark hair and dark eyes. Zsari took it and held it tightly in one fist.

"Here we are," he said. He held it up to Tanry. "This is Myrthe. She died before the rest of us were born. Here is Lizseta, and Laurina, and I. My mother used to wear this every day."

The rest of the jewels, though more valuable, were of less interest to Zsari. He shared them out among his companions. Bridget took Lizseta's diamond hair pins and her collection of rings. Matfey had Laurina's earrings and brooches and one emerald bracelet that belonged to an ancestor Zsari couldn't name. Valentin, to his chagrin, was left with the imperial tiara and a string of pearls.

"What am I going to do with this?" he asked.

"Ask Athalie," joked Zsari. "I would cut it into pieces and sell the gems in different towns."

At the princess' name, Valentin blushed deeply. "Do you think I could see her again?" he asked, his tone so hopeful that it was painful.

"I don't know," said Zsari. "Introduce yourself again. See what she says."

Tanry and Matfey fetched clothes for them. Tanry begged

Cook for a packed lunch, claiming that she could not face eating with her father.

It all came together rather quickly. Bridget dressed in one of Tanry's tweed suits, and Valentin in one of her father's old suits, his own clothes having been destroyed. They both packed a small bag, and when the sun went down and the villagers had returned to their beds, they walked through the woods to the road that bordered Taltois. Tanry passed an alchemic lantern to Bridget.

"Send a letter," said Tanry.

"I don't think that I can."

"Just write. Say that you arrived in Karda Ven, and naught else." She spun to Valentin. "That goes for you as well."

"I can't bear not hearing from you again," said Matfey. "Say that you will."

"It's all so uncertain," said Valentin. "But I will try. Take good care of Beck."

Tanry waited as the impostors bade a long goodbye to one another, briefly holding each other tightly. She stood by Zsari. After he had hugged Matfey, Valentin turned to Zsari. They waited for a moment, saying naught to one another, before Zsari raised his arms and threw them around Valentin.

"Where will you go?" asked Valentin.

"I've no idea."

"You should have taken more of those jewels."

"The past only weighs me down. Good luck."

Valentin let go of Zsari. He nodded at Tanry. She saluted him in return.

"Goodbye then. I don't know what else to say." Valentin laughed. "The next life begins." He moved down the road, towards the north, while Bridget turned southwards.

"I'll write to Taltois," she swore. "But I won't sign it."

"Tell us when you have found Idonea," said Matfey, and Bridget blushed.

"Best not mention me to her," said Tanry.

"Look after my dog, Matfey," said Bridget.

With naught else left to say, Bridget began to walk south, and Valentin north. Matfey, Tanry, and Zsari waited on the road until they were no more than bobbing lights in the distance.

CHAPTER THIRTY-FIVE

The Guardian of the Land

Following the death of a husband, a lady must enter mourning for a period of four years. For two further years, she must be in half-mourning, and wear muted colours, such as grey and charcoal. Any less time would be a disrespect to the husband's memory, and will limit her chances of marrying again. — Margrit Bellere's Manual for Young Ladies

The funeral was a rather muted affair. Tanry had not cared to advertise it. She worried over a letter to Athalie, detailing the deaths of Cezsario and Lizseta, for a week. The messenger only set off to deliver it to Athalie on the morning of the funeral.

In the mausoleum, Matfey and Cotterall sat on the front row holding hands. A gold ring glinted on Matfey's finger. The wedding – ill-timed – had been quick, and with only Tanry in attendance.

Behind them, the guests began to filter out. Tanry's eyes were fixed on the marble plaque newly fixed to the wall above her mother's tomb. In a rather humble manner, it mourned the death of the archduke and the archduchess. It was nothing like the gilded effigies they would have received in the empire of Karda Ven. A note at the bottom explained that the archduke was the loving husband of Tanry Teneri.

Beside her, Matfey and Cotterall stood.

"Are you coming?" Matfey asked. Idonea-dog, who had been sleeping under the bench, began yapping and circling Matfey's feet.

"Give me a moment to sit here," said Tanry.

Matfey put a hand on her shoulder as they walked away.

Tanry waited until the mausoleum had emptied entirely. There was food and drink waiting for her indoors, where all the halls smelled of brick dust and plaster and charcoal. She stood, and instead of going to pay her respects to the new plaque, she turned to her left, where a statue of a mourning figure loomed in an alcove. Trevor's tomb was resplendent in its sadness. At the time of its design, she had thought it an embarrassing expense, and she had warned her father against commissioning the crying young man in marble. Perhaps now she understood the expense a little more. She pressed her palm to the cool surface of the tomb.

"I miss you," she whispered, "and I am so angry that you left me here alone."

For some time, she stood there and cried.

Indoors, Tanry tried to avoid all the guests who wanted to speak to her. With limited exception, none of the attendees had known Valentin or Bridget. They had no notion of what it was to lose them. She found a decanter of whiskey and drank, pretending not to hear the entreaties of those around her. It was only when she heard Cole's voice that she looked up.

"Your father wants to speak to you," he said, "in the library."

Or more accurately, where the library used to be. She meandered her way there and with care, opened the temporary door to her father's most sacred space. The walls were as black as her funeral suit. There was a hole in the floor where her father's work bench had been.

Labourers had already been through, assessing the damage and shoring up the structure of the building. Through the hole in the ribcage of the roof, Tanry could see the fading sky. Duke Teneri was there, looking at his library with more sadness than he'd displayed at the funeral.

"What is it?" Tanry asked.

"I wanted to discuss your future."

"A fine time for it, during my husband's wake. My most immediate plans involve repairing the damage you caused."

"It was her," he insisted again.

The feeble claim made Tanry more furious than she could describe, though she held her jaw tightly instead of shouting.

"Let the dead rest and take ownership of your actions, Father," she said, in a far more measured tone than he deserved.

He tutted. "Without an heir for Taltois, the duty is still upon you to create one."

"What can you be suggesting?"

"I am back in talks with Duke Archibald, though he is demanding a far higher dowry now that you're a widow and spoiled, so to speak."

"You cannot be serious."

"You will have a period of mourning of course, but then you will marry, and I will make sure that your intentions are carried out this time. You made a fool of me before. It will not happen again."

"You really have no notion of my feelings, do you?"

"I will hear no more about it." He waved his hand, as if Tanry was that easy to swat away.

"You burned down my house. You cannot send me away from it."

"My house was burned by the harlot that you brought here. I have also decided to limit your credit. It is time you accepted your position, Tanry."

It was all Tanry could do not to push him out of the window, or laugh, or spit at his feet. She knew very well her position – at least, the one she'd chosen for herself. She was the rightful Duke of Taltois, guardian of the land, a hunter and a groundskeeper. She would not be bought and sold.

"Then perhaps it is time you accepted your ability. You are a shoddy alchemist and an incompetent duke. Without me, you will fall into debt, I guarantee it," she said.

"You will marry, Tanry. You will give me heirs. I survived the death of my spouse. So will you."

"You are perhaps the worst person I've ever known," said Tanry. "I will not marry again, unless by my choosing."

"You, alas, have no right to refuse."

His words hung heavily on the air. Tanry thought for a moment of revealing the truth. The real archduke was not dead in a fire. He was in Taltois, though he looked nothing like a gentleman anymore. Yet, she was certain that her father would not be convinced of his identity. What was more, she could not proclaim that he would be her husband without his knowledge, and without his consent. It was a mistake, she knew, to do that again.

Tanry found an expensive vase and threw it off the landing herself. She heard the cries of shock from below and didn't care. She marched down the stairs and into the drawing room. A desperate plan was forming in her mind, and if she stopped to think she would never succeed.

She found Matfey and Cotterall in conversation with the priest. Tanry ignored him and spoke directly to Matfey.

"Pack," she said. "Take the deed to the townhouse from Russeau."

"What is happening?" asked Matfey.

"I am disobeying my father again. I don't want you to be caught up in it. Pack and get out of here. You have everything out there waiting for you."

"What are you doing?"

"Don't worry about it."

She ran away and up to her bedroom, pulling on the cord. Uma appeared through the servants' door with Cole behind her, both sporting concerned expressions.

"My lady, what can we do?" asked Cole.

"Pack up the discernment engine," said Tanry as she threw open her wardrobe.

"May I ask why?"

"I'm taking it somewhere. Don't tell my father. If you don't want to answer to him, get out now. I can pen you a quick reference, though I'm afraid my word isn't worth much among the aristocracy." She hunted out her most important belongings: her mother's hairbrush, Trevor's long riding coat, a collection of the jewellery that Caterina had favoured for her. She stuffed it into a sack and turned to Cole.

"Can you tell the groom to take two horses to the caravan? Tell him Rusty and Ink."

"Is he expected to hitch these horses up? That caravan has not moved in years."

"It will move. I will make it move."

She suspected that her urgency made him take the situation seriously. Uma summoned help, and they wheeled the discernment engine away. She could not stop moving. She could not stop and think about how this might be the last time that she was in this room, that it had already been the last time she'd slept in this bed. She found all the money she had to hand and her best work boots.

Ignoring the hubbub in the drawing room, she dashed down the grand staircase with her bag over her shoulder. There was one more thing she needed to do.

The frost had all but melted from the lawn. Spring was well on its way and soon the daffodils would be in bloom all over Taltois. It was usually a treasured time of year for Tanry. She ran as fast as she could down the lawn to the caravan. She beat her fist against the door.

"Zsari, I need you."

He threw the door open. He was dressed for walking, having wrapped a scarf around the bottom half of his face.

"Were you leaving?" she asked.

He pulled the scarf down. "I was hoping to get away without anyone seeing me," he admitted.

"Including me?"

"Tanry, I—"

"I want to come with you. If you'll have me."

"I— Of course I would. But how would that ever happen?"

"My father is going to marry me off. There is nothing I can do. I love my home – it is the thing I love most – but I cannot stand to be bought and sold. There is no recourse for that. I have no option but this. So much of what I value will be taken away, so I will take what I can with me."

"Including me?"

"You, and a machine that can tell absolute truth."

"What?"

"I want to be with you. Can you help me get this caravan mobile?"

He laughed.

"I should have known there would be some taxing task."

"Do you want a place to live or not?"

He laughed again, and she kissed him to shut him up.

It took most of the day to encourage the caravan from its resting place. They greased the wheels and cleared away the brambles that had grown underneath. Cole gathered the grooms and stable hands to come down and dig a path to free it.

Mrs Button and Cook arrived with a basket filled with bread, cheese, dried meat, and preserves.

"I don't know how well you'll survive on your own," said Mrs Button. "But if there was anyone who was going to try, it would be you."

Somehow, Russeau caught wind of what was going on and

walked down the lawn with his wife on his arm.

"It's not going to be the same without you," he said. "Your father and I haven't worked together in years."

"Do your best with him," Tanry said. "Though he is doomed."

"I had Uma fetch something for you," he said. "I thought your father wasn't going to use it."

Uma appeared, her cheeks flushed, clutching Trevor's alchemic rifle. It was a clever device that fired strange, sound-based missiles. Since his death, Tanry hadn't had cause to go hunting. She took the gun, which felt heavy and familiar in her hands.

"I thought you would make a good poacher," said Russeau.

"You aren't disappointed that I'm running away and robbing my father in the process?"

"Who am I to cast aspersions, my lady?"

As the sun was setting, they moved the caravan onto the drive. Either her father had not noticed what was occurring, or he'd no interest. The two shire horses, both named for their colour, shook their heads and pawed the ground. Tanry shook hands with the staff, most of whom she'd known since childhood, those good souls who had cared for her when her father did not.

"I might even come back one day," she said. "Who knows?" She wasn't confident of this sentiment. She'd well and truly alienated the future queen, so Tanry could not hope that the law would change in her favour.

She sat on the front seat, next to Zsari, who held the reins and the whip in his hands.

"Maybe we go to Nessa Spa," he said.

"Let us go, before I lose my nerve entirely."

Tanry gave a final wave to Cole before he began to usher the servants back up to the house, then took the reins from Zsari's hands. She clicked her tongue, flicked the whip, and said, "Walk on."

The horses moved, the caravan swaying behind them. Zsari glanced behind them, and Tanry allowed herself one look back too. The sun dipped over the ridges dug by Competency Green, and sparkled off the lake, and winked through the scorched beams of the hall's roof. They rode on, and the trees blocked Taltois from view.

CHAPTER THIRTY-SIX

The Engine Cannot Predict the Future

Princess Athalie has the most delightful new wardrobe for the season. Rumours are that she has employed a young, fresh-eyed seamstress, who will soon have a client list as long as her arm. — Pherson's Courtly Hearsay

Summers in the city were always exciting, and a welcome reward for Caterina's years of exile in the countryside. Especially now she had the budget to truly take advantage of the city. She visited three haberdasheries and met two drapers, so she felt prepared to fit the princess in the latest fashions for the season. As they stepped out of the last shop, Caterina ordered both of her maids to deposit their purchases in the carriage.

"I shall meet you there," she said. "I've an idea to get a pastry before we return to the palace."

She set off at a light pace, enjoying the feeling of sun on her face. She had a bakery in mind that made the most divine apricot croissants; to get there, she needed only to cross the square at the end of the street. She adjusted her parasol and strode in that direction.

The square was lined with coffee houses with striped awnings where men in light-colored suits and ladies with floral hats sipped from porcelain cups. Caterina strolled her way through the crowd, but stopped short when she heard a familiar voice.

"It can indeed answer any question. But be warned – the engine cannot predict the future. Don't waste your precious coins on a question to which there is no answer."

Caterina changed her direction. She wove through a crowd gathered in the centre of the square.

In the centre of the throng was a gaily painted caravan. It had a window open on one side, through which Caterina could see familiar brass tumblers and dials. Tanry Teneri stood at the centre of the crowd, holding court. She was much the same as she always had been, though perhaps more rugged. Her rust-coloured suit wasn't ironed, and it was fraying at the hems. Her tie sat loosely around her neck and her cuffs slipped out of her sleeves, unbuttoned. It suited her.

She turned to a youth with a spotted face at the front of the crowd. "You sir, you had a question."

"Yes, I wanted to ask if Davina had any feelings for me. Romantically speaking."

"It's good to be specific. That will be three coppers." She held out her hand and waited for the young man to hand over the payment. Money acquired, Tanry swung her arm to the caravan.

"Zsari, if you will." A scruffy man hopped down from the seat of the caravan, where he had been tending to two carthorses. He turned the dials on the discernment engine. It spun as it did when it was in thought, then it popped out a very short answer.

"I'm afraid it's bad news, lad," said Tanry; the youth looked rather like he was about to cry. "Of course, it's actually good news in disguise. Now you know that this Davina is not worth your attention and you can look elsewhere. Do we have any other seekers of knowledge?"

Caterina stepped forward.

"I have a question," she said.

Tanry's eyes landed on her and a small smile crept onto her face. "What question might that be?"

"My employer, she has changed my life, but she's not been happy," said Caterina.

"I'm sorry to hear that," replied Tanry with faux sincerity.

"She had a love. A very sincere one. She thinks that he will never return to her, but I have a feeling that he will. When will that be?"

"Now, you know that the engine cannot predict the future."

"I know that well." She hadn't watched that damned machine turn its cogs and its wheels for hours for nothing. "But I do not need the engine to know that he is already on his way."

THE END

ACKNOWLEDGEMENTS

I'd like to thank my absolutely wonderful editor, Adie Hart! Without her, this book simply wouldn't be what it is. She's the editor of Indie Bites, a fantasy anthology for indie writers, where I've had the pleasure of seeing my stories included. Incidentally - she has many stories published there too, and you should absolutely go read them. If you are a social media type of person, check them out on instagram using @indiebitesanthology (or @adiehartauthor). I would never have been confident enough to publish and share my work without seeing other indie writers out there, and knowing that there was a path to being an author.

This also wouldn't be possible without my writer friends, who have travailed through many hours of me talking about my work: Charlie, George, and the Little Jester Man. They have gone through many hours of me talking about the mechanics of a magical search engine, and debating names for a fictional imperial family.

I also must send huge thanks to my amazing beta readers, Eleni and Mia Delic! It's a joy being able to share work with other writers and hopefully help one another improve.

ABOUT THE AUTHOR

Ash Parker was put on this earth to do two things: make mischief and write stories. Fortunately, they're not out of stories yet.

When they're not writing, they spend all their time taking up new crafts, playing the sims, and visiting niche museums.

If you liked this book, the best place to keep up to date with Ash Parker's work is on their newsletter. Sign up to hear about new releases, cover reveals, and bonus content: http://ashthehermit.substack.com

Alternatively, you can follow them on social media using the handle @ashthehermit.

You can also keep up to date with Tanry and friends in
The Tales from Karda Ven.

The next installment:

PRINCESS ATHALIE'S TREATISE FOR ABSOLUTE TRUTH

will release in 2025.

If you liked this book, try:

WINTER'S CHOSEN

by Ash Parker.

If you were chosen to save the world, would you do anything it takes?

Ifry is the long suffering clerk to the wealthy and demanding Thomas Townsend. When the latter takes Ifry to the mountains to build a ski resort, they have their work cut out for them. The mountain town is overrun with carnivorous monsters and Ifry is woefully unprepared, but he finds help in Jos Nothernine, the reserved but charming local hunter. Yet the town is plagued by more than just monsters: it is home to Solyon, the god of summer himself. Each year, Solyon chooses a townsperson to defeat a sacrifice chosen by Lady Winter. If the chosen fails, winter will continue endlessly, meaning disaster for the world at large.

A sacrifice must be made, and this year Jos has been chosen to kill someone, lest summer never return.

BV - #0064 - 280825 - C0 - 203/127/21 - PB - 9781068754135 - Matt Lamination